THE DUKE'S INCONVENIENT BRIDE

JAYNE RIVERS

Editing by Hot Tree Editing.

Proofreading by Proof It Write.

Oops Detection by Anne Victory.

Cover design by EDH Professionals.

To my sister,
For being my #1 fan
(besides Mum).

CHAPTER 1

London,
October, 1819

Vaughan Stanhope, the Duke of Ashford, had never wanted a wife. Unfortunately, one could not get heirs without a wife, and without an heir, his title would pass to his bullying cousin, Reginald, and his brood of entitled brats.

Thus, here he was, in his best carriage, bedecked in his finest evening wear, and accompanied by his long-suffering friend, Andrew Drake, the Earl of Longley, on the way to a ball.

"I always knew you'd be the first of us to find a wife," Longley said, glancing out of the window as they arrived outside the Earl of Wembley's townhouse.

Vaughan scoffed and resisted the urge to look for himself. He was anxious enough without laying eyes on the crush of society that would no doubt be turning up tonight.

"Yes. After growing up with such a splendid example of matrimonial bliss, how could I possibly resist?"

Longley rolled his eyes. "Not because of your awful parents. Purely to spite that loathsome jackanapes, Reginald."

"Ah, yes. Him."

"Darling Reggie" as Vaughan's dearly departed mother had called him, had spent years tormenting him behind their parents' backs. Calling him names, mocking his shyness, and telling everyone who'd listen what a joke it was that he'd one day be a duke.

"He is the reason we're here, is he not?" Longley asked.

"In a roundabout way." At that moment, the carriage came to a stop. The door opened, and Vaughan climbed out, only too eager to be free of the conversation.

They made their way up the stone steps to the house's main entrance and stepped inside the foyer, where they were met by their hosts.

"Your Grace." The Earl of Wembley greeted Vaughan with a nod, then turned to Longley. "Lord Longley. Welcome to Wembley House."

"Felicitations. It seems as if you have a success on your hands," Longley said, and Vaughan shot him a look of gratitude for taking the lead. He was so much better in social situations than Vaughan was. Longley took the countess's hand and bowed over it. "My lady."

"Lord Longley," the countess demurred, then smiled slyly at Vaughan. "Your Grace, please allow me to introduce my eldest daughter, Lady Henrietta."

Vaughan acknowledged the girl with a tilt of his head. "Lady Henrietta. It's an honor to make your acquaintance."

Lady Henrietta's blond curls bounced as she angled her head back to look up at him, a friendly smile on her face. "The honor is all mine, Your Grace."

He glanced at Longley, who discreetly bumped him in the ribs with his elbow.

"I hope you will save me a dance," Vaughan said, the words difficult to get out past the lump in his throat. Still, this was what he was here for. To find a wife. Lady Henrietta was both pretty and suitable in terms of her connections. He could do worse.

"I would be delighted." She offered him her dance card and he filled a spot.

"We must move along," Longley urged as more guests arrived behind them. "Until later, Lady Henrietta."

They moved into the ballroom, which was massive, with high ceilings, white walls gilded with gold, and a polished wooden floor. It was also packed. Vaughan grew warmer, and not only from the mass of bodies pressing in around him. He and Longley seemed to have attracted a lot of attention with their arrival. Many young misses glanced their way, while their mothers studied the men more openly.

Heat prickled at the back of Vaughan's neck. He had the unmistakable feeling that he was being hunted. He drew in a shaky breath, his nostrils filling with the scent of the shrubbery somebody had felt the need to drag inside. He shrugged, trying to shake off the sensation of his skin being too tight for his body.

"Your Grace." A redheaded woman appeared in front of him with two younger ladies in tow. "Ah, and Lord Longley too." She looked like the cat that had eaten the canary.

"Lady Bowling," Vaughan replied, glancing over to make sure Longley hadn't beaten a rapid escape. His friend may be kind enough to have accompanied him tonight, but he had no desire for a wife of his own.

"May I present my daughter, Lady Esther, and her cousin, Miss Rose Hawthorne. They are new to society this season."

Vaughan blinked at the girls, one of whom wore a ridiculous feather construction in her hair, and the other of whom seemed to have been cinched so tightly into her ball gown that she might pass out at any moment.

"Charmed," Longley said, covering for Vaughan's hesitation. "I daren't hope that either of you lovely ladies have any space on your dance cards for His Grace or myself?"

3

The cards were proffered with much giggling and glee, and Vaughan dutifully added his name to each. They bid farewell to the group but had only made it another five paces before they were intercepted yet again.

By the time they reached the stairs leading to the upper balcony that overlooked the ballroom, Vaughan felt as if he hadn't drawn in a full breath for hours. A male voice called his name, but fearing yet another introduction to an eligible lady, he hurried up the stairs with Longley trailing behind him.

"Good lord, Ashford," Longley puffed as he drew even with Vaughan at the top of the stairs. "You're far less likely to find a wife up here than you were down there."

Vaughan surveyed the throng below, his pulse pounding madly in his temples. Even several feet above the revelry, he could hear the giggles, the inane chatter, and felt gazes following him.

"I did not realize it would be so...." He waved his hands, searching for a suitable descriptor. "Intense."

Longley chuckled. "'Tis the biggest ball of the season so far, which means every marriageable miss is seeking to make an impression. The fact that you are an unmarried duke, who has apparently decided to rectify your lack of a wife, makes you the plumpest catch here tonight."

Vaughan snorted. "You make me sound like a grouse."

"To the mamas of unwed young women, you might as well be."

Vaughan shook his head. "There must be a better way to find a wife."

Longley shrugged. "If you find one quickly, you won't have to subject yourself to many of these ghastly affairs. How many dances have you scheduled?"

"Almost half of them." His tone was morose. He enjoyed dancing, but not in cramped quarters such as this, and especially not with so many eyes on him.

Longley leaned on the balustrade. Vaughan followed his example, gazing out over the shining jewels of the ton.

"What do you want in a wife?" Longley asked. "Perhaps we can hasten the matter by being selective about the ladies to whom you offer your remaining dances."

Vaughan nodded. That made sense. "She must be well-mannered and respectable." His duchess would need to be able to smooth over his own occasional social missteps. "She does not have to be wealthy or from a titled family."

He pursed his lips, trying to quiet his thoughts, but it was difficult with the ruckus below. "She would ideally be popular and able to entertain herself, as I don't intend to spend much time together after we are wed."

There was a moment of silence, and then Longley asked, "Are you truly sure you wish to do this?"

BEING LADY VIOLET CARLISLE'S TWIN SOMETIMES MADE EMMA feel invisible. Especially on nights such as these, when gentlemen were practically getting into fisticuffs to determine who would have the honor of dancing with Violet whilst seeming not to notice Emma at all. It made it difficult for Emma to find a man to fall in love with when they all wanted her sister.

With a sigh, Emma shrank back against the wall beside the refreshments table, watching as Violet spun across the dance floor on the arm of a viscount. She surveyed the gathering, searching for her mother, but her attention was halted by the sight of the square-jawed and remarkably well-built Earl of Longley, who seemed to be making his way directly to her.

Emma straightened, pushing her shoulders back and smiling in welcome. She had always liked the earl. Not only was he handsome, but he was also clever and kind. Perhaps he would spare her from another evening spent as a wall-flower by asking her to dance.

"Lady Emma," he said, stopping in front of her. "You look well tonight."

She dropped into a curtsey. "As do you, my lord."

When she rose, he gestured toward the dance floor.

"Do you know when Lady Violet will next be free? I have someone to whom I'd like to introduce her."

Emma's heart sank. Of course the earl had not come over here to see her. As always, it was her sister whose company was desired.

"I believe she is free in two dances' time, my lord."

"Very good. My thanks, Lady Emma." He sketched a quick bow and left.

Emma turned to the table beside her and poured herself a drink. She sipped the lemonade and eyed the tiny pastries and cakes set out nearby. They had not eaten dinner prior to departing from Carlisle House because their mother had wanted them to look slim in their gowns.

Unfortunately, being hungry made Emma lethargic, which meant she lagged even further behind Violet in the beauty department than usual. She edged closer to the table and reached for a pastry, slipping it into her hand and quickly raising it to her lips. She glanced around, checking whether anyone had noticed, but of course, nobody was looking at her.

Nobody ever was.

She took another pastry and spied one of her acquaintances dancing with her new husband. Their heads were ducked close together, their gazes locked on each other. Emma sighed. They looked as though they were aware of no one else in the room.

How she wanted that.

Emma sipped her lemonade, wishing it were laced with something stronger. Something that would make the evening more tolerable. It wasn't that she didn't like balls. She rather thought she'd enjoy them if she weren't such a wallflower.

"Emma!"

Emma flinched and spun around. Her mother, Lady Carlisle, was making a beeline toward her around the edge of the ballroom, past the row of chairs where the spinsters and chaperones sat, drawing even with the refreshments table. Her eyebrows had climbed impressively high and her eyes were narrow as she appraised her erstwhile daughter.

"What on earth are you doing all the way over here?" her mother demanded. "Nobody will ask you to dance if you do not remain near the dancing."

Emma pursed her lips. She thought there were likely other, more pressing reasons she was not asked to dance, but far be it for her to say so.

"Sorry, Mother. I shall return with you momentarily."

She tried to finish her lemonade, but Lady Carlisle plucked the glass from her hand and put it on the table.

Emma sighed. "Very well."

Lady Carlisle took Emma by the arm and guided her back into the fray. Emma nodded at an acquaintance of hers who was, likewise, not particularly popular with the males of the aristocracy.

"Doesn't Violet look brilliant tonight?" Lady Carlisle asked, watching her other daughter with such pride stamped across her face that Emma had to look away. It was difficult to bear the knowledge that she never brought her mother the same level of joy.

"She does," Emma agreed because it was true. Violet sparkled tonight, as she did every night. The song ended, and there was a brief pause before the next one began. Violet was making her way toward them across the dance floor on the arm of a handsome gentleman Emma did not recognize.

The music started again, and Emma tapped her foot,

wishing somebody would ask her to dance. Even an elderly bachelor or a homely one would do. She did so love to dance.

"Mother," Violet said as they drew near. "This is Mr. Bently."

"Cousin to the Earl of Longley," Mr. Bently added—presumably to make himself look like a better catch to the Carlisle matriarch.

"He's quite a dashing dancer," Violet exclaimed.

Emma felt a pang of envy. She tried not to be jealous of Violet, but sometimes it was difficult.

"Lady Carlisle." The voice came from behind Emma and startled them all. Emma's hand flew to her chest as she turned toward it.

Lord Longley smiled broadly. He tipped his head. "Lady Emma. Lady Violet. Bently."

"Lord Longley." Violet's smile was beatific. Lord Longley was on her shortlist of prospective husbands. While Emma wanted to find a connection before she married, Violet was much more pragmatic. A title and a fortune would do nicely for her.

Lord Longley waited for the greetings to finish and then gestured to the man beside him, an austere-looking fellow with an immaculately tailored waistcoat, dark hair, and eyes the color of the sky on a cloudy morning.

"Please allow me to introduce you to my good friend, the Duke of Ashford."

Emma heard her mother's quick intake of breath. Violet was more subtle, but her eyes still widened. Emma didn't know why they were surprised. She wasn't. If the rumors were to be believed, the duke was looking for a bride, and Violet would make a remarkable duchess.

There was a chorus of "Your Graces" followed by curtseying, during which Emma surreptitiously watched the duke. His eyes were unusual and quite stunning, but he didn't have the same amiable air about him that Lord Longley did. In fact, while his mouth twitched slightly during the introduction, he didn't even smile.

When Emma found a husband, she'd want one who smiled regularly and laughed easily.

"A pleasure." The Duke of Ashford's voice was cool and cultured. He reminded Emma of what she imagined the character of Mr. Darcy from the novel she was reading would sound like. He turned to Violet. "Lady Violet, may I have this dance?"

Violet fluttered her eyelashes—dark, unlike Emma's overly pale ones—and smiled. "It would be an honor."

She took his hand and allowed him to lead her away. As soon as Violet left, Mr. Bently made his excuses, and the earl melted away into the crowd.

"Would you believe it?" Lady Carlisle asked, hushed but excited. "A duke."

"They look lovely together," Emma said. The duke had an intriguing dark handsomeness about him that did not appeal to her, but she knew many young ladies would go crazy for it. In conjunction with Violet's pale blond hair, strawberries-and-cream complexion, and dark eyebrows and eyelashes, they were a striking pair.

The song picked up, and Emma's foot tapped as she watched the dancers.

"Oh, Emma, please stop that," her mother snapped.

Emma scowled, but stilled her foot. All she wanted was to dance. And perhaps to eat a few more of those pastries.

When the dance finished, the duke returned Violet to them. His expression gave nothing away, but Violet appeared to be in raptures.

"His Grace is truly accomplished at the cotillion," she said.

The duke seemed to shrink an inch, and Emma frowned. She'd have expected him to either preen at the comment or not acknowledge it at all.

"It was a delightful dance," he said with all the enthusiasm Emma saved for when her governess had made her practice her sums as a girl.

He turned to Emma, and those pale gray eyes met hers. He hesitated, actually pausing to look at her, whereas many people simply swept straight over her. His lips parted, and anticipation fizzed in her stomach. Would he ask her to dance too?

CHAPTER 2

Attraction punched Vaughan in the gut as Violet Carlisle's sister met his gaze. He tried to recall her name, but he'd already been introduced to so many young ladies today that it had dropped from his mind.

He released Violet and took a subtle step to the side, thanking his lucky stars that society did not dictate he ask both sisters to dance. Perhaps doing so would be good manners, but he had no wish to get closer to the woman with those soulful blue eyes.

He shifted his weight from one foot to the other, then reminded himself that dukes did not fidget. Instead, he took a moment to study Violet's sister. Violet's white-blonde hair curled artfully around her shoulders, whereas her sister's was golden and pulled back. Violet's vivid cornflower eyes sparkled with life. In contrast, her sister's were darker and impossible to read.

But the most marked difference was in how they presented themselves. From only one dance, he could already judge that Violet was a lively conversationalist and would brighten any place with her presence. She reminded him of a bubbling brook.

Her sister was a still pond.

Ordinary at first glance, but he suspected there was more to her than appeared on the surface.

"Please excuse me," he said. "I am engaged for this next dance."

"Thank you, Your Grace," Violet said, her pretty lips lifting at the corners.

Vaughan glanced at the stairs as he left them, briefly considering whether he could escape to the upper level once again. Nobody would call him out on his behavior if he missed a few dances. He was a duke, after all.

But no. Like it or not, he needed a wife.

He hunted down the young lady to whom he owed a dance and spent the next hour being shepherded from one marriageable miss to another until he struggled to recall which of them was which.

He wasn't good at meeting new people. Especially not when he was so overwhelmed already.

His shoulders sagged with relief when Longley finally agreed he'd had enough, and they said their goodbyes and summoned the carriage. They sauntered down the front stairs, and Vaughan shivered, shoving his hands into his pockets to ward off the chill from the cool wind.

After a few minutes, the carriage trundled into position in front of the house, and the footman held the door open while they entered. The dark interior wasn't much warmer than outside, but at least they were sheltered from the blasted wind.

"So?" Longley asked, rubbing his gloved fingers together.

Vaughan huffed. "Give me a minute to recover."

They lurched into motion, and Vaughan laid his hand against the polished wood of the wall to steady himself.

"I forget, sometimes, how tedious you find social outings," Longley said.

Vaughan rubbed his throbbing temples. "That's because

we spend most of our time alone or at the club. These affairs are completely different." He sighed. "It's amazing that most of the ton aren't abed for days following every ball."

Longley shook his head. "Most of the ton aren't like you, my friend."

Vaughan didn't take the comment as an insult. He knew it wasn't intended as such. It was true. He was a homebody, preferring the company of horses and dogs to people.

They rode the rest of the way to Ashford House in silence. Vaughan gazed out of the window, allowing himself to decompress, grateful that Longley knew to give him space to gather his thoughts.

When they arrived, they were greeted by servants, who helped them disembark and guided them into the warmth of the house. Many large city homes could be cold, but Ashford House had been well-constructed and retained heat from the sun long after it had gone down.

By unspoken agreement, they headed down a hallway lit by a half dozen candles to Vaughan's office. He removed his coat as they entered and hung it from a hook near the door, then struck a match and lit the candles in a holder to his left.

They illuminated the space well enough for him to cross the room to the oak desk positioned in the center and light the candles in the brass stand along one side. In another month or so, the ornate marble fireplace behind the desk would remain in use most of the time, but for now, it was unnecessary.

"Brandy?" he asked Longley, who'd sat on the brown leather chair on the opposite side of the desk and crossed his legs.

"Please."

Vaughan went to the side table and poured brandy from the decanter into two crystal glasses, then passed one to Longley and took the other around the back of the desk. He sank into the cushioned seat with a sigh of relief.

"You look like you need that." Longley gestured toward the brandy.

Vaughan tipped the glass back and sipped, enjoying the burn down his throat. "Badly."

"Are you sure you wish to take a bride this season?" Longley asked. "There will be many more evenings like this one, and no one would blame you if you wanted to put it off."

Vaughan tossed back the remainder of the brandy in his glass, then closed his eyes and briefly allowed himself to indulge in the fantasy of doing exactly that. He opened his eyes, got up, and refilled his glass.

"There's no sense in delaying." Doing so wouldn't magically make him more amenable to social outings or quell his lack of desire to actually have a wife.

Longley held out his glass, and Vaughan filled it, then returned the decanter to the side table. "In that case, did any of tonight's candidates interest you?"

An image of the second Carlisle chit's dark eyes and full lips flashed through his mind, but he banished the vision as quickly as it arrived.

"I imagine any one of them would make a fine duchess," he said honestly. All of the girls he'd danced with had been well-spoken, attractive, and from good families. "Am I correct in assuming that Lady Violet Carlisle is likely to be the most sought-after bride on the market this year?"

Longley nodded. "I really do think she would be perfect for you, Ashford. I don't believe she would expect much of you, other than for you to keep her in the manner to which she is accustomed. She is an excellent foil for you. Quite the social butterfly. She seems to have a good head on her shoulders, and I'm sure her mother has trained her in what it takes to manage a large household."

Vaughan swirled his brandy. "Are you sure I should marry her? It sounds as if you'd quite like to."

Longley scoffed. "I don't intend to shackle myself to any female in the near future."

Vaughan raised the drink to his lips and drank again, a sense of calmness already stealing over him. "Is there a reason why you introduced me to Lady Violet rather than her sister?" he asked. "I assume they are equally eligible."

"Lady Emma?" Longley gazed into his amber-colored drink. "On the surface, she and Violet may appear similar—although Violet is obviously more beautiful."

Vaughan pursed his lips. He could see why Longley would say that, but he didn't necessarily agree.

"Emma is quieter. More reserved. If not for Violet, she would be considered a wallflower. She is not someone who would cover for you so well in social settings." He hesitated, then added, "I have also heard a rumor."

Vaughan leaned forward, intrigued. "What kind of rumor?"

"That she"—Longley lowered his voice—"intends to marry for love."

"Oh." Vaughan sat back, a shudder running through him at the thought. His father had married for love, and it had turned out abominably. "Then she's obviously out of the question. I will call on Lady Violet tomorrow."

"Good." Longley raised his glass. "Let's toast to your future bride."

Vaughan grinned. "And to Cousin Reggie never setting foot on Ashford land."

Longley stayed a while longer. After he left, Vaughan rested his elbows on his desk, his chin on his palms, and closed his eyes.

A memory overtook him.

"Mother?" Vaughan crept into the duchess's bedchamber, drawn by the sound of her giggles.

The giggles stopped abruptly, and someone made a shushing noise.

15

Vaughan tiptoed further into the room, squinting in the dimness. Only a single candle burned on the nightstand.

"Yes, darling?" Her voice was terse. Impatient.

"I can't sleep." As his eyes adjusted, he could make out the shape of her in the bed. But she wasn't alone. "Is that father?"

He'd thought his father was visiting one of their country properties.

"It's no one," she replied. But then a face appeared above the blankets. One that was decidedly not his father's. "Go back to bed. You're a big boy now. You shouldn't need cuddles to sleep."

Vaughan opened his eyes, shame burning through him. That may have been the first time he'd known his mother to flout her marriage vows, but it certainly hadn't been the last. And his besotted father hadn't done a thing about it.

He'd said he loved her, but Vaughan knew better. Love was a fallacy. One he'd never fall victim to.

∾

"Turn around, my lady."

Emma did as her maid requested, presenting her back so Daisy could make quick work of her buttons. She'd already unlaced the front of Emma's gown, and Emma was more than ready to be free of it so she could collapse into bed. She was exhausted after another night of watching Violet be the belle of the ball.

"Emma!" Violet breezed into the room, clad in her night-gown but with her hair still curled and styled. "Tonight was such a dream. Can you believe it?"

Her smile was filled with so much joy that Emma half expected her to float away from sheer happiness.

"I danced with a duke." She spun in a circle, her hands clasped in front of her chest, before dropping onto the edge of Emma's bed.

"And two viscounts, an earl, and a man richer than them

all," Emma pointed out. The Duke of Ashford was impressive, but Violet's night would have been a raging success even without him. He was simply the brightest feather in her plume.

Daisy slid the gown down Emma's shoulders, and she stepped out of it, then removed her underthings and accepted the maid's help in putting on her nightgown.

"A duke," Violet exclaimed, grinning at the ceiling as if she'd gone quite mad. "Even in my wildest fantasies, I never imagined I'd become a duchess."

Emma sat in front of her mirror and allowed Daisy to remove the pins from her hair.

"I don't know why you're so surprised," Emma said as Daisy began to brush the thick mass of her hair with soothing strokes. "You're beautiful, you have a good dowry, and you are the daughter of an earl. It makes perfect sense that the duke would be interested in you."

She shivered, recalling how cool the duke's eyes had been. How unfriendly.

"Are you cold, my lady?" Daisy asked.

"Only a little," Emma replied rather than admit the truth. "Don't worry, I shall be in bed soon."

"So you shall." Daisy narrowed her dark eyes at Violet in the mirror. Violet didn't notice, but Emma did. For some reason, her maid had never warmed to Violet, although she was fiercely loyal to Emma, ensuring she was kept apprised of everything that happened in the house—something her family often forgot to do.

"Perhaps you'd be warmer if you'd danced more often," Violet said. "Is there a reason you did not?"

Emma clenched her teeth so as not to point out the obvious. Violet was the reason she hadn't been asked to dance, since any woman standing near her was rendered invisible to the male eye.

"I wasn't asked," she said simply.

"Hmm." Violet did not say more.

"All done, my lady," Daisy said, placing her hairbrush on the dresser. "As beautiful as ever."

Emma turned and smiled at her. "Thank you, Daisy. You may be excused for the night."

"Wait." Violet sat up. "Can you undo my hair, please, Daisy? I dismissed Jane earlier because I was eager to talk with Emma."

"Of course, my lady."

Emma stood and changed places with Violet. While Daisy began working out the tight curls, Violet met Emma's gaze in the mirror.

"If I become a duchess, it will be the talk of the town." She winced as the brush snagged in a knot. "Do you think the duke is very handsome?"

Entirely too much so.

But not the sort of handsome that was meant for Emma.

"He is," Emma said. "But he seemed too cold to me."

Violet cocked her head, scowling when Daisy repositioned her. "How do you mean?"

Emma shrugged. "Just that I got the impression he would be a difficult person to know."

Violet's eyes lit up. "A challenge. My favorite thing."

Emma forced herself to smile and tried to forget the flare of interest she'd felt when the duke had looked at her. Really looked at her, as few people did.

It's useless, she told herself. *He wants Violet.*

Violet delicately cleared her throat. "You know, you could make a good match too, if you tried a little harder. Maybe not a duke, but you could snare a title. I'm certain of it."

Despite the backhanded compliment, Emma laughed. "I do not wish to snare a title. I want love."

Violet pulled a face. "But why? With money and a title, everyone in the ton would respect you. You would be invited everywhere, and you could afford whatever gowns and trinkets you wanted. Or," she added, perhaps sensing how futile that argument was, "all the books you could dream of."

"A never-ending supply of books would be nice," Emma acknowledged. "But not nice enough to change my mind."

Daisy finished with Violet's hair, and Violet bounced over to the bed and joined Emma.

"Good night, Daisy," Emma said as the maid smoothed her skirts and left.

"Good night, my lady."

"Explain it to me," Violet said after the door closed. "Help me to understand why you want love over status."

Emma slipped beneath the covers. "I just...." She tried to figure out how to put her desire into words. "I want someone who cares for me. Someone good and kind to whom I mean more than a healthy dowry or a pretty face who can play hostess. I want someone who likes and respects me."

She pulled the blankets up and imagined her perfect suitor. "I want to feel butterflies in my stomach when I see him and for him to always kiss me before he leaves the house. I want endearments, sweet touches, and private jokes." She sighed. Really, it boiled down to one thing. "I want to be the most important person in someone's world."

Violet gazed at her with an open mouth, and for a moment, Emma thought she might have gotten through to her, but then her sister flashed a mischievous smile.

"Then I will marry my duke, and you can marry your doting pauper," she said. "We shall see who is happier."

Violet made her way to the door and hovered in the doorway. "A piece of advice, though? You won't find any match—love or otherwise—unless you put more effort into your appearance and manners." She scrunched her nose. "I know you can be charming, and you are quite pretty when you try."

Emma's mouth was dry. Fortunately, Violet left, because Emma didn't know what she'd have said otherwise.

The thing was, Violet wasn't wrong.

But if Emma gave her all to finding a potential husband and failed, she didn't know how she'd handle the rejection. At least for now, she could pretend that men might notice her if she tried her hardest.

If she showed her best self to someone and they rejected her, she'd be crushed.

CHAPTER 3

EMMA GAZED AT THE THREE NEW DAY DRESSES SHE'D YET TO wear and ran her finger along the soft fabric of the pale blue one.

"What do you think of this?" she asked Daisy.

The maid cocked her head, her dark bun bobbing as she studied Emma and then the dress. "It will look very fetching with your eyes, my lady."

"Do you think it may garner me a suitor?" After her conversation with Violet last night, Emma had come around to the idea that in order to attract a potential husband, she should at least put in more effort than she had been.

"Yes, indeed." Daisy glanced around, then spoke quietly. "If I may be so bold, it is a wonder you don't already have suitors lining up around the block. The gentlemen of London must be dim-witted."

Warmth filled Emma's chest, and she barely resisted the urge to hug Daisy. "Thank you." She blinked rapidly as emotion threatened to spill from her eyes. "That is most kind of you."

Daisy's eyes crinkled at the corners. "Just calling it how I see it, my lady. Come along, let's get you into this dress."

Emma donned her petticoats and thanked her lucky stars that she would not have to be stuffed into a corset this morning. Daisy took the dress from the hanger and positioned it so that Emma could step inside, then she lifted it into place. The fabric whispered over Emma's skin, and she allowed herself to check her reflection as Daisy began fastening the row of buttons on the back.

She smoothed her hands over the skirt, admiring the color, which was similar to the bedchamber's wallpaper. The same blue as a bird's egg, but while the wallpaper was threaded with gold, the dress was trimmed in white.

"How would you like your hair?" Daisy asked, finishing the buttons and then ushering her into the chair in front of the mirror.

"Perhaps something similar to the way Violet usually wears hers," Emma suggested. Her own taste was simpler, but hadn't she learned that men preferred the extravagant?

Daisy scrunched her nose. "You know you don't have to look like Lady Violet to find a suitor. You're beautiful, my lady."

"And you are biased," Emma retorted. Many ladies would not allow their maids to address them so impertinently, but she and Daisy were of a similar age, and she liked to think they had a friendship of a sort. At least, as much as one could be friends with their staff.

Daisy brushed Emma's hair, and she closed her eyes, enjoying the gentle ministrations. "No curls," Daisy said. "We don't have time. But perhaps we could pin it like this."

She gathered the hair to show Emma what she meant.

"That looks nice." Emma's stomach grumbled, and her cheeks heated with embarrassment. She hadn't had the chance to eat yet, and she was hungry.

As per Lady Carlisle's decree, looking pretty for their callers was top priority the morning after a ball. Emma could eat once Daisy had finished with her hair. If she had time.

She bit her lip when Daisy accidentally pulled too hard.

"Sorry, my lady."

"It's all right, Daisy."

Emma clasped her fingers together, nerves rioting in her gut. Even if their callers came to see Violet, perhaps one of them would be blown away by the sight of her in this dress. If even one man came for her, she would be happy, but she was scared to hope.

Footsteps padded down the hallway, and Violet whisked into the room, bringing the scent of lavender with her. When her gaze landed on Emma, she stopped abruptly and clapped, a smile spreading across her face.

"You took my advice to heart," she said. "You look lovely, sister, and I'm sure I won't be the only one to notice it."

Emma smiled. "Thank you. Your dress suits you well."

Violet took the compliment as her due and swept over to look out the window. "Who do you suppose will be the first caller?"

Emma pursed her lips. "I'm not sure."

"Imagine if it's the duke." Violet moved away from the window. "What a coup."

Daisy put the last hairpin into place, and Emma watched in the reflection as she examined her hair.

"Very nice," Violet said, and for once, Daisy smiled in her presence. "Let's go to the drawing room. Mother will want to speak to us before the suitors arrive."

Emma stood and linked her arm with Violet's. Their shoulders bumped together as they made their way along the hall, down the grand staircase, and around a corner into the drawing room that Lady Carlisle used to receive guests.

Their mother looked up from her needlepoint to greet them. "Good morning, girls." Her skirt pooled around her, a shade somewhere between pink and orange. She patted the cushion that was nearest to the empty fireplace, indicating for them to join her.

Violet did so immediately, but Emma's attention was caught by the scent of freshly baked scones. She started toward the small refreshments table in the opposite direction, only to stop when Lady Carlisle tutted.

"Emma, leave those scones alone," she said.

Emma eyed the scones longingly. They were smothered with jam and topped off with clotted cream. Her mouth watered, and her stomach gurgled again.

"But Mother—"

"But nothing," Lady Carlisle interrupted. "You cannot greet suitors with a mouth full of scone. God forbid you scatter crumbs all over your dress."

Emma pouted and turned to face her mother. "I haven't eaten yet."

Lady Carlisle shrugged unapologetically. "You should have risen earlier, then."

"Fine." Emma huffed and lowered herself onto the chaise opposite Violet and Lady Carlisle. The silvery-blue seats were stunning to look at but decidedly less comfortable. "Will Sophie be joining us?"

The door burst open, and the youngest Carlisle sister hurried in, her cheeks flushed and her ginger hair bouncing around her face.

"Did someone mention my name?" she asked.

"I was just asking whether you'd be sitting with us," Emma said.

"I would be delighted." Sophie headed straight for the scones, and when she took one, their mother did not scold her. Of course, Sophie wasn't out in society yet, so Lady Carlisle was not trying to find a husband for her. Sophie was only fifteen. Much too young for that.

"Is it true that you danced with a duke last night?" Sophie asked Violet breathlessly.

"It is," Violet said. "He was most adept, although not as skilled as Mr. Bently."

24

"However, Ashford is a duke, and Bently is a mere mister," Lady Carlisle said. "His talent for dancing is far less relevant than his title, wouldn't you say?"

Violet lowered her head. "Of course, Mother."

A knock at the door announced the butler's arrival. He cleared his throat. "Viscount Tredwell and Mr. Bently are here to call on Lady Violet."

Lady Carlisle waved her hand imperiously. "Show them in." She turned to Sophie. "Make yourself useful, dear."

Sophie glanced at Emma, and her expression clearly said she wanted to stay with them and eavesdrop on the conversations, but she knew her role, so she crossed the room to the pianoforte and flipped through the pages of music. A moment later, she began playing a gentle melody.

"Lady Carlisle," the butler intoned, having returned with their guests. "May I present Viscount Tredwell and Mr. Bently."

"Thank you, Samuels."

The butler excused himself and closed the door.

Viscount Tredwell parted his lips in a slightly frightening display of teeth. He had a lot of them—and large gums as well.

"Lady Violet, these are for you." He offered her a bouquet. As he drew near, the scent of lilies hit Emma, overpoweringly sweet. Her nose twitched.

Do not sneeze.

"Thank you, Lord Tredwell," Violet said, rising to accept the flowers. "They're lovely."

"Not as lovely as you," he said.

Emma and Sophie exchanged unimpressed glances, but their mother cooed, and Violet seemed pleased.

"I bought you violets." Mr. Bently sounded entirely too smug as he passed them to her. "Violets for the most beautiful Violet of them all."

It was a good thing Mr. Bently was so handsome, because

25

he wasn't terribly original. Emma had lost count of how many gentlemen had brought the tiny purple flowers for her sister. She wouldn't be surprised if Violet was single-handedly responsible for a resurgence in their popularity.

While Mr. Bently was making cow eyes at Violet, Viscount Tredwell claimed the seat beside Emma, filling the chaise so that his competitor had no choice but to drag over a seat from the refreshments table.

Emma smiled at Viscount Tredwell. "Are you well, Lord Tredwell?"

He nodded distractedly. "Quite."

She tried again. "I've heard your stables are strong this year."

Viscount Tredwell bred racehorses.

"They are." Apparently, even broaching one of his favorite topics could not tear his attention from Violet, who had sat opposite them and was arranging her skirts just so.

Emma bit her lip. All right, so Viscount Tredwell was unlikely to transfer his affections from Violet to her. Perhaps one of the others would.

An hour later, her spirits were lower than the floorboards. Plenty of suitors had visited Violet, and only one of them had responded to Emma's attempts to engage him in conversation—and promptly began questioning her about her sister.

She gritted her teeth and glanced at the clock, wondering when she could escape with a book. Her pride could only take so much rejection. Surely one gentleman in all of London might look past Violet's bright light to see the subtler glow of Emma's.

Samuels stepped into the room. Everyone quietened, waiting to see who their latest caller was.

"The Duke of Ashford."

～

Vaughan had known he wouldn't be the only man calling on Lady Violet Carlisle this morning, but he hadn't anticipated such an audience. He opened his mouth, then promptly closed it. There was no way he could be smooth and flirtatious in front of this many people.

He stepped into the drawing room, surveying the assembled guests—noting a girl behind the piano who must be a younger sister of the Carlisle twins and his future bride on a chaise beside her mother.

Across from them, Lady Emma appeared to be trying to vanish into the furniture while a man a few years older than Vaughan sat beside her, staring intently at Violet.

Jolting into action, Vaughan forced his feet to cross the distance between himself and the chaise, where he presented Lady Violet with his bouquet. He had no idea what the flowers were, but they were pink and the most expensive ones the florist had on offer.

"They're beautiful," she exclaimed. "Thank you, Your Grace."

He inclined his head in acknowledgement and tried to find his voice. "May I have the honor of accompanying you for a walk in Hyde Park?"

It was a spur-of-the-moment idea, but quite a good one. With no one else to worry about, he'd be better able to woo her.

Lady Violet bit her lower lip. She glanced at her mother, who was visibly torn. It was only then that Vaughan realized he'd probably committed a faux pas in issuing the invitation. If she accepted, it would mean asking her other callers to leave. Blast. This was why he liked to have Longley around to smooth things over. He was too apt to mess it up on his own.

Still, he didn't rescind the invitation, and he saw the moment when Lady Carlisle decided that the opportunity to snare a duke as a son-in-law outweighed the risk of offending everyone else.

"What do you think, Violet?" she asked her daughter. "The weather is amenable, is it not?"

"It is." Violet bestowed a smile upon him, and several of the other men glared daggers. "Perhaps we could receive guests tomorrow as well, for anyone whose visit today has been cut short?"

Lady Carlisle's face softened with relief. "Wonderful suggestion, my dear."

A man standing near Lady Violet's shoulder protested his dismissal. "This is hardly the done thing."

"I'm sorry, gentlemen," Lady Carlisle said. "You're more than welcome to return tomorrow." Her intense blue gaze, more faded than her daughter's, landed on Vaughan. "Lady Emma will accompany you as a chaperone."

On the chaise, Lady Emma blanched. She grabbed a handful of her skirt, and her gaze darted sideways. He could have sworn it lingered briefly on the refreshments table.

The butler ushered the men out, and the girl at the piano stopped playing. She watched Vaughan out of the corner of her eye as she joined the other women and exchanged a few words with Lady Emma. When the girl left the room, only Vaughan, Emma, Violet, and Lady Carlisle remained.

"I must get my pelisse," Violet said, rising to her feet. "I will be down momentarily."

"As will I." Lady Emma's voice was a pleasingly soft timbre.

While the twins were gone, Vaughan made awkward small talk about the weather with Lady Carlisle. Relief bloomed in his gut when they returned.

"My carriage is parked out front," he said.

"Wonderful," Violet said. They left the room together.

Violet fell into step with Vaughan.

"Do you enjoy walking?" he asked, hoping to establish some common ground.

"Only in parks," Violet replied. "I confess, I am not fond of the outdoors."

Vaughan's mouth twitched, and he forced himself not to grimace. The outdoors wasn't for everyone. It didn't matter if he preferred to ride his horse across wide open spaces to dancing in a Mayfair ballroom. After all, he didn't intend to share a life with his wife.

The butler opened the main door and held it while they exited. As he'd hoped, his carriage was parked a short distance away, his coachman still in place. When he saw Vaughan, he urged the horses into motion and stopped in front of them.

"Oh, what a lovely carriage," Violet exclaimed.

"Thank you." Vaughan didn't think it was much different from any other carriage, but if Violet liked it, so much the better.

The footman opened the sleek back door, and Vaughan assisted Violet into the carriage. Emma stepped up behind her, and something fizzed through him as she laid her gloved hand on his to steady herself as she followed her sister.

Vaughan swallowed and told himself not to be silly. The touch had been feather soft. It was ridiculous for it to affect him so.

Nevertheless, he'd have to steer clear of Lady Emma.

He climbed inside and sat stiffly on one of the padded leather seats while the footman closed the door and took up his position on the rear of the carriage. Lady Carlisle waved from where she stood outside the house, and her daughters waved back.

The drive to Hyde Park was mercifully brief, but he and Violet quickly exhausted their supply of conversation about the weather and current events—although that wasn't saying much, since her grasp of current events was based around who was courting whom rather than politics or economics, the topics he cared for.

The carriage pulled up outside one of the park's entrances, and they disembarked. Vaughan offered Violet his arm, and dimples popped up in her cheeks as she took it. He escorted her to the path into the park, which was already busy.

Several courting couples strolled arm in arm near the stream, while clusters of women stood about, talking. Birds sang in the trees, and the air was fresher here than in the more urban parts of the city. Vaughan inhaled deeply, a dull ache in his chest. He rubbed it, wishing he could be in the country, with no one around for miles.

"Do you enjoy games, Your Grace?" Violet asked as they wandered along the path. People watched them, and she seemed to bask in the attention, lighting up and holding her shoulders straighter.

Meanwhile, Vaughan wanted to slink off somewhere private so none of them could see him. Unfortunately, he wasn't in the mood for a scandal today. Instead, he kept pace with her, trying not to notice her sister, who followed a few yards behind. Close enough to hear their conversation, but not close enough to be a part of it.

"What sort of games?" he asked.

An uncomfortable lump formed in the back of his throat. Poor Lady Emma. Forced to accompany them and to watch her sister become the toast of London. Vaughan could be wrong, but he doubted any of those callers this morning had been for Emma. They'd all been far too attentive to Violet, the more conventionally attractive of the two.

"How about pall-mall or lawn bowls?" Violet replied.

"Both are enjoyable," he said.

"Do you have horses?" she asked.

"I do." The tightness in his chest eased. Finally, something he could talk about. "My personal horse, Thunder, is a gorgeous black gelding."

"Is he in London?" she asked, her forehead smoothing. Perhaps she was as relieved to find a topic of conversation as he was.

"No, he stayed in Norfolk. The groom is taking care of him while I'm gone."

"Oh."

"I have other horses," he said, knowing this was something he could happily talk about for hours. He started giving her a summation, but after a few moments, he realized her eyes had glazed over, and she was nodding absently but not really paying attention.

Damn it.

He'd bored her.

"Ashford!"

He looked around at the call and spotted Longley striding toward them across the grass. Longley doffed his hat as he approached and inclined his head to the ladies, who both dropped into curtseys.

"Lady Violet, Lady Emma, what lovely visions you are today." He flashed his teeth at them.

Vaughan's eyes narrowed. This was absolutely not a coincidence.

Violet's dimples made an appearance again. She was clearly glad of the interruption.

"Good morning, Lord Longley," she said.

He returned his hat to his head.

"Good morning," Emma murmured from behind them.

"Lady Emma." Longley directed the full force of his smile at the unsuspecting woman.

Vaughan scowled. What was his friend about?

"Walk with me," Longley said. "It's been too long since we spoke."

"But…" Emma sounded bewildered.

He winked. "We'll stay close behind Ashford and Lady Violet to ensure your sister's virtue remains intact."

"All right, then." Her tone had warmed considerably.

"By all means, join us," Vaughan muttered, not that anyone had asked him.

Longley gave him a meaningful look and passed them to join arms with Emma. Vaughan suspected his friend was trying to allow him time alone with Violet to improve upon their acquaintance, but that was the opposite of what he needed.

Violet gently brushed his arm, indicating for him to resume their stroll. Vaughan did so, but his mind remained woefully blank. How was he supposed to charm the woman when he could hardly think of anything to say to her?

Behind them, Emma laughed, low and husky. His gut tightened. What had Longley said to make her laugh? She'd been completely silent until now.

Of course she was silent. She was the chaperone.

His subconscious didn't care for logic. It was strangely upsetting that someone else had broken through Lady Emma's reserve when he hadn't.

He glanced over his shoulder. Longley's and Emma's heads were close together, and they were both smiling. Vaughan's lips pressed into a firm line. Perhaps he and Violet weren't the ones who needed a chaperone. Was Longley flirting with Emma?

"Shall we get ice cream?" he asked, loud enough for them all to hear.

"Oh, I couldn't." Violet touched her chest. "I must be careful of my waistline."

Vaughan frowned. There was nothing wrong with her waistline. He could hardly say so, though. It wouldn't be appropriate to comment on her figure.

"I would love an ice cream," Emma said.

When Vaughan turned to face her, her tongue darted over her upper lip. He stared, entranced, until Longley cleared his throat.

Don't lust after your future sister-in-law, he berated himself. *You can't have her.*

CHAPTER 4

"THANK YOU SO MUCH FOR AGREEING TO COME WITH ME," Emma said to Violet as she rolled on a long white glove.

Violet patted her shoulder. "What are sisters for if not to provide support while husband hunting?"

"I hope you won't be too bored." Emma enjoyed poetry, so she'd be happy at a poetry reading, but Violet usually preferred parties and balls.

"Nonsense." Violet touched one of her curls, which was perfectly positioned, as always. "I'm expanding my horizons. Who knows what manner of gentlemen may attend a poetry reading whom I might not otherwise meet?"

"I guess we shall find out." Emma knew at least one of the gentlemen who'd be attending. Mr. Mayhew was the respectable second son of a viscount, with a fondness for poems by Lord Byron.

She had met him at the opera, but they'd only been able to speak for a few moments. She hoped she'd be able to get more time with him today. He was exactly the type of man she could imagine herself falling for, and quieter events such as the one today provided more of an opportunity for her to shine.

Hopefully he liked what he saw.

"Is that another new dress?" Violet asked as they walked down the corridor together and into the foyer inside the entrance of Carlisle House. Violet's maid was waiting, and she bobbed a swift curtsey as they arrived.

Emma ran her hand over the supple pink fabric. "It is."

Violet studied her critically. "It isn't terrible, although it could be cut a little lower and fitted more tightly."

"I like it as it is." Emma didn't intend to attract a husband with her body. She knew she wasn't unattractive, but she was also no great beauty. Besides, she'd prefer to find a man who saw beyond appearances.

"Suit yourself."

The main doors opened, revealing the carriage waiting outside. The sisters walked down the stairs together and accepted the footman's help inside. Violet sat looking forward, as she always did, while Emma's back was to the coachman. Violet's maid sat beside her.

"What is your plan to beguile Mr. Mayhew?" Violet asked, placing her hands neatly on her lap.

The carriage bumped over a rough section of road, jolting them all.

"I'll talk to him and find out whether I feel a connection," Emma said. "I already know he's handsome, but attraction isn't everything. I want to know whether it goes deeper. I want to come alight when I'm near him. To feel everything."

Violet sighed. "That does sound lovely." Her tone was surprisingly wistful. "Do you think a reaction like that is instantaneous, or can it grow over time?"

"I don't know." Emma glanced out the window, watching the street roll out behind them.

"I hope it can grow." Violet spoke so softly that Emma almost didn't hear her.

When they arrived at the townhouse owned by Lord Mayhew—Mr. Mayhew's father—the reading was almost about to start. They hurried up the stone stairs, and the butler showed them around the corner and into the largest drawing room.

Lord and Lady Mayhew stood just inside the door.

"Welcome," Lady Mayhew said, a smile sweeping across her pretty face. "You're just in time."

"Thank you for the invitation," Emma said. "We're looking forward to the reading."

Lord Mayhew harrumphed. "You'd be one of the few."

"Shush, Nigel," Lady Mayhew chided him. "Please take your seats, ladies."

The array of chairs was about half full. The front row appeared to be reserved for those involved in the reading. Unmarried misses filled the second row. No doubt they'd had the same idea as Emma. She and Violet claimed a pair of seats in the third row on the nearest side of the room while the maid stood near the wall.

Mr. Mayhew turned in his chair and smiled at Emma, his warm brown eyes twinkling—in pleasure at the thought of her company? She hoped so. His gaze traveled to Violet, and one of his eyebrows rose. Emma's answering expression contained more than a hint of amusement. She was as surprised by her sister's presence as he was.

Mr. Mayhew rose. "Welcome, all. Thank you for coming to our poetry reading. Today, we have a selection for you from Lord Byron. I will begin and then introduce you to our next speaker."

Without further ado, he broke into a recital of "She Walks in Beauty," one of Lord Byron's most iconic poems. His voice was rich and dripped with emotion.

Emma leaned forward, enthralled. He spoke with such passion, and she could imagine him bringing that same passion to his marriage. If he loved a woman, he would love her with his whole heart. She was certain of it.

And oh, she so badly wanted to be that woman. What would it be like to be the subject of such devotion?

To her left, the door clicked open and gently closed again. Emma didn't look around to see who had arrived late, too preoccupied with the gentleman pouring his heart out for them all to see.

When Mr. Mayhew finished, he bowed jauntily. She clapped, wishing there was more she could do to show her admiration. His gaze landed on her, and he winked.

She melted inside. Surely that reading must have been meant for her.

Another gentleman took Mr. Mayhew's place and read from a book. He spoke well, but he didn't have the same depth of feeling that Mr. Mayhew did, nor had he memorized the words. Still, Emma enjoyed the remainder of the reading. It ended too soon for her liking.

She stood, hoping to get to Mr. Mayhew before any of his other admirers did, only to be intercepted by an acquaintance. While she made small talk, she noticed that Violet had joined Mr. Mayhew, and they were conversing animatedly.

Emma relaxed a little, confident that no other debutantes would try to compete with Violet for his attention. Even at this very second, Violet might be telling him what a good match he and Emma would make.

As soon as they'd finished conversing, she forged her way through the guests toward Violet and Mr. Mayhew. When she drew near, Mr. Mayhew's pleasing voice reached her ears.

"I was thinking of you," he said.

Emma looked up, expecting to find him gazing at her, but he was focused on Violet.

"Whatever do you mean?" Violet asked.

He angled himself toward her. "While I read the poem, I was imagining that she was you. You are the perfect muse."

What?

No. It couldn't be. Emma must have misheard. Mr. Mayhew wasn't interested in Violet; he was interested in her. He'd extended the invitation to her.

"A muse?" Violet sounded intrigued. How could that be? She wasn't any more interested in Mr. Mayhew than he was in her.

"A source of inspiration," Mr. Mayhew said, clearly assuming that Violet did not know what a muse was. "Beautiful. Charming." He lowered his voice, his tone becoming far too familiar. "Captivating."

Emma froze. Someone bumped into her from behind and cursed her clumsiness, but she hardly noticed, too preoccupied with the fact that Mr. Mayhew was flirting with Violet.

The back of her throat burned, and she quickly turned away so he wouldn't see her staring. She waited for Violet to dismiss his remark or redirect his attention to Emma, but instead she just giggled.

"You find me captivating?" she asked breathlessly.

"You are captivating," Mr. Mayhew said. "It is an empirical fact."

"Oh, my."

Something cracked inside Emma. Mr. Mayhew was supposed to be hers. She'd told Violet she was interested in him. She'd found him first. All she wanted was one man who'd see something in her that exceeded what they saw in Violet.

Just one.

Surely that wasn't asking for too much?

Tears pricked in her eyes, and she swiped at them furiously. She would not cry. Not here.

She skirted a group of women speaking with one of the men who'd done a reading and darted through the door leading into the corridor. Glancing around, she spotted a door just across the hall that was ajar and hurried through it, gulping mouthfuls of air.

She just needed a moment of privacy to get her emotions under control. But how could she face Violet after this?

～

"MR. MAYHEW READ WELL," VAUGHAN SAID TO LORD Mayhew, with whom he'd been speaking in the rear of the room while he waited for Violet to notice his presence.

He hadn't told her he'd be in attendance, but when he'd heard she'd be present, it had seemed a good opportunity to solidify their connection. Assuming she even realized he was there. She seemed quite preoccupied with another man.

"He did," Mayhew agreed. "He's always been more interested in the arts than business." Mayhew was an astute businessman, and his older son took after him, while his younger son clearly didn't.

Vaughan bared his teeth in an approximation of a smile. It was difficult to summon anything more genuine when he had a first-row seat to watch the woman he intended to marry flirt with another man.

"At least you have James," he said.

"I suppose there's that," Mayhew agreed.

Vaughan's gaze was still locked on Violet and the younger Mr. Mayhew, and he reminded himself that he didn't have any feelings for Violet, nor had he an official claim on her.

He didn't intend to develop romantic feelings for her, now or ever. Watching his mother cuckold his father time after time had put him off the concept of love. Seeing her flutter her eyelashes at another man stung, though.

This is exactly why you're choosing a convenient bride. If she isn't attached to you, so much the better, as long as you aren't attached to her either.

A flurry of movement caught Vaughan's attention. Lady Emma Carlisle had come to an abrupt stop halfway across the room. She raised her hand to her mouth, focused on

Violet and Mr. Mayhew. She seemed to freeze for a long moment, and then she spun around and rushed out of the room.

"I wonder what that was about," Mayhew said.

Vaughan had a suspicion he knew. Emma was probably interested in Mr. Mayhew for herself.

Mayhew cleared his throat. "I'd better circulate, or my wife will tell me I'm not doing my duties. Good to see you, Ashford."

"You as well." Vaughan nodded respectfully and lingered in place while Mayhew moved on.

Minutes passed, and Emma hadn't returned. Vaughan noticed Violet's maid, who must have accompanied them, standing by the side wall, deep in conversation with another maid. She seemed oblivious to her charge's absence.

Before he'd fully thought out his actions, he found himself following Emma out of the room. The corridor was empty, but a muffled noise came from Viscount Mayhew's office. His feet carried him across, and he knocked gently on the door.

The noise abruptly cut off.

"Hello," he murmured, unsure what on earth he was doing. One didn't follow unmarried ladies into private rooms. He should turn and leave immediately. Yet he couldn't bring himself to do so. Not when he was so sure that Emma was in there, and she was upset.

"I'm coming in," he said, just in case he'd read the situation wrong and was about to interrupt an illicit rendezvous.

He eased the door open and stepped in. The faint scent of cigar smoke greeted him. Lady Emma sat on a chair in the corner, her shoulders slumped and her dark blue eyes gleaming with moisture. Her eyebrows—a shade somewhere between blonde and brown—scrunched together.

"Your Grace." She sounded confused. "What are you doing here?"

A good question, and one he didn't have an answer for.

He stood stiffly in the doorway, debating whether to come in properly and close the door, or if that was just asking for trouble.

"I came to check whether you are all right. You seemed distressed when you left."

"Oh." She sniffed and folded the handkerchief, tucking it into a pocket in the folds of her skirt. "That's very considerate of you, but I am fine."

He drew in a slow breath, wishing he knew how one was supposed to handle a situation such as this.

Delicately, he supposed.

"With all due respect, you don't look fine."

He winced. Probably not like that.

She scowled, the sadness in her eyes heating into something else. Something angrier. "Do you make a habit of telling young women that they don't look well, my lord?" Her cheeks flushed, and she clapped her hand to her mouth. "My apologies. I don't know what came over me."

Vaughan stared at her, shocked into silence. If he'd believed Lady Emma to be mousy, he'd been wrong. She may be more reserved than her sister, but she was not timid.

"Don't apologize. I phrased that poorly." He glanced around the room, seeking a way to escape this conversation, but none presented itself. "What happened to unsettle you?"

"Nothing." She stood, her purple skirts swishing around her ankles. "I won't keep you."

He didn't move from the doorway, so there was nowhere for her to go. They stood at an impasse.

"Allow me to guess?" he said.

She lowered her gaze, and thankfully, she no longer seemed on the verge of tears. "If you must."

"I theorize that the man you are interested in is more interested in your sister."

Her mouth dropped open, and she reacted as if he'd

slapped her. "How—" She cut herself off and folded her arms over her chest. "I am not interested in you, Lord Ashford."

"I know." His gut tightened, and he told himself it wasn't disappointment. If the rumors were to be believed and she indeed wanted love, then he was the last man for the job. Still, he moved closer and lightly touched her gloved forearm. The warmth of her body radiated through the fabric, and he was seized by the impulse to pull her closer.

He did not.

"I'm sorry," he said instead and removed his hand. The touch was fleeting, and yet it impacted every part of him.

"Thank you."

To his surprise, she seemed to mean it.

"Please let me pass." Her voice was low. "If someone comes upon us, neither of us will enjoy the results."

She was probably right, but he couldn't bring himself to move. At least, not yet.

He glanced sideways, making sure they were alone. "Not all men will prefer Violet."

The loose curls bracketing Emma's face swayed as she tilted her head. A light had appeared in her eyes, and it made him nervous. It was... hopeful. As if she thought perhaps he preferred her to Violet.

Damn. This wasn't at all what he'd intended.

"You're right," he said. "I should leave."

As he beat a hasty retreat, he caught a glimpse of her crumpled expression, and guilt lanced through him. He'd been trying to help, but it seemed he'd only made her more miserable.

CHAPTER 5

EMMA LAUGHED THROUGH GRITTED TEETH. THE DUKE HAD escaped so quickly that anyone would have thought the devil was on his heels, not a lonely Mayfair miss.

She'd read too much into his kindness, and now she'd scared him off. Hopefully there wouldn't be any long-term awkwardness if he decided he'd like to marry Violet, which seemed likely given his prior behavior.

She dabbed underneath her eyes and, finding the skin dry, stepped through the doorway and into the corridor. A cool breeze wafted through the air, and she shivered. Perhaps a door had been left open.

She wished she had a mirror in which she could check her reflection, but, lacking that, decided to brazen it out. She inhaled deeply and reentered the poetry reading. Several guests must have departed, because the room was emptier.

Emma surveyed the collected people, her gaze immediately landing on Violet, a blonde beacon among her darker-haired companions. She and Mr. Mayhew were no longer alone, thank goodness. The duke stood between them, and they had been joined by another gentleman.

You can do this.

Gathering the discarded scraps of her dignity, she crossed the room. Violet turned and stepped aside to invite Emma into their group, but she stayed back.

"My head is aching," Emma said softly enough that only Violet could hear. "I need to return home."

Violet's forehead creased with concern. "Is it bad?"

"Enough." It was hardly even a lie at this point.

"Then let us depart." Violet made their excuses and summoned her maid with an imperious wave.

They bid their hosts farewell and headed outside. Emma rubbed her temples as they waited for their carriage.

"You're very pale," Violet said.

"I can imagine." Emma's tone sounded as mournful as she felt.

Violet raised her chin as the carriage stopped in front of them, and then the footman leaped down to open the door. "You didn't speak to Mr. Mayhew before we left."

Emma waited for Violet to board the carriage and then followed.

"I wouldn't have made a good impression in my current state," Emma said.

The maid sat quietly beside her.

Violet sighed. "Well, there's always next time."

Emma's fingers curled into her skirts, her knuckles white as she battled not to lose her temper. It wasn't Violet's fault that men adored her, although it would be nice if she'd rebuffed the one man whom Emma had told her she wished to get to know better.

Part of her knew she wasn't being fair, but the rest of her screamed that life wasn't fair, and she just wanted one person to herself.

Very well, so maybe it wasn't going to be Mr. Mayhew or the duke, but surely one man out there would see her and think: that's my future wife.

They didn't speak as the carriage rumbled through the

neighborhood, returning them home. Violet eagerly watched people pass outside the window while Emma turned her thoughts inward.

At home, Samuels informed them that their mother was out shopping. Emma was grateful for that because it meant she could retreat to her bedroom without being questioned.

She curled up in the most comfortable chair in the house, which was hidden in the corner of her room, since her mother and Violet considered it ugly, and rested her head on a cushion. She considered taking a nap, but that would require changing her outfit, which was entirely more than she had energy for.

"Emma?"

She turned at Sophie's quiet voice. Her younger sister hovered in the doorway, one hand on the frame and the other on the door.

"Violet says you don't feel well," she said.

Emma groaned. "I don't."

Yet apparently she wasn't going to get the peace and quiet she'd hoped for. At least Sophie's company was the next best thing.

Sophie closed the door softly behind herself and padded into the room on stockinged feet. "What's really wrong?"

Emma's lips twisted. Trust Sophie to know there was more to the matter than she'd admitted to Violet. For her age, Sophie was remarkably perceptive.

Folding her legs with one over the other, Emma rearranged her skirt. She scooted sideways so Sophie could join her on the chair.

"The poetry recital didn't go how I wanted it to," Emma said as she sat. "It would seem that Mr. Mayhew has eyes for Violet rather than me."

She still didn't understand why he'd invited her to the recital if it was Violet he wanted, but perhaps he'd guessed that she'd invite her sister to accompany her.

The reason didn't matter anyway.

Sophie pulled a face. "Sometimes I'm pleased I don't have a twin."

"Sophie!" Emma exclaimed.

Sophie rolled her eyes. "I love Violet—you know I do—but I've seen how difficult her presence can make things for you."

Emma wrapped her arm around Sophie's shoulders. "It isn't intentional."

Violet would never mean to hurt her.

"That doesn't make it easier," Sophie said.

Emma didn't argue because she was right.

"Nor does it help that Violet is so oblivious," Sophie added. "She's very canny when it comes to men and to managing Mother, but there's a lot she doesn't notice."

Emma opened her mouth to reply but then stopped. Someone was walking in the hall. A moment later, Violet glided into view. She paused at the sight of them and arched one of her eyebrows.

"You two look cozy," she said. "Are you gossiping?"

Sophie tensed beside Emma. "It's nothing."

Emma stroked the back of Sophie's head, hoping to calm her. "Sophie had a question for me about Miss Austen's work. She and her governess have been reading *Mansfield Park*."

"That's right." The tautness dissipated from Sophie's muscles, and she relaxed against Emma.

"Where is Mansfield Park?" Violet asked, moving toward them so gracefully, Emma could have sworn she was floating. "Is that in Suffolk?"

Emma laughed. "No, Vi. It's a fictional place in a novel by Miss Jane Austen."

"Ah. A book." She said it with the same distaste she held for asparagus. "I have something more interesting to discuss."

She turned the chair in front of the mirror toward them and settled onto the seat.

"May I stay?" Sophie asked, since Violet sometimes preferred to dismiss her from what she considered to be more "adult" conversations.

Violet waved her hand breezily. "Yes, you may." She touched her hair, as if to check whether it was all in place. "I would like to discuss love."

"Love?" Emma repeated. She hadn't expected that. "But why?"

Violet shrugged. "Because it matters to you, and I'm intrigued by the concept."

Emma pursed her lips. "Just remember, I'm not an expert."

Her lack of gentleman callers proved that.

"But you believe in it," Violet said. "You want it."

"I do."

"I should also like to find love." Sophie sighed wistfully. "Preferably with a handsome foreign prince."

Emma's lips twitched, but she hid her amusement.

Violet leaned forward, her bright blue gaze even more intense than usual. "What do you think love feels like?"

Emma was so caught off guard that she gaped at her sister. "I-I cannot be certain. I haven't felt it."

"If you had to guess," Violet said.

Clasping her hands together, Emma tried to collect herself. "I would imagine that I'd feel giddy in his presence. That being with him would bring me joy. There is a quote by Miss Austen that you might appreciate." She cleared her throat. "'There could be no two hearts so open, no tastes so similar, no feelings so in unison.' That's what I believe love is. When two hearts are as one."

She thought Violet might tease her, especially for reciting a quote from a novel by heart. In the past, she certainly would have done so. But instead, Violet's eyes shone.

"That's beautiful," she said. "I—"

A hiss from the doorway cut her off. "Lady Emma."

All three Carlisle sisters turned toward Daisy, who blushed bright red.

"What is it, Daisy?" Emma asked.

"The Duke of Ashford is here," Daisy said. "He's asked to speak with Lord Carlisle."

Emma's heart sank. If there had been any doubt whether she'd imagined her brief moment of connection with the duke, it vanished.

His asking to meet with her father could mean only one thing: he'd come to request Violet's hand in marriage.

VAUGHAN PASSED A BOUQUET OF ROSES TO A FLUSTERED LADY Carlisle, who'd arrived on the doorstep of Carlisle House at the same time he did.

"Lady Carlisle," he said. "Can you make sure these are taken to Lady Violet? I need to speak with the earl in private."

"Of course." Lady Carlisle took the bouquet and blinked at him owlishly. "Lord Carlisle will be in his office. Would you like me to get him for you?"

Vaughan shook his head. "I can show myself in."

"Are you sure?" Her voice rose in pitch.

He frowned. Did she consider it inappropriate to allow a duke to wander freely in their house? He'd rather thought dukes could do whatever they pleased.

"Very," he said and swept inside, walking past the wide-eyed butler and toward the ground-floor room he knew that Lord Carlisle kept as an office.

He was aware he was behaving abruptly, but if his encounters with both Lady Emma and Lady Violet at Lord

Mayhew's home had taught him anything, it was that he needed to act quickly.

There was no reason to delay moving forward with Lady Violet. He'd recognized from the outset that they were well suited. She would not bother him after they were married; she would be more than able to entertain herself.

Besides, the sooner they were wed, the sooner he could escape his inexplicable draw to the intriguing Lady Emma. Staying far away from anyone he might be romantically interested in was at the top of his priorities list.

Vaughan knocked on the solid wooden door. He couldn't hear anything from within—probably because of the thickness of the door and the fact that it was firmly closed.

A moment later, it swung inward, and Vaughan met Lord Carlisle's piercing gaze.

"Ashford," he said, his polished vowels as aristocratic as his high cheekbones and thick gray hair. "Are you here about my daughter?"

"I am," Vaughan said, noticing that Carlisle did not ask which daughter.

"Very well. Come in." He stepped aside and went to a crystal decanter atop a small writing desk set against one wall. "Brandy?"

"No, thank you." One brandy was unlikely to dull his wits, but he didn't want to take the chance.

"Please, sit." Carlisle gestured at the elegantly carved wooden chair on the visitor's side of his desk.

Vaughan took the seat, wishing it had upholstery that he could rub his damp palms on.

Lord Carlisle sat in his own chair, which was much larger and made of black leather. Vaughan briefly wondered if the two chairs had been chosen strategically to put the earl at an advantage over whomever he was meeting with.

"I understand you've been courting Violet," Carlisle said.

"Yes. I believe she's an excellent match, and I would like to ask her to be my duchess." Vaughan was proud of how steady he sounded.

Carlisle smiled, and there was something a little smug about it. "She will make a fine duchess, and I am happy to give you my blessing. I looked you up as soon as I heard you were sniffing around, so I know you aren't a fortune hunter or considered to be a scoundrel. In fact, I couldn't have found a better match for her myself."

Ah, yes. The earl was definitely pleased to have a duke joining the family.

"I assume we can come to an agreement on the details later?" Vaughan asked, referring to the dowry and any settlements made upon Violet.

"Absolutely. I'm sure you are eager to speak with Violet first." Carlisle stood and came around the desk. "Follow me to the drawing room. I assume my wife will have already summoned her."

Lord Carlisle led Vaughan to the room he'd been ushered to when calling on Violet previously. Their surroundings were very feminine, from the pale pink patterned wallpaper to the strong floral scent that hung in the air.

Violet rose from a chair and curtseyed as he entered.

"Lady Violet," he said in greeting. "It's lovely to see you again so soon."

Her skirt swished around her ankles as she moved toward him. "I could say the same, Your Grace. After seeing you this afternoon, I did not expect to have the honor of a call today."

"Yes. Well." He coughed, his throat suddenly tight. "I have something important to ask you."

A faint squeak drew his attention to Lady Carlisle, but her expression was carefully neutral, so he wondered if he'd imagined it.

He inhaled slowly, the scent of the bouquet tickling his nose. He resisted the urge to sneeze. One did not sneeze on beautiful young ladies. He was certain that would be considered bad manners.

"May I get you some tea, Your Grace?" Lady Carlisle asked, and he realized he'd gone for too long without saying anything.

"Oh, yes please."

He sat on the nearest chaise, feeling like a lumbering bull in comparison to the dainty piece of furniture. Both Carlisle women sat. Lord Carlisle did not move from his position near the doorway.

"How do you take it?" she asked.

"A splash of milk, no sugar," he replied.

Lady Carlisle poured tea into three delicate cups and passed him one.

"Thank you." He took a sip. A bit too milky for his taste, but nice enough otherwise.

"You said you have a question for me," Violet prompted.

"Er." His collar was too tight. He tugged at it. "Lady Violet. I have enjoyed getting to know you. I think you are a woman of great character and beauty, and I would be most grateful if you would do me the honor of becoming my wife."

"I'd be delighted," Violet said almost as soon as the words had passed his lips. She blinked, and made a small sound in the back of her throat, as if startled by her swift reply... and uncertain whether she meant it.

"Of course you would," Lady Carlisle said, covering for her daughter's blunder. "Do you intend to hold a large wedding, Your Grace?"

Vaughan shrugged, studying Violet, trying to figure out what was going on in her head. "Whatever you think is best, Lady Carlisle. I give you free rein."

He was rich enough that she could invite the entire ton to St. George's in Hanover Square, followed by a wedding breakfast and luncheon, and the cost would barely register against the vast Ashford fortune.

"When?" Violet asked, seeming to have recovered.

"I would like to marry quickly, but not so quickly that there is any hint of a scandal."

The sooner this whole thing was over with, the better. He wanted nothing more than to leave London and its society behind. Nevertheless, he didn't want to damage his future bride's reputation.

"Would a month suit you?" Lady Carlisle asked. "That will give me sufficient time to plan."

Vaughan reached for Violet's hand. It felt dainty in his, but there was none of the zing he'd experienced with her sister. Thank God.

"Are you happy with a month?" he asked her.

She nodded.

"Then a month it is."

Perfect," Lord Carlisle said. "If you'll excuse me, I have work to do."

He left the room, and Vaughan wished he could do the same, but Lady Carlisle's eyes were lit up like those of a cat who'd spotted a succulent bird, and he didn't think his escape would be so swift.

"Your Grace, would you like to accompany Lady Violet and me on a walk so we can discuss the details?"

He supposed it couldn't be avoided. "Very well."

"May I come, Mother?" The redheaded girl he'd identified as Violet's younger sister was leaning around the drawing room door. He couldn't help wondering whether she'd been eavesdropping the entire time.

"No, Sophie. It's your job to take care of Emma." She turned to Vaughan. "My other daughter is unwell."

Upset was more like it. He didn't say anything, though. If Lady Emma wasn't prepared to be honest with her family, it was none of his business.

Even if he had contributed to her distress.

Guilt churned in his stomach, but he did his best to ignore it. She wasn't his problem.

"Fine." Sophie pouted and disappeared back around the doorframe.

As they prepared to depart, Vaughan took Violet's arm. She smiled up at him, but he couldn't help thinking that it was missing some of the brightness he'd become accustomed to seeing from her.

"Will you be attending the Hampstead ball tomorrow night?" she asked, allowing him to guide her down the corridor, her mother following closely behind.

"I'm afraid not. I have business that I must attend to." That "business" involved drinking brandy and thanking his lucky stars that his bride hunt was over and he no longer had to attend such events.

Violet huffed. "Then I shall have to entertain myself."

His stomach rolled sickeningly at the recollection of how his mother used to do that. Preferably with handsome men, and often right under his father's nose. He hoped Violet Carlisle had more discretion than his mother.

CHAPTER 6

SOPHIE CHASED AFTER EMMA AND VIOLET AS LADY CARLISLE hustled them out of Carlisle House and toward the waiting carriage.

"Three," she called to Emma. "You promise?"

"I promise," Emma called back. "I'll dance with at least three eligible gentlemen."

"I'll make sure of it," Lady Carlisle muttered, not loudly enough for Sophie to hear, but Emma understood her just fine.

Sophie waved. "Have a good time."

"We will." Violet laughed. "She's going to be a handful during her season."

"Fortunately, that won't happen for another three years at least," Lady Carlisle said.

A footman assisted her into the carriage, and Violet and Emma followed. The interior was unseasonably warm. Someone had probably placed hot bricks beneath the seats.

Emma smiled to herself as she looked out the window at where Sophie stood silhouetted in the house's entrance. Her heart was light and hopeful. With Violet betrothed, Emma might finally have an opportunity to meet a suitor of her own.

"You look nice tonight," Lady Carlisle said to Emma as the carriage jostled away. "Is that one of the gowns we ordered from Madame Baptiste at the start of the season?"

"It is." Emma fingered the skirt, which was cream but trimmed with the palest green. She thought it brought more color to her face, and she hoped the men who'd be at the Hampstead ball would agree.

"Do you like my dress?" Violet asked, rearranging her skirt around herself.

"It complements your eyes perfectly," Lady Carlisle replied. "It is almost the exact same shade of blue."

"You look lovely too, Mother," Emma said. It was true. Lady Carlisle may have silver hair threaded among her blonde, but she was an elegant woman. Emma hoped she aged as well as her mother had.

"Thank you, dearest."

They'd timed their arrival so that the rush of guests was over. Therefore, their carriage was able to stop outside Hampstead House without delay.

Lady Carlisle whisked Violet and Emma inside, one of her daughters on each arm as she greeted their host and hostess. After Lady Carlisle finished conversing, and the three women moved into the ballroom.

Emma surveyed the ballroom, her lips parting as she took in the view. The walls were plain white trimmed with maroon, but dozens of gilt-framed mirrors reflected back the colors of dresses and suits as several pairs of partners engaged in a country dance.

The effect dazzled her.

A string quartet played, and despite the number of people packed inside, the space smelled like a garden. Of course, that might be due to the enormous number of shrubs that seemed to have been relocated inside.

"Lady Carlisle."

Emma turned toward the male voice, and her eyebrows pinched together. Mr. Mayhew had broken off from a group of men and was approaching them.

"Lady Violet and Lady Emma," he added. "The evening has improved by your arrival."

"That is very kind of you," Violet replied, fluttering her dark eyelashes at him.

Emma murmured something—she didn't know what, but it seemed to be satisfactory, because no one looked at her twice.

"It's just the truth." He sounded as though he meant it. "May I have the next dance?"

A little of Emma's hope leeched away. Violet was engaged —word had already spread to most members of the *ton*—and somehow, she was still the one he'd asked to dance. Not that Emma particularly wanted to dance with him after hearing him dote on her sister, but it was the principle of the thing that mattered.

Don't let it get to you.

"You may." Violet took his hand and allowed him to lead her away.

Lady Carlisle harrumphed. "A lot of good that will do him. She's to marry a duke."

Emma hid a laugh behind her hand.

"Come along," her mother said. "Let's find you a dance partner."

Emma kept stride with Lady Carlisle, surprised by her attitude. So far, she hadn't concerned herself with Emma's prospects at any of the balls they'd attended. Perhaps Violet's successful engagement had motivated her to seek an alliance for her other daughter too.

"Ah, look. There's Mr. Bently." Lady Carlisle raised her hand in greeting.

Mr. Bently glanced behind himself and, seeing no one there, slowly came toward them.

"Good evening, ladies," he said, and clearly realizing his duty, added, "Lady Emma, would you like to dance?"

Excitement fluttered in Emma's belly as she set her hand on his. Perhaps Mr. Bently would be more capable of changing where his affections lay than Mr. Mayhew was.

"I would love to."

The strains of another song began, and Mr. Bently led her in a minuet. He moved with perfect grace, and she practically floated across the floor with him.

"So," he said as they came closer to each other. "Is the rumor of Lady Violet's engagement to the Duke of Ashford true?"

She crashed down to earth.

"Yes, it is." Her jaw tightened. Good lord. Even now, when Violet was betrothed, was every gentleman in Mayfair more interested in her than in Emma?

"What a shame," he said.

"Not for her or the duke," she said tartly.

He looked taken aback, and they didn't speak again during their dance. She was grateful when he returned her to her mother, but her mood sank lower when she realized Lady Carlisle was not alone. Violet and Mr. Mayhew stood with her.

"You and Mr. Bently danced beautifully," Violet said to Emma.

"Lady Violet." Mr. Bently was breathless, and Emma doubted it had anything to do with their dance, since he'd seemed fine a moment earlier. "Would you grace me with a dance?"

Violet beamed, took his arm, and let him lead her away.

"Lady Emma," Mr. Mayhew said, not to be outdone. "A dance?"

Emma went with him because she knew it was expected

of her. A few days ago, she'd have been ecstatic to dance with him, but now it felt empty. She winced when he stood on her foot.

"Sorry," he muttered.

He held her stiffly. She tried to relax and enjoy the moment, but it was impossible when he repeatedly trod on her toes and stumbled over nothing.

An awkward silence fell between them. The first time they'd met, she'd conversed with him easily, but now she couldn't think of anything to say.

At least she'd danced with two gentlemen already, even if both had been disappointing. She'd imagined being swept off her feet by a gorgeous dark-haired man who'd suddenly real-ized he was unable to live without her.

"No such luck," she whispered.

"What was that?" Mr. Mayhew asked.

"Nothing," she said. "I was counting steps."

He chuckled. "Thank goodness I'm not the only one who has to do that. You ladies always make it look so easy."

She softened. Perhaps all was not lost. She did tend to be overly dramatic.

"You are doing very well, sir."

Mirth sparkled in his eyes. "Not as well as you. Or your sister." His expression turned rapturous. "Dancing with her is like waltzing with an angel."

She pressed her lips together. Or maybe not.

Perhaps her third dance would be magical.

When she separated from Mr. Mayhew, Violet was nowhere to be seen, so Emma sought out their mother. She stood near the refreshments table, drinking punch.

"That looks good," Emma said, reaching for a glass.

Lady Carlisle intercepted her and handed her a lemonade. She leaned forward and murmured, "The punch is laced. If you wish to keep your wits about you, drink only the lemonade."

Emma sipped the lemonade, savoring the tang on her tongue. "I can't help but notice that you are drinking punch."

Lady Carlisle's mouth curled. "That is one of the benefits of being a married lady. One day, you'll be able to have the punch too."

They finished their drinks and passed the glasses to a servant.

"Now." Lady Carlisle took Emma's arm. "Let's get you your third dance. Are there any gentlemen here whom you have not already met?"

Emma surveyed the room, her gaze drawn to a pair of men standing near a wall. The taller of the pair tilted his head back and laughed. He ran his hand through his tousled brown hair, and one side of his mouth hitched up in response to whatever his companion had said.

"Them," Emma said. The men looked similar enough to be brothers, and she had no doubt her mother would know who they were. Her knowledge of the ton was frighteningly encyclopedic.

"Jonathan and Marcus Adair, the sons of Baron Marwick," Lady Carlisle said, leading Emma toward them. Jonathan is the second son, and Marcus is the third."

So neither was the heir. Not that Emma cared either way.

Lady Carlisle called out to the men as she and Emma came closer. Both turned, and the taller fellow broke out in a smile brighter than the midsummer sun.

Introductions were made, and the taller Mr. Marwick—incidentally, the younger of the two—claimed her for a dance.

"I have not seen you in London before," he said as he guided her expertly through the steps of the waltz. "I would remember."

His chin stayed high while he turned her, but his rich brown gaze followed her movement, and when his hand landed on her waist, a shiver rippled down her spine.

"This is the first season I'm out," she said. "I spent most of my life in our country home in Essex before this year."

His smile widened. "You hail from Essex?"

"From a small town called Shelton," she confirmed, her skirt swirling around both their legs as they turned. Marcus Adair was a wonderful dancer. Even better than Mr. Bently. Or perhaps she was biased because he was much better company.

"My family home is also in Essex," he said, the warmth of his hand soaking through her gown to sear her skin. "Perhaps twenty miles from Shelton."

"Really?" Her heart lifted. "I'm surprised we never met."

He shifted closer, and her cheeks heated. "I am the youngest of our family, but I suspect I am still quite a bit older than you."

"You're not old," she protested. He could not be more than thirty.

"But you are as fresh as a daisy." Somehow, he didn't make the comparison sound like a bad thing. "Tell me, what did you like to do when you were at home in Shelton?"

Emma considered her reply, knowing that Violet or her mother would coach her to be mysterious, the better to hook him, but if she wanted a man who loved her for who she was, then that man needed to know her.

"I read a lot," she said. "On warm days, I took long walks outside. Sometimes my father's dogs would accompany me."

"Do you like dogs?" he asked.

"Very much so."

"As do I."

They locked eyes, and Emma's breath caught. It took several seconds before she realized the music had stopped.

"The dance has ended." Yet she did not want to let him go.

Mr. Adair was precisely the type of kind, friendly man

she would like to marry, and while she didn't want to get her hopes up, he seemed to have enjoyed her company.

"I hope I will see you again soon," he said, echoing her thoughts.

She linked her arm with his and walked alongside him as they returned to their family members. "I will look out for you."

She released him reluctantly and accepted the elder Mr. Adair's invitation to dance. While he was pleasant to talk to and a reasonable dancer, she experienced no flutters of delight while in his arms. Her heart did not race, nor did she yearn to see his smile.

But his brother....

He had potential.

The dance over, she found her mother once again. Lady Carlisle radiated pride, and Emma wanted to bask in it. She and her mother didn't have a lot in common, so Violet was usually the primary recipient of that heady approval.

"I predict that both of you will be wed before the season ends," Lady Carlisle said, handing Emma another lemonade.

"I hope so." They walked a circuit of the ballroom, and Emma couldn't resist peering into each mirror they passed. They were quite distracting.

Dozens of tiny cakes and desserts covered the refreshments table. The tart scent of lemon filled Emma's nostrils, and her stomach grumbled loudly. She glanced at one of the lemon cakes, edging closer.

"Don't," Lady Carlisle warned. "If you intend to keep the attention of any suitors, you can't be seen stuffing your face."

Surely her stomach would put them off if it sounded as if it might consume them. Emma didn't mention that, though. She doubted her mother would find it amusing, and she wanted to enjoy their camaraderie for a while longer.

She'd just have to sneak a cake when no one was looking.

"There's Violet," Lady Carlisle said, nodding toward the dance floor.

Emma reached for a cake while she was distracted, but then she froze. Her hand fell to her side, empty. "She's dancing with Mr. Mayhew."

"Hmm." Based on her mother's tone, she wasn't pleased with that turn of events. "She shouldn't dance twice with a man she isn't engaged to—or does not intend to become engaged to. I'll have to remind her of proper etiquette later. We don't want the duke to have second thoughts."

Did it make Emma a bad person that she found a strange sort of satisfaction in hearing her mother criticize Violet?

Probably. Yet she couldn't seem to help it.

An hour later, during the ride home, she found her sympathy. Lady Carlisle had lectured Violet on the importance of keeping the duke happy until Emma felt quite sorry for her sister.

Meanwhile, Violet pouted and said very little in her own defense. She was subdued, and Emma wondered whether something was wrong.

As soon as they were inside Carlisle House, Violet excused herself. Emma summoned Daisy and went to her room.

"Lady Sophie wanted to stay up and talk to you," Daisy said, removing the pins from Emma's hair. "But she fell asleep."

"I'll see her tomorrow," Emma said.

"She'll want to hear all about any gentlemen you met." Daisy took the brush off the dresser and slowly worked it through Emma's hair. Her scalp was sensitive at first, but gradually the brush strokes became pleasant.

"I met a good-humored gentleman from Essex who danced like a dream," Emma said.

"Was he handsome?"

Emma flushed. "Indeed."

"Then I hope he calls on you tomorrow." Daisy placed the brush on the dresser and started braiding her hair.

"So do I." For the first time, she actually believed it might happen. If Mr. Adair came by in the morning, she would give him her prettiest smile and ask him about his favorite parts of Essex.

Daisy tied a band around the bottom of the braid, helped Emma disrobe, and bid her goodnight.

Emma went to bed and dreamed of wedding bells.

She was woken what felt like minutes later by someone shaking her shoulder.

She rolled onto her side, peering through her lashes. Lady Carlisle stood over her, her eyes so wide that white showed around the iris.

"Have you seen Violet?" she demanded.

Emma blinked, her mind sluggish as she tried to make sense of the sight of her mother standing in her bedchamber.

"What time is it?" she asked.

"The time doesn't matter." Lady Carlisle's voice was shrill. "Violet is not in her bed. Do you know where she is?"

Emma sat up and patted the fluff that always formed on the sides of her head when her hair was braided. "Perhaps she's with Sophie."

Lady Carlisle sat on the edge of the bed and closed her eyes briefly. "Sophie is the one who realized she's missing. She woke early and wanted to ask about the ball last night. Apparently she tried to wake you, but you wouldn't stir, so she went to Violet's room instead. The bed is empty."

Rubbing her temples, Emma wondered why her mother seemed so frantic.

"Maybe she went to get breakfast."

"She hasn't taken breakfast, and none of the staff have seen her this morning."

Emma shook her head, hoping to clear the remaining fog.

"She could be anywhere in the house. Perhaps she went to the library early, and that's why no one has seen her."

Her mother gave her a look. "I searched the library and the drawing rooms."

Emma bit her lip, beginning to understand why her mother was worried. "Could she have gone on a walk and taken Jane with her?"

"Mrs. Wilson woke Jane ten minutes ago. She hasn't seen Violet since last night." Lady Carlisle pressed her hand to her mouth. "What has happened to her? Where has she gone?"

"Let's do our best not to panic," Emma said. "Does Father know she's missing?"

"No."

"Then first, we should speak to him and carry out a full search of the house. I'm sure she will turn up somewhere."

Lady Carlisle lowered her hand. "I hope you're right."

Unfortunately, a full search of the house did not reveal any useful information. There was no sign of Violet, and it didn't look as if her bed had been slept in.

They took a break from searching, and Emma washed and dressed. She went looking for her mother but was intercepted by Samuels at the top of the grand staircase.

"A caller has arrived for you, my lady," he said.

Her heart lifted. "Who is it?"

His craggy face softened. "A Mr. Marcus Adair."

"Send him away."

Emma flinched as the order came from her left. She spun and found her father standing with his hands on his hips.

"We are not receiving this morning," he said. "Not until Violet is found."

"But father," Emma protested. "He—"

"But nothing." His tone was firm. "Samuels, please inform any visitors that they may call on us tomorrow instead."

"Very well, my lord." Samuels took the stairs down to speak with Mr. Adair.

Emma's insides grew heavy. She'd finally met a man she liked who might like her in return, and her father wouldn't let her see him.

She turned away before he could see that he'd upset her.

Why did Violet's antics have to interfere with her prospects? Her sister had probably gone to visit a friend and not mentioned it to anyone. Yes, it was early, but that explanation was more likely than anything else.

"Confirming Violet's safety is our top priority," he said.

"I know." As it should be. She just wished…. Well, she selfishly wished that Violet had chosen a different time to disappear.

Emma trudged down the corridor, but she hadn't gone far before someone called her name from behind. She glanced over her shoulder. Samuels was hurrying toward her, clutching an envelope.

"A missive came for you," he said.

"Is it from Mr. Adair?" Perhaps he'd left a note with the butler.

"I'm afraid not, but it looks like Lady Violet's handwriting."

Emma took the envelope from him, her hands shaking. He was right. The loopy handwriting was Violet's.

"Thank you."

She tore the envelope open and pulled out a letter. She read it quickly, growing colder inside with every word.

My dear Emma,

By now, you will probably have noticed that I have left Carlisle House. I'm sure you are curious where I am, so I shall be direct.

I have eloped with Mr. Mayhew.

We are on our way to Gretna Green, where we intend to be married. I know my actions are reckless and that you are no doubt shocked by my decision.

The truth is, when I met Mr. Mayhew, I felt all of those things you talked about when discussing love. My heart fluttered, and energy seemed to crackle between us each time we touched.

I could think of no one but him. He consumed me.

I considered marrying the duke anyway. I hoped a connection would grow between us, but he is so cold compared to my beloved.

Perhaps if I had not met Mr. Mayhew, I would be content to share a life of comfort and convenience with the duke, but now that I have, I cannot settle for that.

I'm sure you, of everyone, will understand.

Wish me luck with my nuptials.

Yours,

Violet.

CHAPTER 7

VAUGHAN WAS REVIEWING THE ACCOUNT LEDGER FOR ONE OF his estates when a knock at the office door heralded the arrival of his butler, Gladwell.

"Your Grace, the Earl of Carlisle is here to see you," Gladwell said, standing stiffly in the doorway.

Vaughan stretched the kinks out of his back and glanced at the clock. He hadn't expected to hear from the earl today. Perhaps Carlisle wanted to review the settlements prior to the banns being read.

"Thank you, Gladwell. Show him in."

As Gladwell left, Vaughan closed the ledger and set it aside. He made it a practice not to allow anyone to see inside his books other than the estate managers and his solicitor.

When Lord Carlisle entered, warning alarms sounded in Vaughan's head. The earl's shoulders were slumped, and his clothing was rumpled. For a man who was usually immaculately turned out, this was all it took for Vaughan to know something was wrong.

"Good afternoon, Ashford," he said, lowering himself slowly onto the chair opposite, as if his bones were weary. He turned his sunken eyes on Vaughan, who blanched.

"Good God, man. You look terrible." He shouldn't speak to an earl like that—and especially not his future father-in-law—but the situation called for it.

Lord Carlisle's expression was bleak. "I'm afraid I bear bad news."

"What is it? Has something happened to Violet?" That was the only thing Vaughan could think of that may cause the earl to appear so uncharacteristically disheveled.

"Yes, but not in the way you think."

A chill of premonition washed over Vaughan. His gut rolled, and he rested his hands on his lap, out of sight of the earl.

"Tell me," he said.

Lord Carlisle cleared his throat. "You have no idea how sorry I am to tell you that Violet has eloped."

A buzzing sound filled Vaughan's ears, muffling the words.

"I'm sorry," he said. "Could you repeat that?"

Carlisle looked sick. "Violet has eloped with Mr. Thomas Mayhew."

Dear God. No wonder the earl was an unbecoming shade of green.

Silently, Vaughan stood and went to the decanter of brandy stationed on the side table. He poured the amber liquid into two crystal glasses, then picked up one of them and downed it. The drink burned his throat and heated his gullet but couldn't dispel the churning nausea.

He refilled his glass and offered the other to Carlisle, who gulped the brandy as rapidly as Vaughan had.

"Another?" Vaughan asked.

Carlisle shook his head. "Better not. I need to keep my senses in case we get word that my brother has caught up with her."

"He is pursuing her?" Vaughan asked.

"Yes. Violet wrote that they were bound for Gretna

Green. Unfortunately, they had a head start, and if Graham has not caught up with them yet, then I fear he'll be too late."

Vaughan dropped onto his chair, ignoring the slosh of brandy over his fingers. What the hell had happened?

Violet Carlisle was supposed to be his perfect society bride. She'd given every impression of being a practical—if someone frivolous—young lady who would gladly marry a title, produce an heir, and be a hostess that would make him proud.

He'd never have dreamed she was addle-headed enough to jilt a duke.

"How long has she been gone?" he asked.

Carlisle twisted the brandy glass between his fingers. "She left two nights ago and sent word of her plans the next day. Graham departed as soon as possible after we heard of her destination. If he'd found her, he'd have sent word urgently, so I can only assume he's been unsuccessful."

"You cannot be certain." Vaughan didn't know why he was attempting to comfort the earl other than the fact that he looked utterly miserable.

Carlisle shrugged. "Either way, I felt that you had a right to know. Even if we retrieve her, I understand it's extremely unlikely you'll wish to go through with the wedding."

That was an understatement. The only benefit of taking a wife—other than securing an heir—was to have someone who could smooth his way in social situations. When she returned, Violet Carlisle would be disgraced. She would be useless in the role no matter how nice her manners were.

"Why did she do it?" Vaughan asked. "Was she unhappy with our match?"

Carlisle scowled. "Who knows why young girls do anything." He rubbed his temples. "She seemed pleased. She's been saying since we left Essex that she wanted to marry a wealthy man with a title—preferably not someone in their dotage. In that respect, you're perfect for her."

Exactly what Vaughan had thought.

"Her sister put ideas about love into her head," Carlisle said. "Emma wants to marry for love, and I didn't deter her because she has sense enough not to do something like this. Unfortunately, Violet was obviously more susceptible to Emma's influence than we believed."

"Ah." He should have known that Lady Emma would have something to do with this. From now on, he'd not only steer clear of women who wanted love, but their blasted sisters too.

He sipped his brandy. "I didn't know she was well acquainted with Mr. Mayhew, although I did see them speaking at the Mayhew poetry reading a few days ago."

Carlisle crossed his legs. "Then you know more than I do. My wife informed me that she danced with him twice at the Hampstead ball, but that was the first time she'd seen them together other than when they were introduced."

Had they been sneaking around? Hot, unpleasant emotions swirled in Vaughan's gut. Had Violet accepted his proposal knowing she cared for another?

Bloody fickle women. Not one of them could be trusted. If her affections had already been engaged by Mayhew, and yet she'd accepted Vaughan's proposal, it was a miracle that the other man had been able to see past her actions. Vaughan would not have been so forgiving.

"The wedding is off," Vaughan said. "There's no way around it."

Carlisle sighed. "I thought you'd say that."

Vaughan considered pouring himself another brandy, but he didn't want to become sozzled in the middle of the day even if he had every right to.

All of this because of love.

Some people thought love was beautiful, but Vaughan knew it was ugly. Love was nothing more than a way for one person to hold another poor soul in their thrall.

"All I can say in response is that I am incredibly sorry," Carlisle said. "I had no idea my foolish daughter would do this. I apologize for the inconvenience and for the stir it will no doubt cause—if it hasn't already."

"I don't hold you responsible, for what it's worth," Vaughan said, although it would have been nice if Carlisle had kept a closer eye on his daughter. "I can't say all of the ton will agree."

"I appreciate that more than you know." Carlisle rose. "I'll leave you now. Once again, you have my most sincere apologies."

He showed himself out.

Vaughan sat at his desk, staring into space. His mind whirred, the repercussions of Violet's reckless actions ricocheting through it.

He'd need to find another potential bride. Not only that, but some of the young ladies of the ton might be inclined to think there was something wrong with him. Why else would anyone jilt a duke?

He groaned. How much did he really care if the estate went to Cousin Reginald or his brood?

A sour taste filled his mouth. He cared enough not to allow it to happen. After all, Reginald hadn't only been cruel to Vaughan, but he'd been cruel to his father as well, teasing him for the duchess's many notorious affairs. Vaughan had had to watch as his father became more fractured every day.

Shaking away the memory, he stood and left the office, then locked it behind himself. He wouldn't be able to work now.

He summoned his carriage and asked the coachman to drop him off at his club, the Regent. When he arrived, he found Longley where he'd suspected he would, playing cards with two other members of the aristocracy.

"Ashford," he exclaimed, straightening in his brown leather chair. "Didn't expect to see you here."

71

His companions greeted Vaughan with nods.

"Do you have a minute, Longley?" Vaughan asked.

Longley's eyebrows shot up. "Won't you join us?"

"I'm not in the mood." In fact, he wasn't in the mood for much other than shaking Lady Violet Carlisle by the shoulders and demanding to know whether she'd gone mad.

"I'll finish this hand." Longley surveyed the room, then called out, "Adair, want to take my place?"

The eldest Mr. Adair, Marwick's heir, broke off his conversation and strode over. "Happy to."

They finished out the round, and Longley pocketed his winnings.

"Let's go somewhere quieter," Vaughan suggested.

"Lead on," Longley said.

Vaughan found a room across the hall that was empty except for a pair of older gentlemen sharing a decanter of brandy in the corner. His shoes tapped against the tile floor as he chose a seat as far from them as possible and slumped into it. Longley took the chair on the other side of the small table between them.

Not for the first time, Vaughan thanked whatever sensible man had decorated the Regent. Everything was in soothing shades of white and brown. Nothing too overwhelming. Certainly a far cry from the decor at the balls he'd attended recently.

"What's going on?" Longley asked. "I assume it's serious to have broken you out of your routine. Isn't Tuesday when you usually review the estate ledgers?"

Vaughan grunted. His friend had always mocked him for being predictable. He drew in a deep breath, realizing that there was no easy way to say this. It was awkward as hell, and unfortunately, all of the ton was going to know before long.

"Lady Violet Carlisle eloped with Thomas Mayhew the night after the Hampstead Ball."

Longley jolted, his eyes widening. "She did what?"

"Eloped." Vaughan dragged his hand through his hair, relishing the faint prickle of discomfort as he tugged too hard. "They're bound for Gretna Green."

"But... She..." Longley appeared to be at a loss for words. "Seriously?"

Vaughan gave him a look. "I wouldn't joke about something like this."

"Bloody hell." Longley gestured at a servant and indicated that he wanted a drink. "When did you find out?"

"Lord Carlisle visited me right before I came here."

He scowled. "He didn't think to tell you sooner?"

"Perhaps he hoped he'd bring her home with no one the wiser." Vaughan couldn't blame him for putting off the unpleasantness. But he could blame Violet. He could blame her for everything.

"I'm sorry." Longley reached over and clapped Vaughan on the shoulder. "I feel terrible. It was my idea for you to court her, and now this. I honestly had no clue she and Mayhew were involved."

"It's not your fault." Vaughan glanced up as the servant approached with what smelled like brandy and poured them each a glass. "Thank you," he said, and the boy nodded.

"Then why do I feel guilty?" Longley asked.

Vaughan left his brandy sitting there while Longley sipped his. Perhaps he'd drink it later, but for now, he didn't intend to risk overimbibing and inviting even more gossip.

"Maybe because you're an idiot," Vaughan said.

Longley laughed. "Just like that, I'm no longer sympathetic for you."

Vaughan watched a trail of melted wax work its way down the side of a tapered candle in the center of their table.

"You have no reason to feel guilty," he said, growing serious. "I chose to court Violet, I chose to propose to her, and I'm the one who didn't pay any attention to the warning signs."

He could have taken issue with Violet flirting with Mayhew at the poetry reading, raised the subject with her, and potentially avoided this entire debacle. If she'd said she had feelings for the other man, he would never have asked her to marry him. Love was too damn chaotic.

"I hope this won't put you off taking a wife altogether." Longley raised his glass to his lips.

The liquid wax dripped onto the candle holder.

"If I could possibly avoid repeating my performance on the marriage mart, I would, but I can't allow Reginald to inherit, and I'm already here. I have the wardrobe, and I've been introduced to many prospective brides. It makes sense to resume the search."

Longley hummed in the back of his throat. "They will call you cold for doing so soon after Violet's betrayal."

"Damn the girl." She'd made everything so much more difficult. "Females are fickle."

"At least you didn't find out about her attachment after you were married." Longley waved for the servant to refill his glass.

"I might have preferred that," Vaughan mused. "At least I could have gotten my heir."

Beyond that, he had no emotional connection to Violet. He wouldn't have cared if she had affairs as long as she was discreet.

"You'll find another bride," Longley said.

Dread pooled in Vaughan's midsection. Perhaps he would, but the last thing he wanted to do was put himself out there again, especially when everyone would know he'd been jilted.

How utterly humiliating.

～

"Hurry up, Emma," Lady Carlisle barked, hustling her daughter toward the front door.

Emma slunk along, her shoulders down, silently praying that the carriage would break down before they left and she wouldn't have to go anywhere.

They were going to be slaughtered.

"Are you sure we should go?" she asked.

She'd protested when Lady Carlisle had announced her plan to attend the opera. By now, news of Violet's elopement would surely have spread, and everyone would be gossiping about them.

"Yes," Lady Carlisle said. "We need to see firsthand how much damage Violet's selfish actions have caused."

She arched her fair eyebrows as if daring Emma to disagree. Emma kept her mouth shut. Her parents had made it clear they thought Emma was to partly to blame for Violet's behavior, so she was walking on eggshells so as not to make it worse. They already weren't allowing her to receive callers. Lord knew what Mr. Adair thought of her after having been turned away twice.

Her father was waiting by the carriage, which, unfortunately, was in perfect working order. He took her mother's hand and assisted her into the carriage, and then did the same for Emma.

"We will all be on our best behavior tonight," he said as he climbed in and pulled the door shut. "If anyone mentions Violet, we will not react. We'll take the higher ground. Understood?"

"Yes, Father," Emma murmured, wondering what else he expected her to do. She never caused a fuss at public events. She didn't even like being the center of attention—although having some attention was nice.

The carriage jostled into motion, and Emma looked out the window, noting Sophie's silhouette in an upstairs window. She'd been subdued the last few days as well.

During the ride, Lord and Lady Carlisle conversed in low voices, and Emma didn't try to participate. Instead, she dreamed of seeing Mr. Adair tonight. Would he like her dress? It wasn't a new one, but she thought the rosy shade of pink suited her well. More importantly, would he forgive her for being unavailable when he'd come calling?

When she could hear the rise and fall of voices outside, Emma knew they must be near the opera house. Her parents stopped talking. Her chest tightened, and her stomach rolled sickeningly. They shouldn't be here. They would not be welcome, and she knew it.

Yet she had to watch as her parents exited the carriage and follow behind, her feet leaden as she forced herself into what was sure to be a disaster.

The massive doors stood ajar, and as they entered the foyer, silence fell. Emma curled her fingers into her palms, trying to warm them. The air seemed as cold as the eyes that watched their every move.

Emma stared down at the rich red carpet as her mother guided them farther into the foyer, presumably toward an acquaintance.

"Lady Talbot," her mother said. "How lovely to see you."

Emma raised her eyes just in time to see Lady Talbot turn away, giving them the cut. Her companions followed her example, presenting their backs to the Carlisles.

Lady Carlisle gasped.

"Come." Lord Carlisle ushered her through the assembly and into the stairwell, where they climbed to their box.

Emma was numb. She hardly noticed the golden walls or the stunning paintings of English landscapes that she usually couldn't take her eyes off. Despite the gathering of people down below and the dozens in other boxes lining the walls of the theater, she'd never felt so alone.

"We are ruined," Lady Carlisle whispered, as if the full depth of their situation had only just sunk in.

Desperate to distract herself, Emma glanced into the box opposite theirs. She stood straighter as she recognized the tall figure of Mr. Marcus Adair next to his brothers and their father, Lord Marwick.

She met his eyes, and he sent her a kind smile. Perhaps all was not lost. But in the next instant, he turned away too.

CHAPTER 8

THE TENSION AT THE BREAKFAST TABLE MADE EMMA uncomfortable. Forks clinked against plates, knives scraped over bread, and no one said a word.

Lord Carlisle buttered a piece of toast, and the rasp was magnified ten times over by the awful silence of his breakfast companions.

Emma sipped her tea. Her cup was nearly empty, but her throat was still dry. She'd tried to eat scrambled eggs, but they sat like a lump in her stomach, and now most of her meal was slowly congealing on her plate.

Lady Carlisle reached for a strip of bacon, cut a tiny piece off, and declared, "I have thought of a solution to our dilemma."

Emma poked at her rubbery eggs, too scared to ask what she meant.

"Do tell," Lord Carlisle said, folding up the newspaper that was positioned on the far side of his plate.

Lady Carlisle busied herself dissecting her strip of bacon. "Emma must marry the duke."

Everyone stopped and stared.

Emma drew in a shaky breath. "I beg your pardon?"

Lady Carlisle lowered her cutlery and met Emma's eyes. "You can see how it makes sense."

"How?" Emma demanded. Her head spun, and she placed her hands on her lap beneath the table so no one could see them trembling.

"Well." Lady Carlisle moistened her lips. "The duke wants a suitable wife. Violet is no longer a viable option, but you are."

Emma opened her mouth, but her mother gestured for her to let her continue.

"You are sisters, so you are similar enough that if he was satisfied with Violet, he will surely find you to be an adequate bride."

Adequate?

Emma wanted to cry at the prospect. She'd always hoped her future husband would consider her more than adequate.

"But most importantly, if you become a duchess, nobody will dare cut us again, and our status will be restored." Lady Carlisle smiled as if she had not just threatened to destroy the only future Emma had dreamed of.

"You cannot simply ask him to swap from one sister to another," Sophie said. "He will think you've lost your mind."

Emma already thought her mother was mad.

"There's no way the duke will want to marry me," she said. "For one, if he found me as 'suitable' as Violet, then he would have pursued me from the beginning, yet he did not. Secondly, if he were to marry me, my mere existence would constantly remind him of Violet and the fact that she jilted him."

Emma poured herself more tea, ignoring the rattle of the teapot as her hands shook. She wanted to believe that her mother couldn't possibly be serious about this, but based on her expression, she was, and Emma had a terrible feeling about it.

"I agree with Emma," Lord Carlisle said as he scooped

strawberry jam onto his toast and spread it thickly. "The duke is unlikely to want to bind himself to us after what Violet has done."

Lady Carlisle narrowed her eyes at him. "Think of it this way: every man wants a wife who is attractive, of good breeding, and who can manage his home and bear him a child."

"Do they?" Sophie muttered.

Lady Carlisle ignored her. "Emma fulfills all of those criteria. She is the daughter of an earl, pretty enough, well-versed in household management, and of child-bearing age and healthy constitution."

Emma sipped her tea, grateful for the soothing warmth on the parched inside of her mouth. Her mother made her sound like a horse. She half expected her to mention that she had all her teeth and good vision too. She was a person, not a broodmare.

"I am not the same as Violet," Emma said. She knew that beyond a shadow of a doubt. Men fought to court Violet, while they would merely settle for her. "A fact of which I'm sure the duke is very well aware."

"And considering the situation, it is also a fact that is sure to please him," Lady Carlisle retorted without taking her gaze off her husband. "My lord, if he were to wed Emma, it would save him from having to go through the process of finding another wife, and it may help repair the damage to his reputation."

Lord Carlisle bit into his toast, chewed, and swallowed before replying. "How so?"

"There may be rumors that Violet ran off with another man because of a flaw or shortcoming of the duke. If Emma were to marry him, that would assure society that there is no reason to shun or be wary of him."

Emma pursed her lips. She rather thought that no one would shun a duke regardless of what rumors might surround him. If anyone was to bear the brunt of the scandal, it would be they and Violet, not the Duke of Ashford.

"I take your point," Lord Carlisle said. "The idea has merit, but I still don't think that Ashford will want anything to do with us. He was quite upset when I spoke to him."

Emma felt a pang of sympathy. She hadn't spared much thought for the duke's emotions, more concerned with her family's well-being and the repercussions for them. Still, the duke had wanted Violet to be his wife. He'd been as charmed by her as any other man of the ton, and learning of her defection must have hurt.

"Was he heartbroken?" Sophie asked.

"Of course not," their father said dismissively. "He didn't love her. Don't be so fanciful."

Emma met Sophie's eyes, and an unspoken thought passed between them. Even if the duke had not been in love with Violet, he'd probably been infatuated. Men didn't like to speak of such things, but both his heart and his ego were probably bruised.

"If Ashford were to agree, would you be satisfied with an arrangement between him and Emma?" Lady Carlisle asked her husband.

Lord Carlisle nodded. "Such an engagement would certainly help restore our standing."

Emma's stomach roiled, threatening to eject the eggs sitting like a rock in her gut. She didn't want to marry the Duke of Ashford. He'd been cold toward her for their entire acquaintance with the exception of those stolen moments in the office at Mayhew House.

Moreover, she didn't want to marry someone who did not want to marry her. She wanted love. She wanted to be wanted. Was that too much to ask?

"Then if we can make it happen, would you approve?" Lady Carlisle said.

"Yes," Lord Carlisle answered.

Emma placed her hands on the table. "I don't want to marry the duke."

Her mother leveled her with a look. "You should have thought about that before you planted silly ideas about love into your sister's head."

"That's not fair," Emma exclaimed. "I didn't make Violet elope with Mr. Mayhew. I shouldn't be punished for something she did."

Especially not when her damn sister would get the happily-ever-after that Emma had always wanted. It was like Violet was being rewarded for her poor behavior while Emma had to pay for it.

Lady Carlisle laughed mirthlessly. "How do you expect to find someone else to marry you if no one in the ton will even be seen speaking with us?"

"Love matters more than reputation," Emma said, pushing her chair back. She wanted to storm away, but she was afraid that if she left, they'd decide her fate without her.

"Maybe that would be the case if you'd already found a gentleman love," Lady Carlisle said. "But how could anyone fall for you if you are persona non grata? They won't bother to learn enough about you to care."

Emma stared down at the table, willing herself not to cry. Her mother was right. Absent an existing suitor, the scandal of Violet's elopement would make it difficult to secure another.

"Another scandal will come along soon," Sophie said, and Emma flashed her a small smile as thanks for her support.

"It may not be soon enough," Lord Carlisle said. "Even if the scandal blows over after a couple of years—which it may well do, since it's not as if Violet married below her station— you may be too old to have your choice of husband."

"But…" Emma blinked furiously. She would not cry.

"Your mother and I won't force you to marry anyone," he added. "But I would urge you to consider her suggestion. As I said before, he may well turn down the offer anyway, but it could garner goodwill, and if he accepted, it would smooth our path, particularly for Sophie."

Emma rose to her feet. Her knees were weak, but she forced herself not to shake. "I will consider it."

"We would like an answer by tomorrow," Lady Carlisle said.

Emma nodded numbly. "You'll have it."

She turned and left.

She went to her bedroom, where she changed into her riding outfit. Daisy hustled into the room, her eyes wide.

"Is it true that the earl and countess wish for you to wed the duke?" she asked, then clapped her hand to her mouth as if realizing she shouldn't have been so bold with her mistress.

Emma sighed. "Yes, but please don't spread the word."

Daisy mimed fastening her lips. "I'll keep mum."

"Thank you."

Daisy studied her attire. "Are you going riding?"

"Yes. I'll need a chaperone. Will you come with me?" Emma asked.

"Of course, my lady." Daisy dipped into a quick curtsey. "Just give me ten minutes to change."

While Emma waited for Daisy, she sent word to the stables to ready their horses.

When they arrived at the stable a while later, Emma's beautiful bay mare, Heather, was waiting alongside a stockier mare that had been prepared for Daisy. A footman assisted Emma into the saddle, then did the same for Daisy.

Emma urged Heather into motion and guided her along the roads toward Hyde Park. The sky was gray, and there was a cool breeze. She was glad she'd worn several layers of clothing. She gripped the reins tighter but was careful not to tug on them in case she unsettled Heather.

Eventually, they reached the wide-open spaces of the

park. The grass was damp but not wet, and the horses had no trouble traversing it. Emma inhaled the twin scents of earth and horsehair. They calmed her, allowing her to breathe more fully than she had since before she'd received Violet's letter.

She slowed and waited for Daisy to come alongside her.

"I don't know what to do," she confessed.

Daisy scowled. "Forgive me for saying so, my lady, but Lady Violet really ought to have thought of people other than herself before she acted so rashly."

"I agree." Emma's gaze swept the park. It was largely empty at this time of the morning, but a young man and woman sat on a bench near the stream. The woman laughed at something the man had said, and he leaned toward her as if drawn magnetically.

A courting couple.

Emma's heart ached. They looked so joyful. A maid hovered behind them, but they appeared oblivious to her as they talked. The man handed the woman a flower, and she tucked it behind her ear.

Emma swallowed, wincing with discomfort at the lump in her throat. "That's what I want," she whispered.

She urged Heather forward, desperate to outrun the fear of what her future might hold. If her parents got their way—on the slim chance that the duke agreed with their outrageous plan—then she would never know how it felt for a suitor to give her flowers or for love to slowly blossom.

The Duke of Ashford wouldn't nurture her finer feelings. She doubted he'd want anything to do with them. He wanted a beautiful wife. A diamond of the ton. Not just plain Lady Emma, the other Carlisle sister.

Emma breathed heavily and realized she was going too fast. She eased off and rubbed the back of Heather's neck, giving Daisy a few seconds to catch up.

"My apologies," she said. "I was distracted."

"It's fine," Daisy panted, her face flushed red.

Behind the maid, Emma spotted a familiar tall, lean figure standing with an older woman on the bridge over the stream. She straightened in her saddle. Was that Mr. Adair?

She urged Heather to saunter closer slowly enough so as not to startle them. The pair turned as one. Emma's heart lifted. It was Mr. Adair. That could not be a coincidence. She smiled and nodded to him in greeting. He caught her gaze, and for a brief moment, she thought he'd smile back.

But then Lady Marwick raised her chin and turned away, cutting them. After a couple of seconds, Mr. Adair followed suit.

Emma's hope shattered.

Her smile froze in place, and she brought the horse to a halt.

"Forget them," Daisy said. "Whoever they are, they aren't worth it."

Tears swam in Emma's eyes, but she allowed Daisy to guide her and Heather away from Lady Marwick and Mr. Adair.

Despair rolled through her, threatening to swallow her in its blackness. She'd hardly known Mr. Adair, but she'd felt as if he had the potential to become important to her, and now that potential was gone.

Her parents were right. If he—a man who'd shown that he liked her on another occasion—wouldn't have her now, then who would?

Surely no one decent. And if she wasn't able to choose an acceptable match of her own, her parents might force one, and she could end up wed to someone elderly or ill-suited to her.

And what about Sophie?

Sweet, lively Sophie might never get a chance to sparkle in society.

She shifted on the saddle, adjusting her bottom into a more comfortable position.

"Let's go home," she said.

Daisy glanced over her shoulder. "Are you sure?"

"Yes." She'd come out here to get her mind off her problems, but they'd followed her. Staying for longer would accomplish nothing.

As they rode, she summoned an image of the duke to her mind. He was, if nothing else, an exceedingly good-looking man. Those pale gray eyes of his reminded her of rain clouds, and his hair was thick and well-kept. The few times she'd been near him, he'd smelled faintly of oranges, which was a step up from many of the men she'd met.

At the sound of voices, Emma realized they were nearly back at the road. Daisy waited for her to take the lead and fell into step behind her.

Emma thought hard while they ambled along. When she'd met the duke, she'd believed him cold, and she'd been hurt when he'd danced with Violet and rejected her. But despite that, he'd come looking for her at Marwick House, and she'd gotten the impression that he genuinely cared whether or not she was all right.

Perhaps behind that austere exterior lurked the heart of a kind man.

They arrived at Carlisle House, and with assistance from a footman, Emma dismounted. She slipped Heather a treat from her pocket and petted her before allowing the stable hand to take her away.

Emma entered through the front entrance with Daisy trailing behind. Loud voices rang out from down the corridor—perhaps from the direction of her father's office— and Emma stilled. Then, without looking around, she hurried toward the noise.

"Is he certain?" Lady Carlisle's high-pitched tone was as clear as if she was standing right in front of Emma.

"Yes, Mary," Lord Carlisle replied. "He is quite certain. Violet is now Mrs. Mayhew."

Emma raised her hand to her chest just as Daisy gasped behind her.

"The deed is done," he said.

The last bastion of Emma's hope vanished. Violet was married. There was no sweeping this under the carpet. No coming back from it.

Unless she made it happen.

Her heart heavy, she knocked on the office door, then pushed it open and stepped inside. She straightened her back and held her head high. She was strong. She could do this.

Then, later, she'd cry where no one could overhear her.

"If the duke is amenable, I will marry him," she said.

One thought kept bouncing around her mind: *Please don't let him agree.*

CHAPTER 9

"Tea?" Vaughan offered Longley as his friend sat on the opposite side of the desk in the office.

"No, thanks," Longley replied.

Vaughan gestured to the decanter. "Brandy?"

"Oh, go on. The occasion merits it."

Vaughan poured a small portion of brandy each for Longley and himself. It would be rude to make Longley drink alone. He passed one to Longley and cradled the other in his hand as he lowered himself onto his comfortable chair.

"So, you received word from Carlisle that Lady Violet is married?" Longley said.

"Indeed. I'm sure most of London will know soon. Do you think the news will worsen the scandal or lessen it?" Vaughan could never predict society's behavior, and he wanted to know how wary to be when leaving the house.

Longley savored his brandy, his expression thoughtful. "Worsen. For a short time, anyway."

"How do you figure?" Vaughan asked, placing his glass on the desk. He didn't really feel like drinking it.

"If they choose to return to London, it will cause a stir.

Hostesses will not be able to decide whether to invite her to events in order to entertain their guests or to exclude her so as not to offend you."

Vaughan gritted his teeth. "And this will impact on me?"

Longley looked at him as though he was stupid. "Everywhere you go, people will stare and whisper. But it will be short-lived." He hesitated, then added, "Perhaps you ought to resume your wife hunt next season. You know you don't deal well with being the center of attention."

Vaughan eyeballed him. "I also don't deal well with being told what to do."

"Touché."

That said, Longley had a point. The attention would be unpleasant, and it might hinder his progress.

"Do you think it will be impossible for me to find a bride this season?" he asked, valuing his friend's opinion.

"No," Longley said.

Vaughan slumped in relief.

"But finding your second fiancée may take longer than finding the first did," Longley added.

Dread seeped into Vaughan's pores. "Damn."

Not for the first time, he considered how badly he wanted to prevent Reginald from inheriting, but then an image of his cousin mocking his father for crying at the news of yet another affair flashed through his mind. He gritted his teeth.

Reginald would not inherit the dukedom. Nor would any of his devil-spawn offspring.

"Do you have any suggestions?" he asked Longley. "Perhaps a girl I've already met."

Longley started to speak, but a knock at the door interrupted him.

"What is it?" Vaughan called.

The door opened, and Gladwell's gaunt frame appeared.

"The Earl of Carlisle is here to see you, Your Grace."

Vaughan caught Longley's gaze, and a question passed

between them. What on earth could the earl want? Everything was settled between them—albeit unhappily.

"I was just leaving," Longley said, rising to his feet. "Perhaps I will see you at the club later, Ashford?"

"I might come by." Particularly because he wanted to finish this conversation.

Longley departed.

"Show the earl in," Vaughan said to Gladwell.

The butler nodded and excused himself. When he returned a moment later, the earl was in tow. Carlisle stepped inside, and Gladwell closed the door behind him.

"Lord Carlisle, I wasn't expecting you," Vaughan said. "Please have a seat."

Carlisle sat on the chair that Longley had vacated.

He rubbed his hand on his pants leg. "I have a suggestion for an arrangement that might suit us both."

He hadn't met Vaughan's eyes yet, which made Vaughan wonder whether Carlisle thought he might take the suggestion poorly.

"What's that?" he asked.

Carlisle raised his eyes and seemed to take a steadying breath. "I feel terrible for the trouble my reckless daughter has caused. You expected a suitable bride and instead were landed with a scandal. I know nothing can make up for that, but I'd like to know whether you would consider marrying my other daughter, Lady Emma, instead?"

Vaughan's jaw dropped. "Excuse me?"

"It's most irregular of me to suggest it—I'm aware of that —but she is the same age as Violet, has a matching dowry, and is as well trained, if not more so, in household management."

Vaughan simply stared. He didn't know how else to respond.

His immediate reaction was to refuse and to tell Carlisle that he was insane. Based on the way the earl was still having difficulty meeting his gaze, that was exactly what he expected Vaughan to do.

He reached for the glass of brandy and gulped it, his eyes watering as it seared down his throat. Lord Carlisle's lips twitched, but he didn't comment.

"Give me a moment," Vaughan said. "You've startled me, and I need to think."

Carlisle nodded in understanding and turned away from Vaughan, possibly examining the walls and furnishings.

In all of his dealings with his peers, Vaughan had never heard of someone offering the intended bride's sister to the jilted groom as some kind of consolation prize. Surely people would be appalled by what Lord Carlisle was suggesting. After all, if Vaughan had wanted to marry Emma, then he would have courted her originally.

He briefly allowed himself to consider Lady Emma as a prospective bride. Like her father had said, she was the right age to be wed, and she had no doubt been trained in the same ways as Violet. However, she was also more reserved, which wouldn't suit his needs, as she may not take the lead when he was socially overwhelmed.

Emma was also, objectively, less beautiful than Violet, but she was still an attractive woman. Her looks were understated. The more one noticed her, the more appealing she became. He certainly wouldn't be opposed to seeing her face on the pillow beside his.

However, Longley had told him that Emma wanted love, and Vaughan wasn't prepared to give her love.

"What does Lady Emma think of this plan?" he asked Carlisle.

The earl's lips pinched together, then released. "She has agreed to it."

Vaughan grimaced. Agreement was hardly the same thing as actually wanting it.

He should say no. The word was on the tip of his tongue.

But he had to admit, the idea of having a wife handed to him on a silver platter made him pause. He didn't want to go through the hassle of meeting and wooing another appropriate young lady, and Carlisle's proposal would save him from having to do that.

"Don't you think it would cause more scandal if I were to become betrothed to Lady Emma, rather than less?" he asked.

Carlisle shrugged. "Who knows what the ton will say?"

Vaughan murmured his agreement. Society was not always predictable.

"Lady Carlisle pointed out that marrying Emma may put a stop to any gossip that Violet jilted you because of a character flaw," Carlisle said. "It's possible that some gossips will say she did it because she learned you are cruel, or something similar. Becoming engaged to Emma will head that gossip off."

He made a reasonable point.

Vaughan glanced at his brandy decanter but decided he didn't need more alcohol to addle his mind right now.

"I understand if you aren't interested in the match," Carlisle said, leaning forward, his forearms resting on his thighs. "It would be unconventional, and despite their similarities, Emma and Violet do not have the same level of attraction. I told Lady Carlisle that I would talk to you, and now I have, so my duty is discharged."

Vaughan scratched his jaw and considered what Carlisle was and wasn't saying. He didn't think the idea of marrying Emma would have the same appeal as marrying Violet did.

For some reason, that bothered Vaughan. He understood where it was coming from—hell, he'd wanted to marry Violet rather than Emma—but he was wrong to make it sound as though Emma was lesser.

She wasn't.

She was infinitely more interesting than Violet, and

therein lay the problem. He was drawn to her in a way he didn't want to be drawn to his future wife. The attraction was inconvenient, but it didn't necessarily need to be a deterrent.

If he housed her somewhere far away from him and only spent the minimum necessary time with her to get her with child, surely he could put distance between them before he developed any finer feelings.

It would be very convenient to not have to find a replacement bride.

"I need to speak with Lady Emma," Vaughan said.

EMMA CURLED MORE TIGHTLY IN ON HERSELF, CLUTCHING THE book in her hands. She was re-reading *Emma*, one of her favorite novels by Jane Austen, and silently mourning the fact she might never have a Mr. Knightley of her own.

"Emma." Her mother was breathless as she appeared in the doorway. "The Duke of Ashford is here, and he's asking for you."

Emma's lips parted. "Excuse me?"

"Come quickly," Lady Carlisle urged. "He's in the drawing room."

Emma put the book on a nearby table, stood, and shook out her skirts. Whatever the duke wanted to speak with her about, she feared it wouldn't be good. After all, if he'd rejected her father's offer out of hand, he wouldn't need to see her personally, would he?

She followed her mother into the corridor and down the stairs. Perhaps the duke was here to express his displeasure at the fact anyone could think she'd be an appropriate replacement for Violet.

They entered the drawing room, and Emma's stomach twisted as her gaze landed on him. She'd forgotten how handsome he was. His stormy eyes held hers captive as he approached.

He turned to her mother. "Lady Carlisle, may I talk with Lady Emma privately?"

Emma's mother blanched. "T-that...," she sputtered.

"You could summon Daisy," Emma said softly.

Lady Carlisle's eyes narrowed, but she stepped outside, leaving the door wide open, and spoke with Samuels in hushed tones. Emma stared down at her hands, afraid of what she might see if she looked at the duke.

Disdain? Or worse?

A minute stretched by in excruciating silence, and then Daisy moved briskly into the room and sat on a chair in the far corner.

"You may have twenty minutes," Lady Carlisle said before drawing the door closed but not latching it shut.

Emma intertwined her hands and raised her head. "Daisy, could you call for tea, please?"

While Daisy did that, Emma addressed the duke.

"I'm surprised by your visit," she said, figuring that there was no proper protocol for the situation since it wasn't exactly a "proper" situation.

"Will you sit?" he asked, and she realized that he was obligated to stand until she did so.

She went to one of the chaises in front of the fireplace, which was cold and empty. He sat on the chaise opposite, his spine stiff and his expression impossible to read.

"I wanted to talk to you directly about the possibility of arranging an engagement between us," he said.

"Oh." Her gaze flicked to Daisy, and she wished her maid were closer so she could draw comfort from her presence. While Emma was relieved that the duke didn't intend to yell at her for her parents' ridiculous idea, she almost wished he would because the alternative was that he was considering it.

She'd been counting on him being horrified by the idea so she could get out of marrying him without it being her fault, but that didn't seem to be the case.

"Your father said you agreed with the idea," he said. "But—"

The door opened, and the housekeeper stepped inside, carrying a tray containing a teapot, two cups, and several small tea cakes.

"Thank you," Emma said, grateful for the reprieve.

"You're welcome, my lady." The housekeeper left again, and this time the door clicked shut properly as she left.

Emma poured tea for each of them. "Do you take sugar?"

He shuddered. "No."

She added sugar to her own tea and blew across the surface. "I'm sorry, what were you saying before we were interrupted?"

She put her cup down and buttered a tea cake. Her mother wouldn't like it, but then her mother wasn't here to tell her not to, was she? And perhaps a tiny part of her wondered if eating the cake might put the duke off the idea of marrying her, as Lady Carlisle had always claimed it would.

He watched her movements. "Just that I want to hear from you that you're happy with the prospect of marrying me."

She laid the knife aside and bit into her tea cake, which gave her a moment to mentally compose a response.

Did she want to marry him?

Not really. She definitely wouldn't say she was "happy" with it. But nor did she have many alternatives, and doing this could save Sophie and protect her family. Besides, he didn't seem to be a bad man. The fact he'd come here to ask her opinion rather than assuming her father spoke for her said a lot about his character.

"I am," she said, her tone coming across more confident than she actually was.

He held her gaze for a long time but seemed to find whatever he was looking for, because he nodded and then buttered himself a tea cake.

"Do you understand that it won't be a love match?" he asked, not looking up from the platter as he spoke.

"I do." Although given enough time, maybe they could come to love each other. He wasn't heartless, and she was willing to dedicate herself to the endeavor.

He lifted his tea cake to his mouth and paused. "You're amenable to that?"

She pursed her lips. "It isn't what I always imagined, but circumstances have changed, and I will be content with it."

He took a bite and wiped a crumb from his lip. "I don't wish to make you unhappy."

Emma set aside what remained of her tea cake, suddenly not hungry. "Unfortunately, I cannot predict the future, but I can say, based on our current situation, that I think this might be the best chance at finding happiness that I have available."

That was true enough, much as she may wish it otherwise.

He finished the tiny cake with a few bites and wiped his hands on a napkin. "I seem to recall you saying that you have no interest in me."

Her face grew hot. "I shouldn't have said that. I wasn't at my best."

"Quite the contrary." He studied her intently. "I appreciated the honesty."

"It isn't that I find you... unappealing," she said, wishing the floor would swallow her up. "I'm sure you know that you're handsome, and as a duke, you could marry any unwed lady of the ton whom you wanted."

A smile quirked his lips. "Now that you're done trying to soothe my ego, may I make my point?"

"Of course." Her cheeks blazed. She pressed her fingertips to them, wishing she weren't quite so fair.

"Why would you wish to marry someone you have no interest in?" he asked.

She blinked at him, stunned by his directness.

His expression wavered. "Have I overset you?"

"No, not at all." She drew in a shaky breath and picked up her teacup to keep her hands busy so she wouldn't wring them and give away her nervousness. "My initial assessment may have been overly harsh. You are attractive, seem relatively intelligent, and are not involved in any scandals. I could be comfortable with you."

He nodded. "I can give you all of the creature comforts you desire. You would want for nothing as my wife."

Except, perhaps, the love she'd always longed for.

"I would expect an heir," he said, and she inclined her head in acknowledgement. "My duchess will need to be well-presented, respectable, and able to play the role of hostess when required."

"I can do all of that," she told him and sipped her tea. A prickle of awareness crept through her at the thought of creating a baby with him. She wasn't sure exactly what the mechanics involved were, but she was reasonably sure they both needed to be undressed.

He moistened his lips. "She would also need to be discreet if she were to become romantically involved with anyone else."

Emma's jaw dropped. Was he implying that, were they to become wed, he'd expect her to engage in extramarital affairs? Would he do the same? She'd thought he had more honor than to say so to her face.

"When I marry, I shall be faithful," she said through gritted teeth. "And if I were to discover that my husband had not been, I would discreetly pack my things and make sure I was as far from him as possible."

Something flashed through his eyes. Was that a hint of approval, and why did she like it so much?

"Noted, my lady. I think we have reached an understanding. Shall we summon your parents to share the news?"

Emma bit her lip, hard, so she wouldn't give away her distress. "Daisy, please request the presence of Lord and Lady Carlisle."

Daisy went to the door and exchanged words with someone on the other side but didn't leave. A few seconds later, she moved aside, and the earl and countess stepped inside.

The duke stood, and Emma followed suit. They met her parents midway across the room.

Ashford took her arm. "Lady Emma and I have agreed to marry."

CHAPTER 10

London,
November, 1819

THE MODISTE, MADAM BAPTISTE, WAS LOCATED IN A STONE building on the corner of a busy street in Mayfair. The windows were filled with dresses and swathes of fabric, and Emma was eager to see them more closely. It was the only part of her wedding she was looking forward to.

While she was not as fashionable as Violet, she knew what she liked, and she loved ordering new outfits.

Lady Carlisle pushed the door open, and a bell tinkled above it. Emma glanced at Sophie, who was gazing around, wide-eyed. She didn't usually accompany her older sisters to the modiste, but their mother had allowed her to come along today, since Emma had said she would enjoy her company.

After all, it was Emma they were shopping for.

A pair of women stepped out from behind a row of fabrics, and Emma froze. The older of the two, Lady Talbot, spotted them first. Considering that the last time they'd seen her, Lady Talbot had given them the cut direct, Emma wasn't expecting much in the way of a greeting.

To her surprise, a broad smile broke out across Lady Talbot's face. Emma glanced at her mother, wondering how she would handle this encounter.

"Ah, it's the Carlisles," Lady Talbot said, sweeping toward them. "How wonderful to see you."

Emma's mother didn't speak, apparently stunned into silence.

"Lady Talbot," Emma managed to say past the tightness of her throat. "It's a pleasure."

It wasn't. It hadn't been even before the marchioness had insulted them. She was a gossip and a terrible snob, and honestly, Emma didn't like her very much.

Glancing at Lady Talbot's daughter, Margaret, Emma added, "Good afternoon, Lady Margaret."

The tall, sallow girl's mouth pinched. "Likewise, Lady Emma. You look well."

Her expression gave the impression that it pained her to say it.

"Oh!" Lady Talbot raised her hand to her mouth as though she'd just had a thought. "Are you here to order a gown for your wedding, Lady Emma? You will make a beautiful bride. Won't she, dear?"

Margaret nodded dutifully. "Yes, Mother."

"So she will," Lady Carlisle chimed in, finally having recovered enough to speak. "And to think that I have mothered a future duchess."

She looked somewhat smug about this fact. After being cut at the opera, Emma couldn't blame her.

"You must tell us how you secured a duke for Lady Emma," Lady Talbot said, coming closer. "Lady Violet was declared an incomparable at the beginning of the season, so no one was surprised when she landed him, but with Lady Emma…. Well, suffice it to say, all of the mamas shall want to hear from you."

Emma hid a scowl. Why did people say such things when

she was standing right there? Sophie nudged her arm and sent her a small smile, then narrowed her eyes at Lady Talbot. At least Emma knew that Sophie would always support her unconditionally.

"How is dear Violet?" Lady Talbot asked, feigning concern. "Is she returning to London to finish out the season?"

Lady Carlisle straightened. "I'm afraid I can't share Violet's plans at this time."

Probably because she had no idea what they were. None of them did. They didn't even know where, precisely, Violet was.

Madam Baptiste emerged from the back room, and her dark gaze shifted from one group to the other before settling on Emma.

"Lady Emma, we are ready for you," she said, her tone polished enough to almost hide her low birth. "Please come through to the fitting room."

"Excuse me, ladies," Lady Carlisle said.

"Wait!" Lady Talbot exclaimed as Lady Carlisle guided her daughters toward the back room.

Lady Carlisle arched one imperious eyebrow at the other woman.

"Will you be attending the Bevington's ball on Friday?" Lady Talbot asked.

"We will."

Lady Talbot nodded approvingly. "Then we'll talk to you there."

Lady Carlisle pursed her lips. "Perhaps."

Emma's lips twitched as she stifled the urge to laugh.

The Carlisle women passed Lady Talbot and Margaret and followed Madam Baptiste into a private room. Emma was relieved to be out of sight of the others. She'd been rigid since she'd seen them, worried about what they might do or say.

A small wooden pedestal stood in the center of the space they found themselves in. The walls were white, and a massive mirror occupied one of them. Light flowed in through a window near the ceiling.

"Did you see that?" Lady Carlisle asked, spinning around and beaming at Emma. "We are accepted again."

Emma's heart lifted. Perhaps she wasn't getting the husband she'd anticipated, but seeing her mother happy made her think the sacrifice might be worth it.

"More than 'accepted,' I would say," Madam Baptiste replied, her burgundy skirt swishing as she turned to face them. "With a duke as a son-in-law, they will fall over themselves to get into your good graces."

"They had better." Despite the tartness of her tone, Lady Carlisle seemed pleased.

"Don't forget what they did to you," Sophie said. "They were ready to make us outcasts only ten days ago."

"And now everything is better," Lady Carlisle said with determined cheer.

Madam Baptiste gestured to the pedestal. "Lady Emma, would you please stand there?"

Emma complied, twisting the end of her braided hair self-consciously as the modiste circled her. The woman's face never betrayed her thoughts, so it was impossible to know whether or not she approved of what she saw.

"You are to be a duchess, so you will need more than a wedding gown," she said, crossing her arms as she scrutinized Emma from head to toe. "You will need a wardrobe of beautiful gowns to choose from, but we'll start with wedding attire, since that's the most exciting and urgent event."

"Will I get a new dress too?" Sophie asked.

"Yes, dear," Lady Carlisle said. "You and I will both need something for the wedding, but let's deal with Emma first."

"Lady Emma," Madam Baptiste said. "What style of wedding gown would you like?"

"I think—"

"Something exquisite," Lady Carlisle interrupted. "White, obviously, but perhaps with a slight pink sheen. Emma looks good in pink."

Emma cleared her throat and shot her mother a look.

Lady Carlisle wrinkled her nose. "Of course, only if that's what you would like. It's your wedding."

Emma grinned, surprised by how good it felt to get the opportunity to give her opinion. She wasn't sure she'd receive the same level of consideration from her mother if she wasn't so aware of what Emma was giving up for the family.

"I would like something simple but elegant," Emma said. "I don't need an intricate or fussy gown, but I do agree with my mother's suggestion of white with a hint of pink."

"Very nice. Let me get some samples for you."

Madam Baptiste went through the door to the shop. She returned after only a few moments with a selection of fabrics draped over her arm.

"What do you think of this?" she asked, holding a scrap of embroidered white lace up to Emma.

"It's a bit... too much," Emma said. "Lace is fine, but perhaps something more understated."

They tried several more options before deciding on a white fabric for the bodice and underskirt with a fine lace of the palest pink to layer over the skirt.

Emma did her best to stand still while the modiste and her assistant measured her and pinned fabric into place around her, flinching when the assistant accidentally stabbed her with a pin.

Lady Carlisle watched eagerly, but Sophie had retreated to the corner, and she seemed to be deep in thought.

"What color would you like to wear?" Emma asked her sister.

Sophie looked up, but rather than answering Emma, she took her by surprise.

"You don't have to do this, you know," she said. "I'll be fine, and so will Mother and Father even if they don't think so now."

Lady Carlisle gasped. "Sophie!"

Sophie just shrugged.

Emma's chest constricted. "That's very sweet of you, Sophie, but I feel I must. It will be for the best. You'll see."

"Indeed," Lady Carlisle exclaimed, glaring at her youngest daughter as if she'd committed an outrageous sin.

Madam Baptiste laughed. "Who would not want to marry a duke?"

VAUGHAN FLIPPED OVER HIS CARDS, REVEALING A ROYAL FLUSH. "I win."

Complaining under their breath, his companions pushed the winnings toward him. Vaughan gathered them, then collected the cards and shuffled them, ready for the next hand.

Across from him, Mr. Norton Falvey puffed on a cigar. He exhaled and blew the smoke directly toward Vaughan.

Vaughan tried to fan the smoke away. "If you must do that, kindly aim it elsewhere."

Mr. Falvey smirked. "What would be the fun in that?"

Vaughan scowled at him, and Falvey stubbed the end of the cigar on a tray and set it aside.

"I hear you've found yourself a new fiancée," the Earl of Wembley said as Vaughan dealt cards to each of the four men seated at the table in the Regent.

"Yes," Falvey said. "It's a little unusual to take your former fiancée's sister as your betrothed."

Vaughan met Longley's gaze across the table. His friend

had warned Vaughan that he might face comments like this, but honestly, he'd rather that than brave the marriage mart again.

"What do you think of Lady Emma?" Wembley asked, picking up his cards and studying them.

Vaughan checked his own cards. He had two tens and an ace, but nothing else of use.

"She seems pleasant enough," he said.

Falvey barked a laugh. "You were conned. You should never have accepted the less-pretty Carlisle girl as a substitute for the other. There are plenty of pretty chits out there, and you could have had your choice of them."

Aggravation bubbled within Vaughan as they each made their move. How must Lady Emma feel about constantly being compared to her twin and coming off worse? There was no chance that she wasn't aware of the comparisons. Nobody was subtle about it, and really, Emma was quite attractive in her own right.

"Lady Emma is sensible and even-tempered, which can't be said for all pretty chits." Although she hadn't been so even-tempered when she'd snapped at him at Mayhew House.

"Lady Emma is a nice girl," Longley said, a warning in his tone.

Falvey grumbled.

"It doesn't matter what she is, anyway," Vaughan said. "I have no desire to become one of those men who is besotted with their wife. As long as she behaves appropriately, I don't need to know anything else about her."

"You're a stick in the mud," Falvey said. "You only get one chance to choose a bride. You should make the most of it. Not all of us have women tripping over us like you do."

Vaughan scoffed. "Because of the title."

Falvey waved his hand dismissively. "Who cares what the reason is."

"He's not a stick in the mud," Wembley said. "He's cold."

Vaughan frowned. He wanted to protest but then recalled that the earl had a daughter of marriageable age and probably wanted more for her than Vaughan was willing to give Emma. It made sense that he'd be protective of the young ladies. It wasn't personal.

But it still stung.

"It's not that I don't care for her," he said, unable to help wondering whether Emma also thought he was cold, and if he'd be bothered if she did. "I've seen what happens when men get too attached to their wives. You recall my father?"

Each of the men nodded in acknowledgement. Everyone knew the stories about the previous Duke of Ashford. Not only had he been a miserable wretch while his duchess was alive as a result of her many affairs, but when she'd died in a carriage accident, he'd ceased functioning as a member of society.

Some days, he hadn't even gotten out of bed.

"Your concern is understandable," Longley said, then called a higher bid. Wembley folded, but Vaughan and Falvey matched Longley. "You should at least get to know Lady Emma, though. From what I've heard, your mother was something of a hell-raiser before she ever married your father. Lady Emma's reputation is quite different."

"She does seem a decent kind of girl," Wembley said.

Vaughan gritted his teeth. He knew they were coming from a good place, but they needed to trust him to know what was best for his own peace of mind.

"I have no intention of seeing Lady Emma until the wedding, and then, once she's with child, I'll be perfectly happy to live separate lives."

CHAPTER 11

EMMA HAD EXPECTED TO BE EXCITED ON THE MORNING OF HER wedding, but instead she felt faintly nauseous. She hadn't fully come to terms with the fact that she was about to marry the Duke of Ashford. She didn't even know the man's first name. Surely one ought to know the name of the person they were marrying.

She choked down a breakfast of dry toast and tea while listening to her mother exclaim over what a wonderful day it was going to be and then returned to her bedchamber to bathe.

Once she was clean and her hair was dry, she sat on the chair in front of the mirror in her bedchamber while Daisy fussed around her.

Emma's unsettled stomach had been gurgling and rumbling, and she blushed harder each time, certain that Daisy must be able to hear. Thank God she said nothing.

Daisy arranged hairpins on the cabinet and measured out several lengths of the blue ribbon that Sophie had chosen for her. Emma watched her quick, neat movements.

Perhaps she wouldn't be quite so nervous if she'd actually seen the duke sometime over the past month. She'd expected that they would meet, at least semiregularly, to discuss wedding details. If not for the fact that her father had assured her that the necessary papers had been arranged, she might worry she'd dreamed up the whole thing.

"Lady Sophie was right about this shade of blue," Daisy said, holding a ribbon beside her face. "It's a lovely match for your eyes."

"Hers too." At this minute, in another room, Sophie was getting her own hair done by Jane, who'd become her maid after Violet had left.

Emma studied their reflection as Daisy began brushing her hair and gathering it into sections. The room was too quiet. She wasn't much of a talker, and maids weren't expected to make conversation unless invited to. Emma had always imagined that she'd share her wedding day with Violet, and vice versa, but it was not to be.

"Do you think Violet had a nice wedding?" she asked Daisy.

Daisy started pinning her hair into place. "I certainly hope she did, since she caused so much distress in order to secure it."

Yes, she had. Emma had been angry at her for that, but today, she couldn't find it in her to be vexed. She was too numb. Even if Violet had had a simple ceremony with the bare minimum of witnesses and no fancy gown, surely it would be worth it to marry a man she was willing to risk everything for.

Emma would never know.

"I've never gone for so long without her," Emma said.

Being twins, they tended to do everything together. They'd been schooled together, learned to dance together, and emerged into society together. She'd always been a little frustrated by that since Violet always shone brighter than she did, but being apart from her for such an important milestone set Emma on edge.

"You're going to be fine," Daisy said. "And after, I'll be able to tell my family I work for a duchess."

As part of the arrangements, they'd agreed that Daisy would come with Emma to her new home. Daisy had no particular attachment to Carlisle House, and she was loyal to Emma.

"Thank you for coming with me," Emma said. It would be nice to have a familiar face.

"It will be my honor, my lady." She giggled. "Soon I will be calling you 'Your Grace.'"

They sat in silence while Daisy finished Emma's hair. When it was done, Emma stared at herself in the mirror. Her long blond hair was secured in a simple knot on the back of her head with loose curls in the front.

"Are you ready to dress?" Daisy asked.

"Yes." Emma stood, but at that moment, Lady Carlisle entered the bedchamber.

"Daisy, can you give Emma and me a few minutes alone?" Lady Carlisle asked.

Daisy dipped into a curtsey and left.

Lady Carlisle sat on the cream chaise and patted the spot beside her. Emma joined her, her stomach clenching with nerves.

"Emma, before you wed, there is something we must discuss." Lady Carlisle looked uncomfortable but soldiered on. "It's about the wedding night."

"Oh?" Emma straightened. Her lack of knowledge about what to expect tonight had been weighing on her. Fortunately, with how many other things she had to worry about, she hadn't had much time to dwell on it.

"How much do you know about what happens between a man and a woman when they become husband and wife?" Lady Carlisle asked.

"Almost nothing," Emma replied. "I've heard they may undress together."

"Yes." Lady Carlisle turned toward her. "In order to get an heir, the duke will, erm, insert his male parts inside you and plant his seed within."

Emma bit her lip, completely confused. "I don't understand."

Lady Carlisle rubbed her temples and groaned, as if Emma was purposefully being difficult. "You know that men and women have different... appendages, correct?"

"Yes," Emma said. She'd also seen as much herself when it came to horses. It was impossible not to notice that stallions had parts that mares did not.

"Well, your husband will insert his shaft inside you. It will feel good for him, and after a while, he will spurt liquid seed from his shaft into your channel, and that is how you get with child."

Emma cocked her head. "Will it feel good for me too?"

Lady Carlisle frowned. "Why would you ask that?"

"Because you said it would feel good for him." It didn't seem fair that it wouldn't feel good for both parties, although Emma had serious doubts that it would because the idea of anything being shoved inside her orifices did not sound pleasant.

"It may," Lady Carlisle said. "Some women find pleasure in the act, but most don't. If it lasts longer than you would like, I find it helpful to mentally organize my wardrobe."

Emma hid a grin. She hoped her mother had never told Lord Carlisle that.

"Thank you, Mother. I think I understand." She only hoped that the duke had a better concept of the act than she did.

"Good. Good." Lady Carlisle stood and wiped her palms on her dress. "Then let's get you into your gown."

She summoned Daisy, and together they held the dress while Emma stepped into it. Her mother fussed with the front while Daisy set to work fastening the row of tiny buttons that lined Emma's spine.

"You've never looked more beautiful." Lady Carlisle's voice rang with sincerity. "The duke is going to be thrilled to have you as his bride."

Tears pricked Emma's eyes. Her mother wasn't often sentimental, and for her to say something so lovely…. Well, Emma wished she could believe her.

Lady Carlisle glanced at the clock. "The carriage will be ready."

"Good luck, Lady Emma," Daisy said as Emma and Lady Carlisle departed.

Emma took one last look over her shoulder at the pale blue walls and ornate mirror, knowing that this room would never be hers again. Sorrow infiltrated her heart, making it heavy. She would have a new life as a duchess, and it would be full of excitement, but leaving her old life behind was harder than she'd anticipated.

"Come along," Lady Carlisle urged. "We want to be fashionably late, but not so late that people begin to gossip."

Emma's lips hitched up, and she was grateful for the ridiculous statement. They hastened down the stairs. Lord Carlisle and Sophie waited near the main entrance. Sophie glanced up and smiled as she saw them.

"Emma, you look wonderful," she said. "Like a princess."

"Thank you, Sophie." Emma studied her younger sister, whose dress was a darker shade of pink than the lace overlay of her own gown. "So do you."

"Emma." Lord Carlisle offered her his arm, and she took it and allowed him to guide her down the outside stairs and to the carriage. White flowers and ribbons adorned the carriage, making it obvious to anyone they passed that a bride was inside.

The family gathered inside the carriage and rode to St. George's church on Hanover Square. They'd needed a large venue to host the many people that Lady Carlisle had insisted on inviting. Emma would have preferred a small wedding, but her mother seemed to think that having a large guest list would render the union less scandalous.

When they arrived, a footman opened the carriage door, and Lord Carlisle assisted each of the ladies as they exited. From inside the church, music began to play. Emma reached for Sophie's hand and squeezed it, then their mother ushered Sophie toward the entrance.

Emma kept herself out of view as Sophie made her way down the aisle. Lady Carlisle darted around the back of the guests, and then Lord Carlisle held Emma's arm and escorted her into the church.

The almost overpowering scent of flowers wafted through the space. Emma's breath caught at the sight of the duke standing in front of the altar with the Earl of Longley beside him.

Her future husband's gaze locked on hers, and his storm-cloud-gray eyes swirled with unreadable emotion. Emma couldn't look away. She was hardly aware of the floor beneath her feet or of the hundreds of pairs of eyes watching her every move. All of it fell away.

When they reached the front of the church, Lord Carlisle handed Emma to the duke—whose name she really needed to learn. They were told to face each other, and Emma lowered her gaze to the small boutonniere tucked into the duke's pocket. Pale pink, matching the accents of her dress. Was that a coincidence?

She stood still while the minister spoke, but she couldn't make out the individual words over the rushing in her ears.

People moved in the periphery of her vision, but she didn't know who they were or what they were doing. It was all she could do to keep herself in the moment. Her mind wanted to run free and leave her body stuck here.

Somehow, she repeated the phrases the minister

instructed her to say, and the rumble of the duke's voice told her he was doing the same. Then, all of a sudden, he reached for her. She flinched backward, and heat flooded her cheeks as she realized he'd been trying to kiss her to seal the union.

She looked like a fool.

She stuck her lips out, her heart hammering dangerously fast as she waited for his mouth to brush over hers. The touch was whisper soft, his lips silken, and she sighed. A shudder rippled through her, and she closed her eyes. It was… nicer… than she'd expected.

But it also made everything so much more real.

AFTER THEY WERE PROCLAIMED MAN AND WIFE, VAUGHAN escorted Emma back down the center aisle and to the open carriage. He paused to help her up onto the step before climbing in after her.

The wedding guests followed them out, cheering and chatting, but Emma's mind seemed to be somewhere else entirely. When he nudged her, she raised her hand and waved, but her deep blue eyes were oddly vacant.

Maybe she was in shock. It wasn't every day that a woman became a duchess, after all. Or perhaps it was the stress of marrying her sister's former betrothed that had unsettled her mind. He'd been assured that women were delicate creatures—not that his own mother could ever have been considered fragile.

As the carriage lurched into motion, she swayed in her seat, and he steadied her.

"Are you well?" he asked as they moved away from the church toward Carlisle House, where the wedding breakfast was to be held.

"Hmm?" She turned to him distractedly. "Oh, fine."

She did not seem fine.

"Are you warm enough?" he asked because being in an exposed carriage could be a bit chilly.

"I'm a little cold, but we'll be there soon," she said.

He shucked off his jacket and draped it around her shoulders. "Here."

Her eyes widened, and it occurred to him that wearing a man's clothing might seem scandalous to her. He hadn't given it much thought, but her exposure to men was surely confined to ballrooms and other proper society affairs. He doubted her mother would have allowed intimacy like shared clothing.

She hunched, and drew the coat around herself. "Thank you."

When they arrived at Carlisle House, a matronly woman wearing all green greeted them outside. Vaughan vaguely recognized her and assumed she was a relative of the Carlisles.

"Come in," she said. "Breakfast will be ready in half an hour. Emma, you can refresh yourself in your former bedchamber if you wish. Your Grace, Lord Carlisle has made his office available for you."

"I appreciate that." Vaughan walked with Emma to the base of the stairs, and when she continued up them, he turned down the corridor to go to her father's office.

He let himself in and poured himself a brandy, figuring that he deserved it for what he was going through today. Weddings were his idea of torture, especially when he was the main attraction. People everywhere, many of them staring, and all of whom hoped to exchange a few words with him at some point.

Hell.

There was a small bookshelf, so he slipped a book from it —*A Natural History of Surrey*—and started reading. It seemed like only a few minutes later that the door opened and Lord Carlisle let himself in.

"All well?" Carlisle asked.

"Yes." Vaughan closed the book and returned it to the shelf.

Carlisle watched his movements. "Ah, you found some reading material, then?"

"I did. Thank you for allowing me to use your office."

"It is no trouble." The man's face lit with a smile. "You're family now. Speaking of which, we'd better join them in the dining hall before Lady Carlisle comes looking for us."

With a sense of impending doom, Vaughan accompanied Lord Carlisle to the dining hall, where a long rectangular table was laid with silverware and at least a dozen covered serving platters.

"Your Grace!"

He looked up and noticed Lady Carlisle calling for him from midway along the table, where there was an empty seat clearly reserved for him, since Emma sat on the adjacent chair.

A dozen faces turned toward him, and his throat constricted. He struggled to draw in a good breath and surreptitiously dried his sweaty palms on his pants. Fortunately, someone had seated Longley and his mother—the dowager countess—opposite him, so at least he would have a pair of friendly faces amid this group of distant acquaintances.

He marched over to Lady Carlisle.

"Welcome to the family," she said. "We are most pleased to call you a son-in-law."

He tipped his head toward her and then dropped onto the seat. Lord and Lady Carlisle sat to Emma's right, but her younger sister didn't seem to be at the table. He was just relieved nobody had invited Violet—or that she had realized it would be best if she did not attend the nuptials.

He glanced around the table. All of the seats were full, so he assumed mealtime wouldn't be far off. He snuck a look at his wife out of the corner of his eye. Her cheeks were pale, but at least she didn't look as vacant as she had earlier. Perhaps having a little time to herself had restored her.

Unlike her sister, Emma did not strike him as a social butterfly.

"Your Grace," the lady to his left said—the one who'd greeted them upon their arrival. "It's been far too long since I saw you in London."

Across the table, Longley laughed. "Ashford prefers the country to the city."

"Is that so?" The lady crinkled her nose. "I've always preferred the bustle of London myself. It gets too quiet in the middle of nowhere. My husband adores the country, but I get quite bored."

Something nudged his shoulder, and he realized that Emma had leaned closer to him.

"My aunt, Lady Tabitha," she murmured. "My father's younger sister."

He gave her the slightest nod, grateful for the information. He hated not knowing with whom he was speaking.

Servants emerged from the kitchen and raised the covers from the food, revealing roasted birds and a variety of bread rolls and accompaniments. A cake occupied the center of the table. Three tiers high, with white icing and a rose placed carefully on top.

"Do you like pheasant, Your Grace?" Lady Tabitha asked.

"I like most foods," Vaughan replied. Except for mushrooms. There was something about them that made him gag. Perhaps it was how slimy they were. Nasty little things.

"A good way to be," she said.

Vaughan caught Longley's gaze across the table, silently pleading for rescue. Thankfully, his friend got the message.

"I hear your daughters are learning the violin," he said, and Lady Tabitha launched into a long story about how gifted her progeny were and how, if they weren't to be ladies of leisure, they would have made fine musicians.

The meal lasted five painstaking courses.

For the duration, Vaughan and Emma made stilted conversation while others around them tried to gain Vaughan's attention. When it was finally over, afternoon was beginning to turn into evening, and Vaughan was stuffed so full, he couldn't eat another bite.

Most of the guests had departed. Longley and his mother had waited until only the earl's direct family remained before excusing himself—a fact for which Vaughan was grateful.

The family gathered to see him and Lady Emma off. They converged on the roadside outside Carlisle House and Emma hugged each of them, lingering on the embrace with her youngest sister. He wondered whether they were particularly close.

When she'd finished her farewells, they got into the carriage, and Vaughan relaxed, feeling a weight slip off his shoulders. Finally, he'd have some space to quiet his mind.

They rolled away from Carlisle House, and Vaughan looked straight ahead while Emma practically hung out the window to wave until her family was out of sight. He felt a pang of sympathy for her. While having a wife would change his life to a degree, it had completely altered hers.

He extended his legs, thankful that their belongings had been sent ahead of them along with Emma's maid.

Emma settled onto the seat and, blessedly, didn't seem in the mood to talk. However, as they reached the edge of the city, she tensed beside him.

"Are we not going to your London house?" she asked.

He frowned. "No. We're heading for my family's seat in Norfolk."

Had he not told her that?

She turned to him, her eyes wide. "We're leaving London? But I..."

"Yes?" he prompted.

"Nothing." She shook her head and pressed her lips together.

The pang of guilt worsened.

Damn.

He'd made an effort to avoid his bride in the weeks leading up to their wedding, but he'd never meant to blind-side her like this. What a goddamn oversight.

CHAPTER 12

SHE WAS LEAVING LONDON?

How could he not have told her that?

Emma loved the country, and while she'd never been to Norfolk, she was sure it wasn't so different from Surrey. However, if she'd known that she was leaving London, she'd have taken more time to make her farewells. She'd have hugged Sophie for even longer, and perhaps extracted a promise from her to write.

She'd thought that she'd be a short carriage ride away from her family in Mayfair. She'd found comfort in the idea of being able to return to her parent's home whenever she liked. Now, Carlisle House would be more than a day's journey away.

She mentally kicked herself. She shouldn't have assumed they'd be staying in London. She should have asked. Not that she had many opportunities to do so. Perhaps if she'd seen her husband-to-be sometime in the month prior to their wedding, they wouldn't have had this misunderstanding.

"Tell me more about your home in Norfolk," she said. "What is it called?"

He glanced at her, divots forming between his eyebrows

as if he were surprised by the question. "Ashford Hall. It's a large Elizabethan house set on a sprawling property."

"Do many people live there?" she asked, fiddling with the hem of her skirt in an attempt to distract herself from the fact that she was alone in a carriage with a man—her husband—and likely would be for several more hours.

He rubbed at his temples. "I'm afraid I have a headache. I'm exhausted after the day we've had. Do you mind if we don't speak for a while so I can rest my head?"

Emma closed her mouth. He'd made the request so politely, but she couldn't help feeling chastened. Her fists tightened in her skirts. She wasn't a very good traveler. Her mind tended to wander, and she got bored easily. She didn't want to irritate the duke, but without something to occupy her mind, she'd probably bother him more.

"I understand. I don't suppose you have any reading material?" she asked.

He leaned over and, to her surprise, lifted the padded seat off the bench opposite them. Within the bench, where some carriages stored warm bricks, were a stack of books. He reached inside and offered her one. She read the title. It was an adventure novel.

"Will this do?" he asked.

"Yes, thank you."

He put the seat back in place and gazed blindly into space while Emma cracked open the book. It was worn and had clearly been read many times. She should have guessed that the duke was a reader.

Although if she had considered the possibility, she'd have thought it more likely for him to read political treatises and land management books than novels.

The inside of the carriage was dim as the afternoon light faded, and Emma angled herself toward the window to get the most light possible onto the page. She leaned over it and began to read.

She was rapidly engrossed in the story and continued turning the pages for much longer than she ought to have before finally giving in because it was too dark to continue. Her mother would have scolded her for squinting in case it gave her wrinkles, but the duke didn't seem to care.

In fact, he'd hardly moved since they'd started on their journey. If not for the fact that his eyes were open, she might have thought he'd fallen asleep.

"How far are we traveling today?" she asked softly, hoping he wouldn't chide her for breaking the silence.

"There is a small town we will be arriving in shortly," he said without looking at her. "The inn there, the Fox and Hound, is comfortable and we will be spending the night."

She nodded, pleased that they weren't making the journey all at once. It could be done if they changed horses and rode through the night, but it would be quite unpleasant. She'd prefer to stretch her legs and have a room to herself.

Emma looked around for something she could use as a bookmark, but not seeing anything, she attempted to commit the page to memory so she could resume reading from there tomorrow.

She glanced at the duke—her husband—but he still didn't seem inclined to make conversation, so she scooted closer to the carriage wall and rested her head against it. Vibrations from the road buzzed through her cheek, but the soft leather and the padding lessened it to the degree where they didn't bother her as she closed her eyes.

Had Violet traveled with this level of comfort?

For all of the awkwardness between her and Ashford, the carriage was well-appointed, and she couldn't have asked for better traveling arrangements. Especially since they'd be stopping at an inn for the night, where she'd presumably have a soft bed and warm food.

Violet had probably had to ride nonstop toward Scotland so that their uncle wouldn't catch up with her. Emma felt a flash of sympathy before recalling that Violet's actions had led to her being here in a carriage bound for Norfolk, miles away from her family.

Of course, Emma could not hold Violet completely responsible. She had made her own choices. Her parents might have encouraged her down this road, but they hadn't forced her hand.

Still, if Violet had been minorly inconvenienced by less-than-luxurious travel, Emma would draw a smidgeon of pleasure from that.

The carriage bumped over a pothole, and Emma's head bounced against the leather. She winced and sat up straight to avoid it happening again.

Fortunately, she didn't get sick during carriage rides as her mother did. A fact she was grateful for if she was going to be making trips back and forth from London,

Hopefully, Ashford would not mind visiting her family. She wanted to see Sophie blossom into a young woman and to support her during her season so she could have her choice of match—whomever that might be.

She snuck a look at Ashford out of the corner of her eye. Perhaps he would be able to advise her about the character of any young men who caught Sophie's attention.

But she was getting ahead of herself. She had at least two years of marriage to navigate before Sophie would have a season.

The first two years of a long marriage that stretched out ahead of her. She was tied to this man she didn't really know or understand. She would have time to remedy that. Ashford may have said he didn't want a love match, but surely he could have nothing against being friends with his wife. Anything could grow from there.

A faint glow lit the horizon.

"That's our destination," Ashford said, breaking the silence.

"We will be there soon then," Emma said.

Ashford didn't reply. Honestly, Emma wasn't sure whether she'd expected him to. The man seemed to like the quiet.

They drove in silence for another fifteen minutes, the lights gradually growing brighter and more defined. As they arrived on the outskirts of the village, Emma glanced out the window. Small, neat houses lined the street, but she couldn't see anyone out and about.

The carriage turned into a courtyard outside a large wooden building painted dark red that had a sign above the door that read Fox and Hound.

Ashford got out first and offered Emma his hand. Hesitantly, she laid her hand atop his and allowed him to help her out. While she subtly shook the pins and needles from her legs, he exchanged a few words with his coachman, and then the carriage was taken away.

His arm still interlinked with hers, Ashford led Emma into the inn. She gazed around at the brown walls and wooden floor and then smiled at the rosy-cheeked woman who greeted them.

"It's the Duke of Ashford," the woman exclaimed in a broad accent. "And this must be the new duchess."

"Indeed," Ashford said. "Mrs. Lemmings, please allow me to introduce Her Grace, Emma Stanhope, the Duchess of Ashford."

Emma gripped him more tightly to steady herself. She shouldn't be surprised to hear him refer to her by a title she was unaccustomed to, yet she was. She didn't feel like much of a "Her Grace", and to be honest, she wasn't certain she'd known that the duke's surname was Stanhope.

"It is a pleasure to meet you," Emma said.

"The pleasure is all mine, Your Grace." Mrs. Lemmings bobbed a curtsey. "I hope you'll enjoy your stay with us."

"I'm sure we will," Emma said.

Mrs. Lemmings glanced from her to the duke. "Come with me, and I'll show you to your rooms. Your travel bags will be brought in shortly."

Emma didn't think much of her phrasing until they'd been taken up a flight of stairs, walked down a corridor, and were handed the keys for two different rooms. Because the duke had booked them two rooms.

Plural.

Was such a thing normal for newly married couples?

For some reason, Emma had assumed that they would share a room. Or at the very least, that they would have connecting quarters. Instead, her bedroom was across the hall from his.

Mrs. Lemmings was clearly waiting for their approval prior to leaving, so Emma thanked her and turned the key in the lock, conscious of the duke standing somewhere behind her. The room was simple, with a bed, a nightstand, and a small table with a mirror over it. It wasn't fancy, but it was clean.

"It's perfect," she said.

Mrs. Lemming beamed. "Supper will be ready soon. I'll come when it is."

"Thank you."

The other woman departed, but the duke didn't go to his own room yet.

"Does it meet with your satisfaction?" he asked quietly.

"Yes." Having a bed would be lovely. "I will see you at supper?"

He nodded and turned away.

Emma entered the bedroom and closed the door behind herself, wondering again about the separate chambers. Perhaps Ashford was trying to give her space to prepare herself for her wedding night. He struck her as a thoughtful man even if not an openly kind one.

That must be it.

It only took a few minutes to refresh herself. Emma sprawled on the bed and stretched her limbs. She didn't mind being seated for long periods of time, but carriages could be so confining.

She closed her eyes, only to be jolted to attention shortly after by a knock at the door. When she answered, Mrs. Lemmings stood on the other side.

"Supper is served," she said. "The duke is already in the dining room downstairs. I'll take you to him."

Emma followed her down the stairs and into a warm space with a crackling fire in the hearth. Another couple were sharing a meal near the window, and the duke was waiting for her at a round table beside the wall.

Emma crossed the faded red carpet. He stood as she approached and pulled her chair out.

"I only ordered a light meal since we ate so much earlier," he said as she sat. "I hope that suits you."

"It does." Honestly, she could have slept without eating anything at all, especially since her insides were tangled with nerves.

Mrs. Lemmings appeared beside the table, carrying a tray, which she set down. She placed a bowl of stew in front of each of them and a plate containing a couple of thick slices of bread in the center of the table.

"Chicken stew," she said. "Would you like something to drink?"

"Tea, please," Emma said.

"Nothing for me," Ashford said.

When Mrs. Lemmings left to get the tea, an awkward hush fell over them. Emma leaned over her stew and inhaled the delicious savory scent of chicken. She waited until the duke raised his spoon before lifting her own.

Chicken and mild spices danced on her tongue. The stew tasted as good as it smelled, and she broke off a piece of bread and happily dunked it in. As she bit into the soaked bread, it occurred to her that her mother wouldn't be pleased by her manners. She ought to use the spoon to ladle her stew even if it took hours.

An unholy glee filled her at the realization that her mother's opinion no longer mattered in this regard. She was a duchess. If she wanted to dunk her bread in her stew, who would stop her? Certainly not the duke, who had done the very same thing himself.

Emma ate without speaking. There seemed to be a sense of expectancy between them, and she wasn't sure if he was waiting for her to fill the void, but given how he'd asked for quiet earlier and claimed his head hurt, she didn't want to strike up a conversation if it would mean being chastised.

Mrs. Lemmings returned with her tea, and Emma realized she'd forgotten to ask for sugar, but she drank it anyway. She didn't mind bitter tea—she just preferred it sweet.

She thought the duke might eventually say something if she remained mute for long enough, but he didn't, other than to inquire whether she liked the stew—quite unnecessarily, since she'd emptied her bowl.

After they were finished, he escorted her back to her room.

"Goodnight," he said and sketched a quick bow as she unlocked the door and entered.

"Goodnight?" she asked, certain that the night could not be over yet. Unfortunately, he seemed to take it as a farewell rather than a question and departed. She stared at his back until his own bedroom door shut and the lock clicked into place.

"Well, that went swimmingly," she muttered, closing her own door. She turned the lock and then looked around, uncertain what to do. Her mother had made it sound as though her husband would come to her tonight, and that was certainly what she'd expected.

Perhaps he wanted her to clean up and get undressed before he arrived. So thinking, she performed her evening ablutions as best she could without the assistance of a maid. She wasn't certain where Daisy was. Since they'd left earlier, perhaps they had made it farther toward their destination.

Fortunately, Daisy must have been made aware of the travel arrangements at some point, because she'd packed a travel bag for Emma that now sat at the foot of the bed. Emma lifted it onto the bed and opened it, finding everything she should need for a night on the road—except for her maid.

She doubted that the duke had considered whether Emma might need assistance to remove her dress. All of those little buttons along the back were impossible to undo on her own.

She pulled the bellpull, and a young girl responded after a few minutes.

"Can you help me with these?" Emma asked, turning her back to the girl.

"Yes, Your Grace." The girl shut the door, locked it, and got to work on the buttons. Her fingers were less dexterous than Daisy's, so it took longer, but Emma was just relieved that she hadn't had to ask the duke to do it.

When the dress was finally off, the girl helped Emma into one of her new nightgowns, which had been in the travel bag. Emma quickly wrapped a robe around herself and sat on the edge of the bed while the girl removed the hairpins from her hair and brushed it out.

Once she was done, Emma passed her a coin and bid her goodnight. She locked the door behind the girl and went to the mirror. She opened her robe and stared at herself.

The nightgown had been ordered specifically for the wedding night, and the white silk revealed far more of her than any of her previous nightgowns had. In the golden glow cast by the candle on the nightstand, shadows danced across Emma's skin, and a thrill shot through her.

She looked sultry. Seductive.

Would the duke like it?

She found that she wanted him to. Whether or not he'd chosen Violet first, and despite the fact he wouldn't have been her first choice of husband, he was her husband and she wanted him to desire her.

But what should she do while she waited?

She checked the drawer of the nightstand, but the only book inside was a bible. Instead of reading, she began to braid her hair. The movements were soothing, and she'd done it so many times that she didn't have to concentrate.

There was a pink ribbon in her bag, so she used that to tie the end of the braid. Digging deeper into the bag, she uncovered her personal copy of *Emma*. Her heart lifted. Darling Daisy. She'd made sure Emma would have her favorite book in a time when everything else was unfamiliar.

She propped herself on the pillows, cracked the spine, and immersed herself in the world of Miss Emma Wood-house and Mr. Knightley.

When she realized an hour had passed and her husband had not appeared, she began to worry. Perhaps she was supposed to go to him. Had she been wrong to assume that he would make the first move? Maybe he thought it was gentlemanly to allow her to come to him when she was ready.

Uncertain of her actions, she unlocked the door and tiptoed across the hall, glancing left and right to make sure she was alone.

She knocked on his door, and heard a rustle inside, but then all went quiet. She knocked again.

"Your Grace?" she called softly.

There was no response from within.

Her teeth clenched together. He was in there, she'd heard him. Why wouldn't he answer?

She tried a third time, and when he did not respond, she returned to her room.

Fine, if that was how he wanted to be, then she would do the same to him.

She locked the door, removed her robe, got into bed, and blew out the candle. Then she lay awake, staring into the darkness, certain that he would soon realize his error and come for her.

He didn't. And for some reason, the rejection stung.

CHAPTER 13

VAUGHAN HELD HIMSELF STIFFLY AS HE KNOCKED ON HIS WIFE'S bedroom door the following morning. After a night with very little sleep, he was ready to finally arrive home.

The door swung inward, and when Emma appeared in the frame, he momentarily forgot to breathe. She peered up at him with puffy eyes, bloodshot from... dear God, had she been crying?

It was official. Day one, and he was already a terrible husband.

But what had he done?

Yes, perhaps he'd been a little short with her in the carriage yesterday, but she'd seemed fine at supper. He'd stopped for the evening when his preference would have been to drive until they reached Ashford Hall, and he'd made sure she had a separate room so she wouldn't feel pressured or uncomfortable on their first night together.

So there was the little matter of ignoring her knock last night. His head had been killing him, and he'd been certain that if she really needed him, she wouldn't have given up before he'd dragged himself out of bed. She'd shown herself to be forceful when the need arose.

"Are you ready for breakfast?" he asked, debating whether to inquire as to her state. But women didn't like it when men suggested they looked less than their best, did they? His mother certainly never had.

"Yes, Your Grace." Her tone was oddly emotionless.

Guilt prickled in his gut. He must have upset her. He just didn't know how.

She stepped into the hall and closed the door, then locked it and tucked the key away. He took her arm, and a punch of lust hit him as he breathed in her sweet scent. She smelled as though she'd been baking cakes, though he knew that was ridiculous.

He escorted her down the stairs and into the dining room. This time, they were seated in front of the window. He glanced out, noting the empty road outside underneath cloudy skies.

Mrs. Lemmings served them tea, and Emma asked for sugar. Vaughan made a mental note of that. He may not want to live in his wife's pocket, but surely it could do no harm to know a few of her personal preferences. One of the staff presented them with two plates with a little of everything on them.

"Thank you," Emma said, with a smile for the server but not for Vaughan.

He sank his knife into a lump of butter and was about to spread it onto a piece of toast when she spoke again.

"I was surprised not to see you last night." She raised her eyes to his, and the furrow between her brows suggested she was confused. "I thought you would come to my room."

He stared at her for a moment, shocked by her forthrightness, but then his stomach plummeted. Was that why she'd been crying? She thought he'd rejected her?

She couldn't be more wrong. He ached to make her his wife, and that in itself was the problem. He'd never wanted to be attracted to the woman he made his duchess.

131

"I didn't want to disrespect you by claiming our wedding night in an inn," he told her.

That was only partly true. He'd also desperately been trying to gain control of his libido, which wanted him to kiss on her soft, pink lips and not let her out of the bedroom for days.

"I would have liked to know that was your plan," she said, biting into that luscious lip before taking a sip of her tea. Her tongue flicked out to catch a droplet, and heat rushed through Vaughan in response.

"My apologies, Emma." He reached across the table and laid his hand on the one she wasn't using. "I didn't think to mention it."

Her gaze darted from his hand up to his eyes, and her pupils dilated. He smothered a groan. Damn, the last thing he needed was for their attraction to be mutual. That would make it even more difficult to let her go once he'd gotten her with child.

"You're forgiven." She turned her hand over so that their palms met. The touch was so unexpectedly intimate that his insides quivered.

Fortunately, she pulled her hand away and picked up her cutlery. As she began to eat, he surreptitiously calmed himself. Gentlemen did not leap across tables to grab their wives. Even frustrated ones who had robbed themselves of a wedding night.

Vaughan hardly noticed the fact that he was eating his own meal until his fork clinked against an empty plate. He'd been absorbed by Emma and the small sounds of enjoyment she'd been making. She seemed to have liked everything they'd been served, and he got the impression she was someone who loved food in general.

Good. The cook at Ashford Hall tended toward making simple meals. He could cater for society dinners if needed, but for the most part, their fare wasn't fancy, and he'd been worried she might turn her nose up at it.

The silence stretched between them, and it occurred to him that most dining companions would have tried to make conversation by now. He wasn't the chattiest person around, but nor did she seem to be, so hopefully she hadn't taken the omission personally.

"Do you like to travel?" he asked, deciding this was as easy a question to begin with as any.

"I like exploring new places," she said, pouring herself more tea. "But I haven't traveled far. Only between my parents' homes in Surrey and London and on a trip to Bath we took a few years ago."

He winced internally. If she hadn't traveled much previously, then no doubt yesterday and today would be difficult for her. He was a cad not to have thought of asking about this ahead of time or at least making certain she knew what the plan was.

"I hope you will like Norfolk," he said. "I think it's beautiful, but I might be biased."

"Surely not," she teased, draining her cup and then returning it to its saucer.

"Only a little." He rubbed his face, using his hand to mask his smile. It wouldn't do for her to know that he was affected by her. "Is there anything you need before we leave?"

"Only to freshen up in the bedroom," she said. "I can be ready in a few minutes."

"Excellent."

Together, they went back up the stairs. Vaughan's bag had already been collected—presumably by one of the staff—so he checked to make sure nothing had been left behind and then waited outside Emma's room until she emerged.

She had a book in her hands, and he glanced at the title but couldn't make it out. Something by Jane Austen, by the look of it.

They farewelled Mrs. Lemmings with a promise to stay again and got into the carriage. Emma immediately went to the window and picked up the book he'd given her yesterday. She placed the other novel on her lap and opened the adventure book.

The early morning sun streamed through the window and caressed the elegant length of her neck. Her golden hair seemed to glow, and he forced himself to look away. If he wasn't careful, he'd find himself enthralled by his wife, and that simply would not do.

"You like to read?" he asked even though it was self-evident.

"I do." She barely glanced away from the page. "It's one of my favorite pastimes."

"Mine too," he admitted.

This time, she did look up and flashed her pearly teeth at him. "Then we shall get along famously, provided you don't feel the need to disparage Jane Austen as some men do."

"I would never." Vaughan believed that everyone should read what they most enjoyed, and Miss Austen had succeeded in creating readers out of many young ladies who might otherwise not partake in literature.

Emma didn't reply. She was engrossed in her book.

They didn't speak much during the journey to Ashford Hall, and Vaughan couldn't help but wonder if that was partly because of how he'd asked her to be quiet yesterday. He watched the scenery pass by for a while, and when that grew tiresome, he selected a French poetry book from the seat box and began to read.

By the time they passed through Beecham, the nearest town to Ashford Hall, he was itching to stretch his legs. He crossed his ankles and gave himself as much space as the carriage could afford.

Emma closed her book and looked through the window. "Is it much farther?"

"Only another couple of miles," he said. "Before we arrive, I'll summarize who you can expect to meet after we arrive."

"Thank you." Her obvious relief made him feel like an ass for waiting this long. In his defense, he'd assumed that if he left it until the last minute, she'd find the names and positions easier to remember.

"The housekeeper, Mrs. Travers, has been at Ashford Hall since I was young. She runs a tight ship, and I'm sure she'll be pleased to meet you."

She nodded, her face an image of concentration.

"The butler, Mr. Yeats, has been there for almost as long." He preferred the former duke's laissez faire style of management to Vaughan's, but considering the improved financial state of the dukedom—and his corresponding pay increase—he rarely made comments about that anymore.

"Mr. Travers does most of the cooking, and Donald tends to the gardens," he said.

"Is Donald his first or last name?" Emma asked.

Vaughan shrugged. "I can tell you that if you call him Mr. Donald, he'll ignore you. It's Donald or nothing. There are several maids and footmen, who have a variety of duties, a stablemaster, Mr. Jensen, and my valet, Hugo."

She nodded. "So the key players are Mr. and Mrs. Travers, Mr. Yeats, Donald, and Mr. Jensen."

The carriage crested a small rise and Ashford Hall came into view in the distance.

"That's right, and you'll meet them in just a few minutes."

EMMA COULDN'T TAKE HER EYES OFF THE BUILDING THAT HAD appeared on the horizon. The rectangular behemoth dominated the landscape, towering over the gardens and fields and taking up so much space that she imagined she could stand in a room at one end, scream as loud as she could, and still not be heard at the other.

As they drew nearer, she could see grassy grounds surrounding the hall and a pond at its base. Statues adorned the roof, and although she couldn't make out the details, some of them appeared to be holding swords in the air.

"This is Ashford Hall?" she asked breathlessly.

She had expected it to be large, but not of this scale. And now she was its mistress.

Dear God.

She tried not to hyperventilate, reminding herself that she'd been trained for this. She'd seen her mother manage a household for years, and surely the fact that this one was twice or thrice the size of their country home didn't make that much difference. The principles were the same.

She would be fine. Provided, of course, that Mrs. Travers liked her. The message had been drummed into her for years that if the housekeeper respected the house's mistress, then all would go smoothly.

Ashford had said that Mrs. Travers "ran a tight ship," so Emma would need to come across as organized and competent if she hoped to win her respect. She could do that.

The carriage trundled down the path toward the hall, and as they drew nearer, Emma noticed a row of servants waiting outside to greet them. Every one of them was neatly turned out, from the distinguished older man she assumed was Mr. Yeats down to the young men who probably worked in the gardens or stable.

They waited in perfect stillness.

Waited for her.

She'd never in her life wanted anything more than to bury her face in a book and avoid her responsibilities. But she'd agreed to be a duchess, and she was going to be the best duchess she possibly could. So good that her duke would have to fall madly in love with her.

She straightened her posture as they slowed and refused to let Ashford see her nerves. The carriage stopped, and Emma steeled herself.

"You needn't be concerned," Ashford said as he clasped her wrist and helped her to the ground.

"I am not," she lied.

He didn't confront her about it. Instead, he led her to the woman at the head of the line. The plump figure curtsied deeply.

"Welcome back to Ashford Hall, Your Grace." Her dark gaze lingered on Emma.

"Thank you, Mrs. Travers. This is our new duchess, Emma Stanhope."

"Your Grace," Mrs. Travers said with another curtsey.

"It's a pleasure to meet you," Emma said, relieved by how smoothly the words came out. "I'm sure we will have a lot to discuss over the coming days."

"Indeed, Your Grace."

Ashford cleared his throat. "Mrs. Travers, will you make introductions?"

"Of course." She led them to the head of the line. "Duchess, this is Mr. Yeats, the butler."

Emma nodded to Mr. Yeats, cataloging his piercing blue eyes, salt-and-pepper hair, and neatly shaped mustache. "A pleasure."

She was introduced to Mr. Travers, who was as plump as his wife and had a jolly face, and then to the duke's valet, Hugo, who had traveled ahead with Daisy. She met the head gardener, Donald, the maids, the footmen, the stable boys, and the under gardeners. All told, there was a ridiculous number of staff, and Emma just hoped she'd remember their names.

Daisy stood near the end of the row, and she beamed at Emma when she passed by. Emma wished she could hug her, but that would certainly not be the best tone to set with the staff. She couldn't show blatant favoritism while they all looked on.

When all of the introductions had been made, Emma thanked Mrs. Travers, who dismissed the staff so they could return to their posts. Emma caught a glimpse of Daisy disappearing into the house before she focused on the housekeeper.

"Would you like a tour?" Ashford asked as they stood side by side facing the hall.

"Yes, please. That would be wonderful." In addition to helping her find her way around, it would also give her the opportunity to see how he interacted with their surroundings.

He turned to Mrs. Travers. "Would you show the duchess around?" Without waiting for a reply, he said, "Thank you," and went inside.

"Well, I never," Mrs. Travers exclaimed.

Emma glared at his back so hard that she was surprised he didn't feel it. She'd wanted him to show her around, not Mrs. Travers. Although she supposed this was a good opportunity to engage with the housekeeper.

"Where shall we begin?" she asked.

"How about in the largest common spaces?" Mrs. Travers suggested.

"Let's."

Emma followed Mrs. Travers up the stairs and into the most exquisitely appointed home she'd ever entered. She gazed around, awed by the plush maroon upholstery and the dark panels of wood that comprised the walls and floors.

A chandelier hung above the staircase, its sharp angles so severe that Emma feared it would impale someone if it ever fell.

"The ballroom is through here." Mrs. Travers gestured to the right. Obediently, Emma headed in that direction. The room dwarfed her and featured a stage against the far wall that was arranged for musicians to play upon. A grand piano occupied the center.

"Does Ashford Hall regularly host dances?" Emma asked.

Mrs. Travers tsked. "Not since the previous duchess was alive, rest her soul. The duke isn't a particularly social sort."

"I've noticed that." Emma wasn't either, although she was beginning to think she might have the duke beat.

"He has a good heart, though," Mrs. Travers added, as though her comment had been disloyal.

Emma hoped the housekeeper was right. She also hoped that the duke's "good" heart was available for stealing.

It took over an hour for Mrs. Travers to guide her through the house, pausing in each room to give a quick description of what it was used for and allowing Emma to look her fill.

"I shall need a nap after that," Emma said upon the completion of their tour. "There are so many rooms."

"It requires a lot of effort to keep the hall in order," Mrs. Travers said.

"I'm certain it does."

Mrs. Travers pointed at a door—the last on their tour. "Those are the duchess's chambers."

"Thank you." Emma hesitated, then said, "Perhaps we could meet sometime in the next couple of days to discuss menus and so you can explain the workings of the house to me in more depth?"

"Yes, Your Grace. Just tell me when."

Emma smiled. "I will."

Mrs. Travers bobbed her head and swept away.

Emma drew in a breath and entered her new bedroom for the first time. A breeze carried the scent of the outdoors in through an open window, and her spirits lifted. How different this place was from London. Even if the hall overwhelmed her, she could delight in the surrounding countryside.

She walked to the bed, which was recessed into the wall with a door to the left that she assumed led to the duke's bedchamber. A quick glance showed that there was no key in the lock, and hence, no way for her to lock it. Not that she wished to.

She perched on the edge of the bed—it was much bigger than her one at Carlisle House—and looked at the portrait that dominated the wall above the fireplace. She had no idea who he was, but his stare unnerved her. At least he was handsome.

She stood and opened the wardrobe. Her dresses hung from a railing inside, carefully displayed by order of color, exactly how Daisy knew she liked them.

She removed her shoes, lay on the bed, and closed her eyes. The pillow was the perfect height for her head, and birds sang outside, lulling her to sleep.

When she woke, it was to see a maid hovering at the foot of the bed, carrying a tray. Emma tried to recall her name. It definitely started with a 'J.'

"Apologies, Your Grace," the maid said, keeping her head down. "I didn't know you were asleep. The duke asked for dinner to be brought to your room, since you must be weary from traveling."

Emma blinked the sleep from her eyes, suddenly remembering the maid's name. "Thank you, Jessie. You can set it on the writing desk."

Jessie placed the platter on the small desk in the center of the room and excused herself. Emma wandered over, curious as to what she'd been served. She lifted the lid, and the aroma of freshly cooked mutton filled the room.

The breeze stirred the curtains. It had grown cold, so she closed the windows and sat to eat. The mutton was well done, and it was accompanied by boiled potatoes and greens.

She ate hungrily, then checked what was in the other covered bowl, beaming at the sight of a slice of chocolate tart.

She dug her spoon into the tart and scooped it into her mouth. Oh, that was good. Dark and rich but sweet enough to make her want more. She had a feeling she was going to enjoy eating Mr. Travers's meals—especially without her mother here to control her intake of sweets.

Soon after she finished, Jessie returned to collect the tray. Emma read for a while, but set her book aside when Daisy pushed the door open and peeked around the corner. When she spotted Emma, she entered. Emma hurried over and hugged her maid tightly.

"It's so good to see you," she said.

"It feels like it's been more than two days," Daisy said. "I was surprised to hear we were bound for Norfolk, but so far, I like it here. The house is amazing, and the servants have been nice to me."

"I'm glad you're taking it in stride. I was surprised too," Emma admitted.

"How was the wedding?" Daisy asked.

Emma cringed. "Honestly, I don't remember much of it."

While Emma told her what she did recall, Daisy helped her undress and change into a nightgown. She selected one of her new ones, wondering whether her husband would see it this time.

Daisy brushed her hair until it shone and then left her alone to nervously await the arrival of the duke. She half-expected him not to appear, but unlike last night, he didn't leave her waiting. There was a knock at the door between their rooms soon after Daisy had departed.

Emma went to the door and paused for a moment to summon her courage before opening it.

"Hello." She brushed a nonexistent strand of hair away from her face.

"Good evening." The duke shifted his weight from one

141

foot to the other. He'd removed his cravat, and her gaze was drawn to the vee of chest revealed by the open two buttons of his shirt. A few chest hairs peeked through, and she couldn't look away. She'd never seen a man's chest before. Especially not a duke's.

CHAPTER 14

Norfolk,
November, 1819

"What's your name?" Emma blurted because really, she ought to stop thinking of him as "the duke," and "Ashford" felt too distant for a man she'd share her life with.

He cocked his head. "It's Vaughan. Haven't I told you that?"

She blushed, a little embarrassed not to have known.

"Vaughan Stanhope," he said with a bow. "The Duke of Ashford, at your service."

She hid her amusement, grateful he hadn't been annoyed by her blunder.

Vaughan. She liked the name. It suited him. Very firm.

She offered him her hand. "Emma Stanhope, the Duchess of Ashford. Pleased to make your acquaintance."

He grinned. "We are doing all of this rather backward, aren't we?"

"So it would seem." She backed away from the door. "Would you like to come in?"

He stepped through. "Thank you. May I sit?"

"Please do." God, this was excruciatingly awkward, but at least he hadn't left her waiting and wondering what she was supposed to do again.

He glanced around and then sat on the small wooden chair beside the dresser. Emma was surprised it could bear his weight, but she supposed it must be well-made. She took the chair behind the writing desk.

"Since we don't know each other well and aren't yet comfortable with each other, I thought it might be appropriate to ease into any physical intimacy," Vaughan said, his aristocratic cheekbones dusted with pink that let her know she wasn't the only one who found this conversation challenging.

How on earth were they supposed to procreate when they struggled to even talk about it?

"How do you propose we start?" she asked.

He swallowed, his throat rippling, entrancing her. "Perhaps with a kiss."

Her breathing quickened. Oh, yes. She'd like that.

She'd enjoyed it when he'd kissed her during their wedding. In fact, it was the only part she had enjoyed.

She stood and moved toward him. Since he'd raised the subject, it would only be polite for her to make the first move. He rose from the chair as she drew near, and she forgot how to breathe altogether. He was so tall, and this close, his chest seemed broader than it had from a distance.

She paused, realizing she didn't know what to do next. Fortunately, he laid his hands on her hips. His palms scalded her through the sheer fabric of her nightgown, and she gasped. His eyes darkened, and he lowered his head toward her slowly enough for her to be able to stop him at any time.

But she didn't want him to stop. She wanted to feel his lips against hers again.

They brushed gently at first. Barely touching. She inhaled, and her chest pressed against his. He exhaled, and his breath gusted over her mouth. She'd had no idea how intimate this would feel. She'd seen her parents kiss and hadn't thought much of it, but the sensation was exquisite.

His lips firmed against hers and his fingers dug into her hips, but not enough to hurt. She stretched onto her toes, angling herself toward him as heat pooled low in her core.

They broke apart, then met again. His lips parted, and when his tongue darted along the seam of her lips, she moaned into his mouth.

He pulled away and took his hands off her. "Wait."

"What?" The word was thready.

He dragged his hand through his hair, his jaw working. "I think that's enough for one night."

He moved backward, toward the door connecting their rooms.

"Did I do something wrong?" Emma asked, bewildered.

"No." His expression softened. "You've done nothing wrong."

But when he fled like the devil was on his heels and shut the door behind himself, she couldn't help feeling as if she had. She just didn't know what.

WHEN EMMA ARRIVED AT THE BREAKFAST ROOM THE NEXT morning, she was disappointed to discover it empty. The food had been disturbed, indicating that her husband had already been and gone.

She served herself toast and eggs, frustrated that her plan hadn't panned out. She'd wanted to catch him before he'd gotten busy so she could get to the bottom of what had gone wrong last night.

She ate alone, ignoring the footman who hovered in the corner, pretending she couldn't see the sympathy in his eyes.

145

She was a newly wedded bride. She shouldn't be apart from her husband, especially not this early in the morning.

After she finished, she searched the house for Vaughan. She didn't find him, but that didn't necessarily mean he wasn't present somewhere. The place was so big that while she was checking one room, he could easily be in another—either by coincidence or because he'd decided to avoid her.

Finally admitting defeat, she looked instead for Mrs. Travers, asking around until she tracked the housekeeper down in a room behind the kitchen. Mrs. Travers glanced up from the table she was sitting at, a pen in her hand and a piece of paper covered in writing in front of her. She put the pen down and stood when she saw Emma.

"Hello," Emma said, thrusting her shoulders back to feign confidence. "I'm looking for the duke. Do you know where I could find him?"

Mrs. Travers removed the reading glasses from her face and rubbed her eyes. "I believe he's riding the grounds with the estate manager. They left on horseback a while before you came down for breakfast."

"Oh." Emma frowned. "I didn't meet the estate manager yesterday, did I?"

"No. He was away on business and only returned late last night." Mrs. Travers put her pen down. "His name is Mr. Johnson."

"Has he held his role for long? I know the duke said that you, your husband, and Mr. Yeats have been here since he was a child."

"Only a few years," Mrs. Travers replied. "The duke met him in school and hired him after he gained control of the dukedom. Not a minute too soon, if you ask me. The previous manager should have retired years earlier."

Emma moved farther into the room, driven by her curiosity. "Did he manage the estate poorly?"

Mrs. Travers made a dismissive sound. "Not terribly, but

he was a senile old fool who refused to modernize anything and flirted dreadfully with the maids. They avoided him most of the time, but it's nice not to have to worry about it."

"I can imagine." Even some gentlemen of the ton who had reached their dotage were poorly behaved around young ladies. Fortunately, the ladies of the ton were rarely ever at risk of anything happening against their will because they were never left alone with a gentleman. A maid would be in a more precarious position.

"May I join you?" Emma asked, now close enough to see that Mrs. Travers was working on a menu. "Or are you too busy right now?"

"Please, sit," Mrs. Travers said.

Emma lowered herself into a chair on the other side of the table. "What kind of meals are usually prepared?"

"Nothing fancy." Mrs. Travers's cheeks colored, and she sat too. "Just simple fare cooked well. Meat, potatoes, and vegetables."

"Very nice. What about soup? Dessert? I had a delicious slice of tart last night."

A smile blossomed across the older woman's face. "My Bill makes a good chocolate tart. He's quite gifted with sweets and puddings."

Emma's eyes crinkled in the corners. "I'm very glad to hear that. I have a sweet tooth, but I was rarely able to indulge it at home."

"That's just not right." Mrs. Travers looked astonished. "A girl like you needs plenty of rich food to grow a healthy heir." She covered her mouth. "Forgive me for saying so."

"There is nothing to forgive." Emma had a feeling she was going to like Mrs. Travers.

They discussed the menu for a while, although Emma didn't feel as though she was contributing much. Her own tastes were wide and varied, so there was no reason to ask Mrs. Travers to change much of anything. It felt good to be having the conversation, though. It made her feel as if she was a member of the household rather than a guest.

Which, she supposed, she was.

After they had exhausted the topic of menus and had gone through the general management of the house, Emma racked her brain, wondering what else she needed to do.

She'd always thought that she'd been so well trained, she'd be able to take over the management of a house without any fuss, but the nerves she was faced with now that this was actually happening left her second-guessing herself.

"Is that everything?" Mrs. Travers asked, glancing at the clock.

"Tenants," Emma exclaimed. "We haven't discussed tenants."

"Ah." The housekeeper pursed her lips. "That's more of a matter for the estate manager than me."

"True, but tell me, do you think they would like a gift basket?" Emma asked.

"A gift basket?" Mrs. Travers was obviously bemused.

Emma nodded. "I would like to introduce myself, and I don't want to go empty-handed."

"I believe we can do that. We have baskets in storage somewhere."

Emma leaned forward. "What should we put in them? Perhaps tea, and do we have any biscuits for the children?"

A gleam formed in Mrs. Travers's eyes. "Mr. Travers can whip some up before you go. He'll be happy to."

"Excellent. What else?"

～

VAUGHAN'S THIGHS ACHED FROM A LONG DAY IN THE SADDLE. He dismounted and rubbed his mare's neck.

"Good girl," he murmured, slipping her a small apple from his pocket. "You've done well. Have a treat."

"Do you talk to your wife like that too?"

Vaughan raised his gaze and glared at Cal Johnson, his estate manager. "Do you?"

Cal grinned. "My wife prefers it when I tell her how naughty she's been."

Vaughan winced. That was something he hadn't needed to know about the academically inclined Mrs. Marianne Johnson.

"Spare me," he muttered.

"Seriously, I can't believe you're married." Cal seemed far too thrilled by the fact. "Do you think Marianne would like her?"

"Possibly," Vaughan said. "She likes to read."

"Huh. What else does she like?"

"Erm." He clapped his mouth shut, afraid of looking a fool when he realized he didn't know much about Emma at all. That was how he'd intended it, of course, but it did make him appear to be a bit of an ass. "Food."

Cal gave him a slow clap. "She likes food. How shocking. That renders her not at all like other humans, who generally need food to exist."

"Not everyone actively enjoys food," Vaughan said defensively. "Some people merely eat for sustenance." As seemed to be the case with most women of his acquaintance. Although perhaps they behaved differently when he wasn't around. Who knew?

Cal checked his watch. "I have to meet with one of the tenants now, but I hope you'll introduce me to your duchess soon."

"I will." After all, Cal would probably end up spending more time around her than Vaughan would.

Cal saluted, then got back on his horse and waved before taking off over the grass in the direction of the nearest tenant farm.

Vaughan handed his reins to a stable boy and headed

inside. He was surprised to hear voices in one of the drawing rooms and paused in the doorway, wondering whether they had guests.

He pushed the door open slightly and peered in. His jaw dropped at the sight of Emma seated on the chaise with a basket on her lap while Mrs. Travers folded small blankets into several other baskets spread across the floor. They were a mismatched bunch, clearly collected from wherever they could be found.

"What's going on in here?" he asked, stepping inside.

Emma looked up and her eyes widened, her gaze sweeping down his body. It occurred to him that she'd never seen him in riding gear before.

"Her Grace had the brilliant idea of creating gift baskets for the tenants," Mrs. Travers said as she stood to greet him, apparently pleased as punch.

"I thought I could introduce myself to them this afternoon," Emma said quietly. "To delay might be seen as impolite."

His chest tightened. He should have thought of that. It hadn't occurred to him that his new wife would want to meet the tenants. Perhaps if she'd been the society jewel he'd intended to marry, his assumption would have been correct, but Emma had more depth than that.

"Good thinking," he said. "What are you taking?"

He'd better check it wasn't useless fripperies, although surely Mrs. Travers would have guided her in a different direction if that had been the case.

Emma rubbed her lips together and glanced at the housekeeper nervously. "We have an assortment of tea and sweet treats as well as blankets, and toys for the children that we found in the old nursery. I hope that's all right."

"Of course." He gave her what he hoped was an encouraging smile. They could always buy new toys for their own children.

"Will you come with me?" She looked down at the basket on her lap, avoiding eye contact.

He cursed internally. The last thing he needed was to be stuck in close proximity to her now that he knew exactly how delicious she tasted, but he couldn't in good conscience deny her.

"When do you intend to leave?"

"Perhaps in half an hour?" she suggested.

"I'll meet you at the entrance then." He'd need to organize transportation. They'd need a curricle for the baskets and possibly themselves as well, since he didn't know whether she was an accomplished rider. He got the impression she liked horses, but that didn't always equate to being a skilled horsewoman.

"Will we have time to get to them all today?" she called after him.

"If we make haste," he replied.

When he met Emma and Mrs. Travers at the bottom of the grand staircase thirty minutes later, they were each carrying three baskets. Seeing that they were struggling, Vaughan took one from each of them and led them outside.

A faint breeze ruffled his hair.

"Oh, it's lovely weather," Emma said.

Vaughan wasn't sure he'd go that far. It was mild but hardly warm.

He slid the baskets beneath the curricle seat and took the others from Emma and Mrs. Travers.

"Drive safely," Mrs. Travers said as he helped Emma into the curricle and climbed up after her.

"We will." He picked up the reins and urged the horses into motion along the gravel road.

Beside him, Emma leaned forward, resting her forearms on her thighs and drawing the fabric tight across them. Vaughan did his best not to look, reminding himself that unless they wanted to crash, he ought to focus on the journey.

"We'll reach the Taylors' home first," he called over the rumble of wheels on gravel. "They're our largest landholder. They have one grown son, one who's away at school, and one who's too young for school yet."

Emma nodded but didn't reply. Perhaps she didn't want to shout above the noise. The country roads around here weren't as smooth as the ones she was used to in London, although he supposed her family's home in Surrey might have similar paths.

He slowed his pace when he noticed that her hair was whipping around her face, one section having come loose from its pins. She withdrew extra pins from somewhere within the folds of her dress and fixed it.

Apparently, his duchess wasn't the type of woman to be bothered by a few hairs falling out of place. For some reason, he liked that about her.

Why the hell should it matter what kind of woman she was as long as she gave him an heir?

Yet, he couldn't deny that he felt an odd sort of pride in having married her.

When they arrived at the Taylors' farm, the youngest boy, George, came barreling outside.

"Your Grace." He sketched a quick bow. "My mama will be just a minute. She's making tea."

"Thank you, George." Vaughan jumped down and waited for Emma to stand, then he wrapped his hands around her waist and lifted her to the ground. Her quick intake of breath drew his attention to the curve of her breasts within the modest green dress.

For a moment, he couldn't take his eyes off her. There should be nothing alluring about a relatively simple garment, but she filled it beautifully.

"This is the Duchess of Ashford," he said, squatting so he

152

wouldn't tower above George. "She has just come to live with me."

"At the castle?" George asked.

"At Ashford Hall," Vaughan confirmed. George had always been convinced it should be called a castle rather than a house because of its size.

Emma bent toward him and offered him her hand. "It's wonderful to meet you, George."

He smiled shyly. "You too, Your Grace."

"Excuse my state, Your Graces. We weren't expecting a call," Mrs. Taylor said. She'd bustled out behind George and was fisting her hands in the plain gray skirt of her dress.

"I'm sorry, that was my doing," Emma said. "I wanted to meet you, but I didn't think about sending a message ahead."

"It's quite all right." She hesitated and glanced over her shoulder. "Will you come in? Let me serve you tea. The men are still in the fields. George has been helping me in the kitchen."

"That would be lovely, thank you," Emma said.

Vaughan agreed, content to let her take the lead as much as she felt comfortable doing so.

"We have something for you," Emma said, selecting one of the baskets from beneath the curricle seat. "I hope you don't mind."

"Of course not," Mrs. Taylor said.

"A gift?" George sounded excited. "Can I open it?"

Mrs. Taylor checked with Emma, who readily agreed.

"Go ahead," Mrs. Taylor said.

George took the basket and looked inside. "There are biscuits!"

"Make sure to save some for your brother and father," Mrs. Taylor warned.

George dug one out and then noticed the small wooden carriage with turning wheels.

He grabbed it with a cry of glee and held it up for his mother to see. "Look, it's a carriage."

"That's very kind." Mrs. Taylor took the basket from him now that he was apparently uninterested in whatever remained inside. "What do you say, George?"

"Thank you!" He took a bite of the biscuit and knelt on the ground, running the carriage back and forth over the packed earth.

"Let me get you that tea," Mrs. Taylor said, guiding them inside.

Several hours later, they'd visited all of the tenant farmers, and Vaughan had a whole new appreciation for his wife. She'd charmed every person she'd met. Some of them too much. He hadn't liked the way the older Taylor boy had looked at her when he'd returned from the fields.

Emma might not be as vivacious as her sister, but she was genuinely kind, and people sensed that and responded to it.

Nothing had prepared him for how it would feel to see her holding the Wolseley's baby girl, her expression soft as she clasped the baby against her. His chest had tightened, and he'd been seized by the longing to see her cradling their child. He could already tell she would be a loving mother. Nurturing.

She'd give their children the love and affection he'd never received from his own.

It was growing more difficult to remember that he wasn't supposed to desire her or to be filled with satisfaction at the knowledge that she was his. Arthur Taylor could look all he wanted, but the duchess would never be for him.

He gritted his teeth. That was precisely why he needed to put distance between them as soon as she was pregnant. He'd visit occasionally—mostly to spend time with his child—but that was it. He could not afford to be enamored with his wife. No matter how pretty her eyes or how serene she'd looked holding a baby.

Vaughan paced around his room. Dinner had come and gone, and he needed to go to Emma in her chamber, but he feared that his infatuation with her wouldn't let him maintain the emotional disconnection required for his peace of mind.

He loosened his cravat and tossed it on the bed, then unbuttoned his shirt down to his navel. However uneasy he was, he couldn't stay away from her. She drew him like a magnet, and even if he'd been strong enough to resist, he needed an heir. One did not obtain an heir without engaging in sexual intercourse.

Therefore, he had to go to her. His duty mandated it.

His lips curled. Ah yes, duty was the sole reason he wished to strip Emma Stanhope naked.

Groaning, he marched over to the connecting door between their rooms and knocked.

CHAPTER 15

EMMA OPENED THE DOOR ALMOST IMMEDIATELY, AS IF SHE'D been waiting on the other side. She tilted her face toward his, her cheeks pinkening.

Dear God, did she have to be so damn gorgeous?

"Your Grace," she murmured.

"Vaughan," he said, unable to tear his gaze from her. She'd once again dressed in a barely there nightgown that had been designed to drive a man crazy. The nearly translucent fabric skimmed her curves and stopped at her knees, displaying shapely calves. But it was her nipples that most captivated him as they puckered and peaked.

"Vaughan," she repeated. The word shot straight to his cock. "Won't you come in?"

He ground his back teeth together. Damn, she had no idea what he wanted to do with her when she said things like that so innocently.

He stepped inside and cupped her face in his hands. She went languid in his arms, melting into his embrace. The silk of her nightgown slid over his exposed chest, and he shuddered from the exquisite sensation.

She gazed up at him, her eyes dark pools of blue, her lips

parted so temptingly. What a pretty picture she painted. He could tell she wanted him, even if she herself didn't understand it.

He claimed her mouth gently at first, but grew bolder as she pressed closer to him and opened for his tongue. He dipped inside, tasting her, reveling in her breathy sighs. He backed her up and turned her so that her calves hit the side of the bed. Her eyes widened, but she allowed him to lower her to the mattress and crawl over her.

"How much do you know about the marital act?" he asked.

She moistened her lips. "I know that a part of you goes inside a part of me."

That's about what he'd assumed.

He dropped kisses along the length of her neck, and she subconsciously parted her legs.

He hovered above her. "Did you know it can bring pleasure?"

She looked confused. "For the man?"

"For both parties," he corrected. "Let me show you."

"Yes, please." She came up on her elbows. "What do I need to do?"

"Nothing. Just tell me what you like and what you don't."

She blushed harder. "I will."

Vaughan slipped down her body until he reached the hem of her nightgown. He took hold of the edge. "May I?"

Her teeth sank into her lower lip, but she nodded. He peeled the silk up to reveal the blond curls at the apex of her thighs. She pressed her legs together, then gasped.

"That felt good, didn't it?" he growled.

"Y-yes," she stammered. "No one has ever looked at me there before."

And no one else ever will.

He ignored the overly possessive thought.

157

"You're beautiful." He blew against her soft flesh, and she quivered. So much gorgeous pinkness, all for him.

"Are you sure there's nothing I need to do?" she asked, her tone worried.

He smiled reassuringly. "Trust me, letting me know what you like and what you don't is the only thing you need to do."

He imagined that alone would be difficult for a woman who'd never had to express herself sexually before.

"I want to kiss you down here." He looked up at her. "May I?"

"Yes."

He spread her with his hands and licked down her center. Her hips bucked, and she cried out.

"Good or bad?" he asked.

She kept her eyes trained on the ceiling. He suspected she was too embarrassed to meet his gaze.

"Good."

He tasted her again, and this time she didn't buck, but she let out the sweetest whimper.

"Mm." He moaned against her.

"Oh, God." She clutched the sheets. "Oh, that's wicked."

"But you like it." He didn't have to ask. The way she trembled and rocked, trying to get more, told him everything he needed to know.

"I do," she whispered. "More, please."

He palmed his cock. Fucking hell. This woman would be the death of him.

He feasted on her, teasing her with his lips and tongue, and when she was desperate for him, her back arching, her breaths coming on short stutters, he slipped his finger inside her and curled it.

She spasmed around his finger, whimpers spilling from her lips as pleasure wracked her body.

"That's it," he murmured. "Give in to me."

His cock was harder than iron, but he already knew that

he wouldn't be able to take her tonight. He had promised to ease her into physical intimacy, but if he sank into her hot channel now, he wouldn't be able to control himself.

He was desperate for her.

When she stopped writhing, he eased his finger out of her and covered her with her nightgown.

She struggled to sit up and looked at him dazedly. "I had no idea...."

Primal satisfaction punched through him.

His wife had never experienced sexual pleasure before, and he'd been the one to introduce her to it. Nobody else would ever have that honor.

"I want to do it all," she said, her gaze sharpening. "Now."

"No." He backed away from her, scrambling off the bed, grateful for the fact that she at least wouldn't know what his erection meant.

Her face fell. "What do you mean, 'no'?"

"We can't," he said. "You're not ready yet."

Liar. It was he who wasn't ready.

"But Vaughan, I am. I—"

He strode to the door. "Not tonight."

He entered his bedchamber and shut the door behind himself. A moment later, he heard her sob and cursed himself for the worst kind of cad.

TONIGHT WAS THE NIGHT.

Emma walked the length of her bedchamber and pulled the drapes shut.

Tonight, she would be with her husband properly. She would no longer be a failure of a wife who hadn't participated in the marital act.

Provided, of course, that she could manage to seduce Vaughan.

He didn't seem the type of man who was susceptible to seduction—although his interest in Violet, a famous beauty, might say otherwise. Had he not performed the act with her yet because she was less alluring than her sister, or was something else amiss?

He'd said he wanted to ease her into it, and she appreciated that, but it also made her question why, if that was the case, he'd fled after both of their more intimate encounters without first pausing to check how she fared.

She'd been left alone to wonder what she'd done wrong. Was there something repulsive about her that made him reluctant to go through with it or linger in the aftermath?

That seemed plausible.

Emma undressed without assistance, since she was wearing one of her simplest dresses, and opened the drawer in which she'd stowed her scandalous new nightgowns. Her mission tonight would require something different.

She retrieved the nightgown she'd resisted wearing so far, considering it too risqué. The neckline plunged, as did the back. The silk was so sheer that when she put it on and looked in the mirror, she could see the outline of her areolas.

She studied herself. Her hips were rounded and considerably more ample than Violet's, but on the whole, she was of average build. Her breasts were not so small or so large as to earn the duke's disdain. If there was something blatantly out of place, Daisy had never told her so. Perhaps if she failed tonight, she'd ask.

She donned her wrapper and summoned Daisy to do her hair.

"How do you want it done?" Daisy asked, running her fingers through the long tresses as Emma sat in front of the mirror.

Emma bit her lip, embarrassed. "Seductive," she squeaked.

Daisy's mouth twitched. "We can do that."

She loosely curled a few ringlets around Emma's face and

brushed out the length until it gleamed in the candlelight, then she dressed the hair with something from a bottle. Emma breathed in the scent of jasmine.

"They say it's an aphrodisiac," Daisy whispered.

"Oh." If it were possible to vanish from embarrassment, Emma would have. "Thank you."

"Good luck," Daisy said. "You look lovely. If this doesn't work, his prick is broken, and don't let him tell you different."

Emma laughed, some of the tension releasing from her stiff shoulders. "Never change."

Daisy sent her a cheeky grin. "I don't intend to." She waggled her eyebrows. "Good night, Your Grace."

"Sleep well, Daisy."

When the maid had left, Emma rose and shed her robe. She walked to the connecting door and, before she could talk herself out of it, she knocked.

Nobody answered.

She cracked the door open and peeked through. The bedchamber was empty.

Curious, she looked around. The duke's chamber hadn't been included in her tour, and she'd only caught a glimpse of it yesterday. The walls were a masculine shade of green, and in the center of the room was the bed, which was covered with a navy bedspread and plush pillows.

She entered. Vaughan hadn't locked the door, so presumably he didn't mind her being in here. She completed a circuit of the room, padding silently on bare feet. As in her chamber, a large portrait occupied one of the walls. It looked old enough that she presumed its subject was an ancestor rather than the duke's father.

She wandered to his wardrobe and looked inside. All of his coats and trousers were stored neatly alongside cravats waiting to be worn.

Guilt pinched her for snooping, so she closed the

wardrobe and sat on the edge of the bed. There was no telling when the duke might turn up, so she ought to be prepared. Perhaps she could pose seductively, and when he saw her, he'd have no choice but to ravish her.

She giggled to herself. Now that she knew a little more about what ravishing entailed, she certainly wasn't opposed, although it would be nice for him not to run away afterward.

She clambered onto the bed and lay on her back with her head on a pillow. Was that seductive? It didn't feel as though she was doing enough. She parted her thighs, but embarrassment washed through her, so she closed them again. She rolled onto her side and inched the nightgown up to reveal a little more of her leg.

There. That would do.

She might not be as tempting as some women, but at least she'd be able to look him in the eyes without dying of humiliation.

Time ticked by, and the duke didn't turn up.

Emma adjusted her skirt again and rubbed her fingers together to keep them warm. She didn't want to invite herself beneath the covers, and besides, she didn't think the lump of her body underneath a bedspread would entice Vaughan to make love to her.

After what felt like hours but was probably only twenty minutes or so, the bedroom door opened, and Vaughan strode in. He stopped short at the sight of her. His gaze tracked the length of her body before bouncing up to her face.

"What are you doing?" His voice was tight.

"I'm ready to perform my wifely duty," she said.

He cringed, and she didn't understand why. Was she really that objectionable?

"Don't tell me I'm not ready," she said as he opened his mouth to speak. "That isn't your decision."

162

"Maybe not," he allowed, closing the door behind himself. "But I'm not certain that you fully understand what the act entails."

Emma ground her teeth together, frustrated by his attitude. "Then explain it to me."

He hesitated and then moved a little closer.

"It will hurt," he said bluntly. "For the first time, at least. You will probably bleed too."

Emma swallowed. She'd been prepared for discomfort, but imagining herself bleeding—presumably from the place where he would insert himself—made her head swim.

"It won't feel like it did yesterday?" she asked. Last night, he'd made her fly. She wanted to experience that again.

He lowered himself onto the bed but didn't touch her. "Maybe eventually, but the pain is unavoidable. It might not hurt in the future, but it's my understanding that the first time always does."

Emma thought quickly. She ached to shatter as blissfully as she had when he'd put his tongue on her, and she also wanted to fulfill her role as his wife. If all other wives engaged in this act, then it couldn't be too bad, and delaying would only make her more anxious.

"I want to do it," she said, and then an awful possibility occurred to her. "Unless you don't. If you don't ever plan to undertake the act with me, then please tell me now."

She'd assumed that they would do it eventually, and he hadn't said anything to contradict that, but he wasn't an easy man to read. It was possible he didn't want to be with her at all. The thought made her stomach churn. If that was the case, she was doomed to spend her life childless.

"I do," he hurried to say. He caressed her cheek, resting his palm against her soft skin. "You are exquisite, Emma. I just don't wish to rush you."

Leaning into the gentle touch, she closed her eyes and breathed in the faint scent of oranges that lingered on him.

When he held her thusly, she could believe that he found her attractive and forget the way he'd run from her previously.

His lips feathered over hers, and a shiver rippled through her. When he did this, he made her feel as though he saw her as more than the second-best Carlisle twin.

His lips brushed hers again, more firmly this time. She shifted closer so that their thighs pressed together.

"I will make it pleasurable for you," he said. "At least, as much as I can. I promise."

"I know you will." Her tone was thready. He'd already shown her could play her body in ways she'd never imagined, so she didn't doubt him when he said he'd make it enjoyable.

He shed his jacket, hung it over the back of a chair, and climbed onto the end of the bed. He pressed her knees apart. She squirmed, but he didn't let go.

"Trust me." He bent and kissed the inside of her thigh. "Let me in."

She stopped resisting, and he shuffled upward, his shoulders wedging her thighs further apart. Her nightgown barely covered her softest parts now, and she felt ridiculously self-conscious.

Never mind that he'd had his mouth on her yesterday. Now his gaze locked on the apex of her thighs as he pushed her nightgown the rest of the way up, and she burned at the knowledge of what he could see.

"Beautiful," he rasped, and heat flooded her core.

She wished she could rub her thighs together. She needed the pressure, but with him between them, she couldn't get it.

He sucked his thumb into his mouth, wetting it, and rubbed it down her center, spearing her open and bumping a bundle of nerves that sent tendrils of pleasure rocketing through her.

He circled his thumb around the nubbin, and her hips arched. A moan slipped from between her lips, and she covered her mouth with her hand.

"Don't," Vaughan said, stopping his ministrations to pull her hand away from her face. "Let me hear how much you like my touch."

Oh, God.

How was she supposed to stay calm when he said things like that?

He rose over her and claimed her mouth, teasing her with his tongue and lips until she was boneless, unable to think or to do anything other than feel.

One of his fingers swept through her wetness, then pushed against the place where he'd entered her yesterday.

"Relax, sweetheart," he urged, nuzzling the side of her neck.

It felt strange to have someone touch her there, but she forced herself to release the tension that had gathered and to focus on the sensuous slide of their kiss. He pushed farther in. There was a pinch of discomfort, but when she allowed herself to become carried away by the kiss, it faded.

Soon, his finger was completely inside her. Another joined it. She exhaled slowly, being careful not to tense. His thumb returned to her nubbin and moved in delicious, teasing circles around it. He pulled away from her face and moved fluidly down the bed until he was hovering over her hot center.

He licked her, then swirled his tongue in a way that made her shudder. He repeated the motion, and raised his eyes to hers, dark and hungry.

"Oh, God," she whimpered.

No one had ever looked at her like that before. Like they were starving, and she was a buffet.

He continued to devour her. She struggled to watch at first, finding the visual too obscene, but the longer it went on, the more she raised herself on her elbows for a better view. The sight of his tongue dipping into her made her hot and fluttery inside. He wound her tighter and tighter until she was a hairsbreadth from snapping.

Then he stopped.

"No," she gasped. "Please."

He grinned wickedly and tore at his clothes. He yanked his cravat off and tossed his shirt aside. He unbuttoned his trousers and tugged them down, revealing himself to her.

She stared in awe. His chest rose and fell rapidly, dark hair spearing down the center between two pale brown nipples. His stomach was flatter than hers, and muscle rippled beneath his skin as he knelt to remove his boots—the movement hindered because he'd pulled down his trousers too soon.

As he rose, her breath caught. His thighs were strong and covered with hair, unlike her own. He peeled off his undergarments to reveal the part of him that her mother had tried to describe to her. The flesh was long and thick and jutted out from his body. No matter how imaginative she was, she couldn't have pictured this.

She gulped at the thought that that was going to go inside her. She understood why he'd said it might hurt. It would be a miracle if it did anything other than hurt. His rod was much larger than the fingers he'd already had inside her.

"I've never seen one of those before," she said, somewhat needlessly. Of course, she'd seen the appendages that male horses had, but she had been quite unprepared for…this.

Vaughan's mouth twitched. "I'm glad to hear it."

"What do you call it?" she asked.

He sauntered closer. "Do you want the technical term or my personal term for it?"

"Your personal term," she said, never taking her eyes off it.

"It's my cock."

He crawled over her and grabbed her hand, lifting it to

him. She curled her fingers around him, surprised to find the shaft so hot and silky.

"Your cock," she breathed, stroking it gently.

He groaned. "A bit more firmly, sweetheart."

She did as he said and moved her hand along its length, reveling at the way it pulsed against her palm.

"It's bigger than I expected," she told him.

His lips tugged into a smirk. "You can take it. As I said, it might hurt at first, but I promise, I will make it as good for you as possible."

"I trust you."

CHAPTER 16

HIS EYES FLUTTERED SHUT, AND HE ANGLED HIS FACE TOWARD the ceiling. For a moment, Emma wondered if she'd said something wrong, but then he lowered his head, and his eyes blazed as they raked across her body.

"Take the nightgown off," he said.

Her fingers fumbling, she did as he said, baring herself to his gaze. He cupped one of her breasts and rolled the nipple between his fingers. It tightened into a peak, and heat jolted through her. He drew her other nipple into his mouth, and she thrust toward him instinctively.

"You're ready for me," he murmured.

She rolled her eyes. "So I told you."

"No. Now, you're really ready. Your body is prepared to accept me. Just keep breathing, and try not to become rigid."

She flopped onto the pillow, closed her eyes, and focused on remaining as languid as possible while the head of his cock notched against her and pushed. She gasped as it entered an inch at a time, and immediately stiffened, but then reminded herself to breathe.

Having him inside her was a strange sensation. She felt oddly full. It wasn't bad, and definitely not as painful as he and her mother had led her to believe, but she wasn't sure whether she liked it either. Finally, he was fully seated within her and lowered himself onto his forearms on either side of her face.

He kissed her. "Thank you. You took me so well."

Warmth seeped into her chest at the praise. She was pleased to have made him happy. She stayed still, waiting for her body to adjust. He gave her time, but when she began to squirm beneath him, he drew out and thrust back into her.

"Oh!"

Her eyes widened, and her mouth fell open as he bumped against her nubbin. He eased out and then in, and sparks sizzled through her insides.

"Oh, that's divine." She wrapped her lower legs around his thighs to make sure he kept hitting the spot that felt so good.

Vaughan's gaze burned into her. "That's it, sweetheart. Take what you need."

"I need more." She arched her body toward him, begging. "Please, Vaughan."

His cock throbbed inside her.

"Say my name again," he demanded.

"Vaughan," she breathed, loving the way his muscles contracted and his control faltered.

Had she done that? Could she drive this man as crazy as he made her?

"Vaughan, I need you." She buried her face in the side of his neck, knowing that she was behaving like a wanton, but it was the first time anyone had looked at her as if she was the answer to everything, and she never wanted it to end.

Each glide of his hard shaft pushed her closer and closer to the edge. She clutched his back, glorying in the firmness of him that was so unlike herself.

When he captured her lips in a steamy kiss, she shattered. Pleasure exploded through her, and she cried out his name as she spiraled into bliss.

A moment later, he tensed and groaned, pulsing inside her as he joined her in oblivion.

Emma held him close, snuggled against his muscular body as she slowly came back to herself. She sighed contentedly and kissed his shoulder. She'd happily stay in his embrace forever if she could. But the moment her lips touched his skin, he stiffened.

He drew away, creating space between them, and the slight sheen of sweat on her stomach and chest rapidly cooled. She shivered and reached for him, but he moved further back.

Her insides shriveled up. Not again. What had she done wrong now?

"Is everything all right?" she asked apprehensively.

"Completely." He leaned forward and kissed her forehead, and for a few seconds, she thought everything would be fine, but then he pulled away again. "Thank you for performing your duty. I'll take you to your bed now."

Her eyebrows furrowed, and she drew her knees to her chest. "But I thought—"

"You must be tired," he continued, ignoring her. "You should sleep."

She got off the bed and clutched her flimsy nightgown to herself, covering what little nakedness she could. Why had he turned so cold and formal when they'd been anything but only minutes earlier?

"I'm not tired." She could perceive when she wasn't wanted, though, even if she was unsure of the reason why, so she hurried to open the adjoining door.

"Goodnight, Emma," he called after her.

She didn't reply. She feared that if she tried, her choked-up voice would give her away. Instead, she gently closed the door, crawled into her own bed, the smell of oranges following her, and wondered what on earth had just happened.

They had made love, and it had been wonderful. Then he'd become distant, like a stranger, almost immediately. It felt like a rejection.

At least he made sure you enjoyed it, she told herself. It was more than she'd initially expected, but somehow, it didn't feel like nearly enough.

～

EMMA GLANCED UP FROM HER BOOK AS A FOOTMAN CARRYING a tray of mail entered the morning room.

"There's a letter for you, Your Grace," he said.

She rose from the chaise positioned beside the window to catch the morning light and crossed the room to take it from him. She hoped it would be from Sophie. She missed her younger sister and hadn't yet heard from her, but the hand-writing was Violet's loopy script rather than Sophie's neater letters.

"Thank you," she said, already breaking the seal into which was pressed a large "M."

He bowed slightly and left.

Emma sat at one of the small wooden tables on the oppo-site side of the room from the chaise. She unfolded the pages, curious what Violet would have to say. This was their first personal correspondence since the letter announcing that Violet had eloped.

My dear Emma,

I suppose by now you know that I have become Lady Violet Mayhew. I'm pleased to be able to retain the honorific despite having married without a title, as Mrs. Mayhew sounds far too dowdy for someone like me.

Our journey to Gretna Green was unlike anything I have ever experienced. I have seen so many things and visited so many places that I never thought I would get the chance to experience. That said, I am quite glad it is over.

Mr. Mayhew and I intend to retire to his family's home in Essex for the remainder of the season. His father has offered us a house on the estate, and while you know the country is not my preferred home, I am looking forward to the peace so we can recuperate.

Perhaps you and I will meet again in London next season, both refreshed and free of the mantle of being an unwed lady.

I was surprised to hear of your marriage to the Duke of Ashford. I was not aware that you held him in high regard, but if he gives you the love you have always wanted, then I am happy for you and relieved I did not hinder your ability to be with him.

I will write to you again once I am in Essex. I would love to hear what life as a duchess entails. Is the estate as magnificent as I have heard?

Yours,

Violet

Emma shook her head, amazed at Violet's obliviousness. Was her sister really blind enough to think that Emma's marriage to the duke had been her own idea rather than a consequence of Violet's reckless actions?

Biting her lip, Emma reminded herself not to be too harsh in judging her sister. After all, becoming Vaughan's wife might not have been Emma's original plan, but she was beginning to believe that she could still have the future filled with love that she'd always imagined.

Leaving the letter on the table, she went in search of a pen and paper, then returned and read the letter again before composing a response. She kept it light and pleasant, not addressing the scandal the family had faced after Violet left. Instead, she described her new home and the people who lived within its walls.

She looked out of the window and paused at the sight of the duke trotting across the grass on horseback. She strolled over to the window and raised her hand to her eyes so she could see better.

He guided the horse back toward the stables, his strong body moving in harmony with the animal. She touched her lips, recalling how that same body had strained above her last night. Her cheeks flushed. She'd never imagined that being married would come with such wicked benefits.

Vaughan left her field of view, but she continued to gaze after him. The past week with him had been beyond her wildest dreams. Yes, she'd have liked it if he didn't return her to her own bedchamber after they'd…finished, but hopefully that would come with time.

After all, he couldn't make love to her so passionately night after night without some of that affection spilling over into their day-to-day life, could he?

Turning away from the window, she noticed that the footman had returned and was quietly waiting. She handed him the letter she'd penned to Violet.

"Please ensure this is sent to Lady Violet Mayhew at the Mayhew's Essex estate," she said, and he nodded.

She smiled to herself as he departed. Violet had been foolish to give up her duke. A man like Vaughan didn't come along often.

"Your Grace?"

She glanced up and realized that Mr. Yeats was standing in front of her, his eyebrows furrowed and his back painfully straight.

"Yes, Mr. Yeats?" she asked.

"You have visitors," he said.

Her heart leaped. For a moment, she was certain it must be Violet, but that was ridiculous. Violet was on her way to Essex, or perhaps she was already there.

"Who is it?"

The furrow deepened. "Missus and Miss Snowe."

Emma racked her brain. "I don't recognize those names," she admitted.

"They live on a neighboring estate and are acquaintances of the duke's," he said.

Ah. "Mr. Snowe is a local landowner?"

"That's right, Your Grace," he said.

She understood now. The Snowes must be members—or even leaders—of local society, and they wanted to be the first to report on the new duchess.

"Thank you. Please show them to the gold drawing room."

He bowed. "As you wish."

The gold drawing room was their most impressive. No doubt these people would want to know if she could hold her own amongst them, and she intended to leave no doubt in their minds that she was up to the task.

As she made her way down the corridor, she encountered one of the housemaids.

"Beth," she said. "Could you please make sure that tea and cakes are brought to the gold drawing room? We have guests."

Beth curtseyed. "Of course, Your Grace."

Emma continued to the drawing room and made herself comfortable on an intricately carved wooden seat with plush padding. Only a few moments later, a pair of ladies swept into the room, bringing with them a heavy floral scent. Emma's nose tickled, and she willed herself not to sneeze.

She stood to greet them. "Good morning."

The pair stopped side by side and bobbed their heads. "Good morning, Your Grace."

The woman on the left was clearly older, so she must be Mrs. Snowe. Her brown hair was interspersed with silver, and her eyes were so dark, they looked almost black, sending a shiver down Emma's spine.

In contrast, Miss Snowe was quite pretty. She was tall and slender with eyes a more natural shade of brown and glossy dark hair curled tightly at the front.

"It's wonderful to meet you," Emma said. "I haven't yet met any of our neighbors—other than the tenants, of course. Please, sit."

She reclaimed her chair, and Mrs. and Miss Snowe sat on similar seats around the small rectangular table.

"I'm surprised we are the first to call on you," Mrs. Snowe said, but a satisfied smirk curled her lips. "I am Mrs. Catherine Snowe, and this is my daughter, Miss Susannah Snowe."

Emma couldn't help but think that Susannah Snowe sounded like the name of a heroine from a gothic love story.

"I'm Lady Emma," Emma said. "Or I was, before my marriage. My father is the Earl of Carlisle."

They both nodded, but their bland expressions said that this wasn't news to them.

There was a sound in the hall, and then Beth bustled in with tea. She set it down in front of Emma and left, closing the door behind herself.

"Tea?" Emma asked her visitors.

"Yes, please," Mrs. Snowe said. "With sugar."

"No sugar for me," Miss Snowe added.

Emma poured the tea, stirring sugar into her own and Mrs. Snowe's, drawing comfort from the familiar actions.

"So, how did you and the duke meet?" Mrs. Snowe asked, taking the delicate handle of the cup between her thumb and forefinger.

Emma narrowed her eyes, wondering if they knew the truth. It seemed unlikely that the local gentry wouldn't be aware of a scandal involving someone as well known as the duke.

"We met at a ball," she said simply. Technically, it was true. They'd been introduced. It didn't matter that Vaughan had promptly asked Violet to dance and ignored Emma.

"I heard that he was betrothed to your sister." Miss

Snowe's tone was salacious, and it made Emma uncomfortable.

She should have expected comments like this. She'd just hoped that people would be polite enough not to make them to her face.

"Briefly," Emma said. "But they decided they were not suited."

"So, she didn't jilt him?" Miss Snowe asked.

"Susannah," her mother chided. "We mustn't ask such things."

Miss Snowe ducked her head. "My apologies, Your Grace. As I'm sure you can imagine, we've heard mixed accounts of what took place."

Emma pursed her lips. Despite her apology, Susannah didn't seem sorry for bringing it up. Something about her expression was almost sly.

"There isn't much to discuss," Emma said, willing herself to appear calm and collected. "My sister and the duke were betrothed for a short time, but their engagement ended. After the severance, the duke asked me to be his wife, and I agreed."

They looked disappointed not to have been given more gossip.

"Did you know that at one point we thought Susannah might be the next Duchess of Ashford?" Mrs. Snowe said.

What on earth?

Emma didn't allow her reaction to show. She'd never have expected Mrs. Snowe to blatantly disrespect her by saying such a thing. Most people would be wary of crossing someone with such a high standing in society.

Were they trying to upset her?

"And yet here I am, and there she is," Emma said coolly.

~

Vaughan paced back and forth in front of his mirror.

"You're an idiot," he told himself. "A goddamned imbecile. Why are you still here?"

He'd intended to leave that morning, believing that he'd laid with Emma enough times that she ought to be pregnant, and if not then he could return next month to try again. He'd packed his bags, readied the horses, but not gotten into the carriage. And he had no idea why.

All right, that wasn't entirely true. He had some idea why, and it was all to do with his far-too-tempting wife.

He didn't want to leave Emma. Which, ironically, was exactly why he needed to. Yet he couldn't make himself do it.

"Just tell her," he said to his reflection. "Tell her you're returning to London in the morning."

He scowled at himself. The whole point of taking Emma as his wife had been to secure an heir while impacting his life as little as possible. To that end, he needed to return to his usual habits.

He hummed in thought, wondering if he could persuade Emma to return to London instead of him so he could remain here. He much preferred Ashford Hall to their city residence. But he'd already dragged her all the way here. It would be rude to send her back again so soon.

A knock on the door captured his attention. He opened it and leaned against the frame. Mrs. Travers stood on the other side.

"Your Grace, I thought you'd like to know that you have visitors." She shifted her weight from one foot to the other, visibly uncertain. "Mrs. and Miss Snowe are in the gold drawing room with the duchess."

Vaughan groaned. Wonderful. Just what he needed.

"Thank you for telling me. I'll be down soon." He shouldn't leave Emma to deal with the women on her own. Especially when she was so new in her role here.

Mrs. Travers nodded her approval and left him to his

business. He dragged his hands down his face and wished he could weasel out of what was sure to be an unpleasant encounter.

Miss Snowe had made no secret of her interest in him, and she'd proven she could be conniving—she'd tried to get him on his own, presumably to entrap him, on more than one occasion.

He could have just given in to her and saved himself the trouble of finding a wife in London, but her attitude reminded him a little too much of his mother's.

Vaughan checked that his clothes were in good order and hurried down the stairs to the drawing room. He reached the door just in time to hear Mrs. Snowe make a remark about how close her daughter had come to being the duchess, and readied himself to barge in and defend Emma's honor.

But then she did it herself. Without quavering or losing her temper.

When he entered, Emma's chin was raised high, and she was looking down her nose at Mrs. Snowe like she was an insect Emma had found on the bottom of her boot.

Vaughan silently cheered her on. He should have known that she could defend herself. She may be quieter and more reserved than her sister, but she'd never let him think her weak, so why would she be any different with others?

Pride flashed through him. His wife was an impressive woman.

"Duke," Miss Snow exclaimed upon seeing him. "How charming of you to grace us with your presence."

He greeted them both and joined the group, making sure to position Emma between himself and Miss Snowe, lest the latter attempt anything like she had previously. He assumed his marriage would end her machinations, but one could never be certain.

"We were just getting to know the new duchess," Mrs. Snowe said.

"I'm glad to hear it." Vaughan sent Emma a sidelong look and quirked his lips. "I consider myself fortunate to have her as my duchess."

"Of course," Miss Snowe murmured, batting her eyelashes at him. "She has been a most welcoming hostess."

The door opened again, and Mrs. Travers shuffled in with a tray laden with miniature cakes. She placed them in the center of the table and flashed a quick smile at Emma. Vaughan wondered how he'd failed to notice that Emma had already earned the housekeeper's respect.

"Cakes?" Emma offered their guests.

Mrs. Snowe reached for one, and Emma followed suit, raising it to her lips and taking a bite. Vaughan tried not to picture her mouth closing around something else. His cock took immediate interest.

"I couldn't," Miss Snowe said regretfully. "I must be careful of my figure if I am to find a husband. Too much cake makes ladies soft around the middle."

She shot Emma a pointed look. Vaughan narrowed his eyes. He would not allow anyone to denigrate his duchess in her own home. But just as he opened his mouth to speak, Emma beat him to it.

"Then I am fortunate to be a married woman now, so I need not concern myself with such things." She held Miss Snowe's gaze while she took another bite. "I'm finding there are many benefits to being a duchess. Hopefully you too will secure a husband soon, and then you may eat all the cake you like."

He silently applauded her.

It was not the only time he would do so over the course of their conversation. By the time the Snowes departed, Vaughan had a whole new appreciation for his wife.

He'd known that she'd be trained in how to handle social situations, but he hadn't realized just how adept she would be at managing difficult personalities such as the Snowes without losing her composure.

Perhaps he had been incorrect to assume that she would be less able to smooth his way in society than Violet. Emma simply had a different technique. Where Violet was lively and friendly, Emma was calm and impossible to ruffle.

As Mr. Yeats showed the Snowes to the door, Vaughan stood and held out his hand to Emma. She took it, and he pulled her to her feet.

"Well, I wasn't expecting that," she said, her frosty expression finally cracking. "Are all of your neighbors so...."

"Affable?" he suggested.

She laughed.

"I'm sure the rest of our neighbors will meet with your approval," he assured her.

Thankfully, Miss Snowe was the only girl in the area who'd set her cap for him so aggressively.

"The Holmes, beside the Snowes, are a married couple of a similar age to us. He is the youngest son of a baron who made money in mining, and she is a former governess. The neighbor to our south is a dowager. I'm sure she would be grateful for your company if you ever wished to call on her."

She straightened her skirt, which was slightly rumpled from sitting. "I shall do that."

He hesitated. "You comported yourself very well with the Snowes. I was proud to call you my duchess."

A faint flush highlighted her cheekbones, and a smile broke across her face. Too late, he realized that his praise might have nurtured any misplaced romantic feelings she had toward him.

"Thank you, Vaughan," she said softly. "I am glad to have pleased you."

His cock stirred again, as her words brought to mind other ways she could please him. He gulped. He needed to distance himself from her as soon as possible. It made sense that she would get attached to him. He was her first lover. But he couldn't afford for the matter to go any further.

"Emma…."

She looked at him expectantly.

He tried to make his mouth shape the words. To tell her that he would be leaving tomorrow. But instead, he clasped her shoulders and kissed her.

Her small intake of breath urged him on, and his hands journeyed down her body to settle on the swell of her hips. His tongue delved between her lips, tasting sweetness and a hint of vanilla.

He clutched her tighter.

"Oh!" The squawk came from behind them.

He released her immediately and used his body to shield her from the maid, who'd entered unannounced. The maid excused herself, but the mood had been broken.

CHAPTER 17

Norfolk,
December, 1819

THE FIRST DROP OF RAIN LANDED ON THE TOP OF VAUGHAN'S head just as he guided the horse to a stop outside the stables. He glanced over his shoulder at Ashford Hall and tried to ignore the flash of guilt that arose from the knowledge he'd been avoiding Emma.

He hadn't gone to her last night, and then he'd left to go riding soon after dawn this morning. She didn't deserve that. He needed to get over his dread of having an uncomfortable conversation and just do it.

Thunder rumbled in the distance, and he dismounted. He rubbed the horse's neck and slipped him a treat, then looked up at the sky, where the clouds were rapidly darkening from gray to ominous black.

"Your Grace," the stable master called as he jogged out from the stables, shielding his face with his hand. The rain was still light but growing heavier with every passing moment.

"Here." Vaughan handed him the reins and stroked the horse's soft muzzle before he was led away.

Vaughan hurried toward the house, hoping to get inside before he was soaked. If he got wet, he'd be tempted to delay the conversation with Emma again, and he didn't need any more excuses for doing that. He'd already been cowardly enough.

What did it matter if he liked the warm, open way she gazed at him, or how passionately she came apart beneath him? This wasn't a love match—it was a marriage of convenience, and they both needed to remember that.

He took the stairs two at a time, relieved when he entered the foyer and was sheltered from the rain. He checked the morning room, where Emma liked to spend time, but she wasn't there. Undeterred, he knocked on the door of her bedchamber, and when there was no response, opened it and looked inside. The room was empty.

Knowing he could search the house for hours without finding her, he went to the room behind the kitchen, hoping Mrs. Travers would be there. She was jotting notes on a worn piece of paper, squinting at the words as though having difficulty reading her own handwriting.

"Have you seen the duchess?" he asked.

She rose to her feet, frowning. "She took a hamper from the kitchen earlier and set out on foot to find you. I think she was hoping to share a picnic lunch."

His stomach sank. Emma was out there, somewhere, in the rain?

"She hasn't come back?" He sounded more pleading than he'd have liked.

"I'm afraid not." She pursed her lips. "She isn't in her bedchamber?"

"No."

"Hold on. I'll ask Daisy. If anyone will know, it's her." She hustled out the door on the other side of the room.

While Vaughan waited, he silently cursed his wife. How could she be thoughtless enough to head outdoors—on foot, no less—when it had clearly been going to rain?

Another pang of guilt chased on the heels of his frustration. Damn it, this was his fault. If he hadn't been avoiding her, perhaps she wouldn't have felt the need to pursue him around the estate.

When Mrs. Travers came back, she seemed troubled.

"Daisy hasn't seen the duchess since she left for her walk," she said.

Vaughan sighed. He was going to have to go looking for the careless woman.

"I'll retrace my route and see if I can find her," he said. "Please send word if she returns."

"I will."

Before going back out into the rain, he donned a thick coat and a hat to keep some of the water from his face. He trudged over to the stables, explained the situation, and resaddled his horse. Minutes later, he was riding the same circuit he'd taken around the property earlier.

He moved more slowly than he would usually so he could scan his surroundings in search of Emma. He saw no sign of her, and when lightning flashed above, his horse shifted uneasily beneath him.

"It's all right," he soothed, patting the animal's neck.

When they passed the folly, approximately a mile from Ashford Hall, he peered through the driving rain toward its entrance. Would Emma have taken shelter there? Would she have even known it existed? He couldn't recall if they'd passed it during their visit to the tenants.

He guided the horse toward the folly, which loomed on the horizon, its turrets dark against the clouds. They covered the ground slowly, as the grass was longer here and the earth muddier.

As they drew near, he couldn't see any life from within

184

the boxlike center of the folly. He stopped a few yards away and dismounted. The building was unlocked, so he yanked the door open and strode inside, removing his hat and shaking water from his hair as he did so.

Emma was huddled on a bench against the far wall. She grimaced at him, her teeth chattering.

"You have no idea how glad I am to see you," she said.

A surge of fear flooded his body, leaving him cold, as he realized how much danger she'd been in. If he hadn't found her, she could have become seriously ill.

Hell, she still might.

"What in God's name were you thinking?" he demanded. "Heading off into unfamiliar terrain, on foot, when everyone and their mother could tell it would rain before nightfall."

She lowered her gaze to stare at her hands, and the sense of guilt returned. He shouldn't yell at her when she was already distressed.

"I thought it might be nice to spend time together," she whispered. "I brought lunch."

He glanced at the hamper beside her, which was sodden, whatever food it contained no doubt ruined. He gritted his teeth. He'd been right—she had done this because he'd avoided her. Clearly, they needed to have that conversation sooner rather than later.

"Come with me," he said. "We can ride back together, and once we get there, we need to talk."

~

EMMA WORRIED HER LIP AS SHE STOOD, HER WET SKIRTS clinging to her legs as she approached Vaughan. He was angry with her, that much was obvious, and she feared what he might say once they were home. She wanted to believe he was upset because he was worried, but she might be deluding herself.

She grabbed the hamper's handle and carried it across the hard floor to where Vaughan waited. He held the door open, and she wrapped her free arm around herself, wishing she'd thought to wear something warmer.

Vaughan sighed as she passed, then touched her shoulder before she stepped out into the rain. She turned to face him, and he shrugged off his coat and held it out to her.

"Here."

"Thank you." She placed the hamper on the floor and worked her sodden arms through the coat's armholes. Perhaps she should have protested and told him to keep the coat, but she was cold, and it still held a little heat from his body. She'd be a fool to turn him down.

He reached for the hamper, but she beat him to it, gritting her teeth and walking into the rain. It drenched her almost immediately, and she blinked rapidly, trying to keep the water out of her eyes.

While she was preoccupied, one of her feet slotted into a mole hole, and she tripped, her ankle rolling underneath her. She dropped the hamper and threw her palms out to catch herself as she fell.

Just before she landed, Vaughan grabbed her around the waist, the jolt leaving her gasping. Slowly, he pulled her upright.

"Are you all right?" he asked, turning her to face him.

"I think so." Gingerly, she set her foot on the ground, and pain flared in her ankle. She winced. "On second thought, I might have twisted my ankle."

To her surprise, he scooped her into his arms and carried her back to the folly. He kicked the door open and lowered her carefully onto the same bench she'd been sitting on earlier. He knelt in front of her and cupped one of his hands around her calf, using the other to lift the hem of her skirt.

His hand slid lower, and he gently probed her ankle. She hissed, flames licking at her nerves.

"I suspect you're right about it being twisted," he said.

He met her gaze, and she searched his face for any hint of affection. With how tenderly he'd held her, and the care he'd taken not to hurt her more than necessary, surely he must feel some affection for her. Even a tiny bit.

But as always, she couldn't read his cool gray eyes.

"We need to get you back so we can summon a doctor to make sure it's not broken." He sat beside her and slipped his arm around her shoulders. "I'll help you walk. Lean on me, and let me take your weight."

Awkwardly, they got to their feet. Emma tried using her foot, but the ankle crumpled beneath her, and Vaughan's support was the only reason she didn't fall again.

"This isn't working. I'll carry you, but wait here for a moment."

He strode into the rain and returned with the hamper, which he placed just inside the folly.

"We'll come back for it later," he said.

With a grunt, he lifted her again. She clung to him as he carried her out to a large gelding she'd seen Vaughan riding before. He lowered her gently to the ground.

"Put your good foot in the stirrup." He guided her into position. "Now pull up. I'll hoist you from behind."

Her eyes widened as his hand landed firmly on her bottom and lifted her into the saddle. A moment later, he'd gracefully mounted behind her and was sheltering her with his body.

"Hold on to the front of the saddle," he ordered.

She gripped onto the pommel and steadied herself as he eased the horse forward. They moved more slowly than she'd have liked, but with the rain stinging her face and the wind whipping her hair, she couldn't blame him for being hesitant to go faster.

Each of the horse's footsteps jostled her ankle, and pain flared over and over again. She bit her lip and refused to whimper. Complaining wouldn't get her anywhere. Vaughan couldn't click his fingers and magically have them back at Ashford Hall just because she wished it so.

She inhaled through her nose, then sputtered as water filled her nostrils.

"All right?" Vaughan called near her ear.

"Fine," she yelled back, deciding it would be best to breathe through her mouth from now on.

She shivered. Her fingers were becoming numb where they clasped the pommel, and her knuckles ached. She couldn't feel her toes, and even the press of Vaughan's chest against her back didn't bring her any warmth. She was cold to her core.

Finally, the silhouette of the house loomed before them, and Vaughan brought the horse to a stop. A stable boy raced over—he must have been awaiting their arrival.

Vaughan slid off the horse's back, and Emma swayed in the saddle. She hadn't realized how much she'd been relying on him to keep her in place. But before she could fall, his hands encircled her waist, and he lifted her off and down.

She expected him to set her on her feet, but instead he cradled her in his arms as his long legs ate up the distance between them and the house. Once inside, he called for the housekeeper.

"Summon a doctor," he told Mrs. Travers. "The duchess has twisted her ankle."

Mrs. Travers wrung her hands. "Oh, dear. It'll be a miracle if the pair of you don't catch pneumonia from this too."

"God, I hope not. Can you summon her maid?"

Emma leaned her head against his shoulder and smiled. His voice was rumbly, and she could listen to him all day.

"Are you with me?" he asked her.

"Mm-hmm," she murmured.

She peered through wet eyelashes. They were in front of

the grand staircase. Mrs. Travers had disappeared, but someone in a maid's uniform was hurrying toward them.

"Your Grace!" It was Daisy, and she sounded distraught.

"Draw her a bath," Vaughan said. "We need to get her warm."

"What about you?" Emma demanded. "You're cold too."

"I'll deal with that later."

She wanted to insist he deal with it now, but at that moment, something bumped her ankle, and she gasped.

"Sorry," Daisy said. "I'm so sorry, Your Grace. I'll see to that bath right away."

Then they were moving again. Up and up. The ceiling shifted overhead, making her feel nauseous, so Emma closed her eyes. If she summoned a little more strength, she probably could walk for herself. There was no reason for the duke to carry her like an invalid.

But, well, she did enjoy it a little. It was nice for someone to make a fuss over her.

He lowered her onto a chaise, and when she opened her eyes, she realized they were in her bedchamber.

"Let's get you out of these clothes," he said, shifting her so he could undo the ties down her back.

Suddenly Daisy was hovering over them.

"The footmen are filling the tub next door," she said. "Let me help with that, Your Grace."

"No," Vaughan snapped, then continued more evenly. "I have it."

Emma flashed Daisy a weak smile, hoping she wouldn't take offense at the duke's rebuke. Daisy shrugged, but her forehead was furrowed with concern.

"Would you like me to help her bathe?" Daisy asked.

"I will take care of it. You may return to your other duties."

Daisy gave Emma's hand a quick squeeze as she brushed past, leaving them alone.

Vaughan finally managed to get her dress open, and Emma resisted the urge to point out that Daisy could have done it faster. He wanted to help her, and that filled her with hope and made her insides warm for the first time since the rain had started.

"Can you get your arm through here?" he asked, trying to guide it out of the sleeve. Working together, they peeled the redingote and the dress off her, and then he draped a blanket over her while he unlaced her boots. He tugged them gently, and one came off easily, but the other didn't want to budge.

Emma winced as he pulled more firmly.

"I'm sorry." His tone was strained. "Your foot is swollen. I may have to cut the boot in order to remove it."

She sighed. It was one of her favorite pairs, but she couldn't insist he leave it on. The ankle might become even more inflamed.

"Cut it," she said.

He left and returned a moment later with a small blade in his hand. She stayed absolutely still as he sliced the leather and then grabbed her calf to get leverage so he could get the boot off.

"I will buy you a dozen more," he promised.

Despite herself, she smiled. "One replacement is all I need."

"Nevertheless."

Once she was fully nude, he reached for her as if to carry her again.

"I can walk," Emma said.

He narrowed his eyes. "You may damage the ankle further."

He wound one of his arms around her back, the other beneath her thighs, and lifted her. She flinched when she came into contact with his clothes, which were still soaking wet and chilled.

"You need to get out of those," she said.

"I will as soon as you're in the bath."

He carried her through the door opposite the one that led to his bedroom, into her private bathing chamber. The tub stood in the center of the room, filled nearly to the brim with steaming water. He lowered her into the tub, submerging his arms as he did so, and set her down with the utmost care.

Tears sprang to her eyes. Against all odds, this union was becoming something to cherish. She yearned for his affection and would eagerly gobble up every little sign of it.

She tensed as the hot water started her blood circulating properly again, and her numb fingers and toes became prickly and uncomfortable. She screwed up her eyes so the tears that had gathered in them wouldn't fall.

Suddenly, Vaughan withdrew his touch. She watched as he yanked off his own clothes, apparently not caring that his shirt tore. When he was bare, she saw that goose bumps had rippled over his skin.

The tingling of Emma's extremities was beginning to fade. She pushed herself to one end of the tub and wrapped her arms around her legs.

"Get in," she said. "You need to warm up too."

Under other circumstances, sharing a bath with him might have seemed scandalous, but they were clearly both focused on comfort right now.

"Shift down," Vaughan said.

Instead of getting in at the opposite end of the tub, as she'd assumed, he dangled his feet into the water behind her back, hissing at the contact. When she wriggled down as he'd asked, he slipped in behind her.

His arms encircled her waist, and he drew her backward so that she sat between his thighs, her back pressed to his chest, similar to when they'd been on horseback.

"Damn, that hurts," he muttered. Then, "Excuse the cursing."

Her lips twitched with amusement. He'd said plenty of

other curses during their intimate moments. Strange how he seemed to forget that the rest of the time.

He reached past her to grab the cup from the table beside the tub. He scooped water with it and tilted her head back. She closed her eyes and relaxed as he poured the water over her hair. His fingers worked the tangles out, going slowly so as not to hurt her.

When he'd thoroughly rinsed her hair, he replaced the cup on the table and used the scented soap to work up a lather on his hands.

"Ah, so this is why you always smell of vanilla," he mused, his hands gliding over her shoulders and arms, gently cleaning her.

"I didn't know you'd noticed."

His breath tickled her ear as he murmured, "I notice everything about you."

A thrill shot through her. But just as she tried to turn and kiss him, she put pressure on her ankle, and it throbbed again.

"Careful," he said. "Don't move too much."

Once he'd soaped her, he cleaned himself, and then they soaked in the warm water until Daisy knocked on the door and announced that the doctor had arrived.

Vaughan slung one of his legs over the side of the tub and levered himself out. Emma made to follow, but he gestured for her to stay put. He dried himself briskly, left the room, and came back only seconds later with a change of clothes that his valet must have left outside. He dressed, rolled his sleeves up, and held out his hand to her.

"Let's get you sitting on the edge, so you aren't stressing the ankle," he said.

She allowed him to manhandle her into position, then perched on the edge while he grabbed a fresh towel and ran it over her legs. He helped her stand and took most of her weight while he rubbed the towel over her torso and down her arms.

She bit her lip as his proximity and the sensation of the towel against her nipples caused heat to rush to her core. She counted her breaths, focusing on keeping them regular so he wouldn't know the effect he was having on her. It wasn't the time for that.

"You wanted to discuss something," she said to distract herself. "You mentioned it earlier."

He shook his head. "It can wait."

He dropped the towel and supported her into the bedchamber, where Daisy was waiting with a robe. Between the three of them, they got her into it. She lay on the bed and Vaughan covered her with a blanket.

She stayed there while he left the room and returned with a man she assumed must be the doctor—a nondescript gentleman who could be anywhere between forty and sixty.

"It's an honor to meet you, Your Grace," he said as he moved into the room. "I wish it were under better circumstances. I'm Dr. Edmund."

"Thank you for coming," Emma said. With the weather as bad as it was, the journey must have been difficult for him.

He raised his bushy eyebrows. "My family have served the Stanhopes for generations. A little rain wouldn't keep me away. Now, let me examine this ankle."

He sat on the end of the bed and lifted the blanket enough to reveal her ankle. She gritted her teeth as he poked and prodded the joint.

"Hmm. Not broken," he said. "Possibly sprained, though."

He covered her again with the blanket.

"Is there anything we need to do?" Vaughan asked from where he was pacing beside the bed.

The doctor dug around in his bag and pulled out a small container. "Spread this poultice on the ankle twice a day. It will reduce the inflammation."

Emma took the container when he offered it and popped the lid open. It smelled herbaceous with a strong undertone of oil of wintergreen.

"Do you have any other instructions?" she asked, putting the lid back in place.

"Stay off it for two days," Dr. Edmund said. "I don't want you walking at all unless it absolutely can't be avoided."

Emma's face fell. Wonderful. Two days of being effectively bedbound.

"After those two days, you should limit your movement for another two weeks," the doctor added. "By then, you ought to be back to normal."

"Thank you," Emma said.

She didn't like the idea of being stuck in one place for two days, but she knew it could have been much worse if Vaughan hadn't found her in the folly. She might have become too chilled and gotten ill.

Vaughan stood as the doctor gathered his things, but Dr. Edmund gestured for him to stay.

"I can see myself out, Your Grace," he said.

"You're welcome to stay until after the rain has eased," Vaughan said. "We can have a room prepared."

Dr. Edmund slung his bag over his shoulder. "Thank you. I might very well accept."

As the doctor left, Vaughan turned back to Emma. He studied her, concern evident in his expression.

"I will remain at Ashford Hall until after you are well," he said in a tone that brooked no argument.

Emma's heart lurched. "I didn't realize you intended to leave."

CHAPTER 18

OH, DAMN. HE'D LET THE CAT OUT OF THE BAG.

"Um." He moistened his lips. "Yes. I plan to return to London."

She looked crestfallen, and he felt like a cad for dropping this news on her when she was already injured and upset. He should have kept better control of his tongue.

"Why?" she asked, clutching the bedspread.

He drew in a deep breath. "I have business there."

She nodded, appearing to take this at face value.

"For how long?" The hopeful gleam in her eyes was like a kick in his gut.

"At least a month. Maybe longer."

A horrid understanding lit her eyes. "Until you know whether I'm pregnant. If I am, you'd have no reason to return."

"Emma, I—"

"I don't suppose you planned to invite me to join you?" she cut in.

He hesitated, and when she noticed, she made a bitter noise that was something between a scoff and a laugh.

"Of course not." She didn't sound surprised. "But why?

What have I done to drive you away and cause you to avoid me as you have?"

His chest constricted. He hated that she blamed herself for his own cowardice.

"This isn't your fault," he said. "I have—"

"Business," she finished for him. "So you've said. I realize that you're a busy man, but I also know that it isn't only business that's been causing you to keep me at a distance for the past while."

He couldn't deny that.

She gestured toward the door. "Please leave. I need to think."

His stomach twisted. He didn't want to leave this argument unresolved. Especially not when her eyes were glimmering with unshed tears.

"Let's talk this through." He started moving toward the chair nearest her bed, but she held up her hand to stop him.

"Please, Vaughan." Weariness made her voice heavy. "Not now. If you intend to stay until I'm healed, we can discuss this later."

Reluctantly, he nodded. "If you need anything, call for me."

She agreed, but something in her demeanor made him suspect she'd summon Daisy or another of the servants before asking him for help.

"I mean it," he said. "I don't wish to see you hurt."

Then he passed through the connecting door into his own bedchamber and collapsed onto the bed with a sigh. Why must everything go to hell?

~

WHEN EMMA DIDN'T TURN UP FOR BREAKFAST THE NEXT morning—or lunch—Vaughan went to her bedchamber to check on her. He'd known she'd been upset, but she'd shown how much she enjoyed her meals. It was unusual of her to not at least request a plate be sent up.

The moment he stepped foot in her bedchamber, he knew something was wrong. The room was too still. A cold breeze swept through, rustling the drawn curtains. Had the window been open all night?

He walked to the bed, where Emma was curled on her side, the bedclothes tossed aside. Sweat beaded her face and her cheeks were flushed deep pink. Her chest rose and fell rapidly, and she whimpered in her sleep.

"Emma?" he asked.

She didn't respond. Tentatively, he touched her forehead. It was burning hot.

Oh, no.

He shook her shoulder gently. "Emma, wake up."

She still didn't react.

He rang the bell and asked Daisy to summon Dr. Edmund, who'd spent the night in one of our rooms. He just prayed the doctor hadn't left yet.

He stayed by Emma's side, attempting to wake her. Several minutes passed, and then the doctor hustled into the room. He paled as soon as he set eyes on Emma.

"How long has she been like this?" he asked.

"I don't know." He felt useless. He should have checked on her sooner. No, he should never have left her alone last night.

Dr. Edmund hurried to Emma's side. He tested her temperature, as Vaughan had done, and then pressed his fingers to her neck.

"She has a fever," he said. "Was she injured anywhere other than her ankle?"

"Not that I know of. Certainly none of her skin was broken." He'd have noticed that when he'd bathed her.

"Then it must be a result of being so chilled." He clucked his tongue. "Shut the window. She may have opened it if she began to feel warm, but it will have only worsened the situation."

Vaughan strode to the window and closed it immediately, chiding himself for not having done so sooner.

"What can we do?" he asked. "Is it serious?"

Dr. Edmund's weathered face scrunched. "It is impossible to know for certain. All we can do is monitor her and control her temperature."

Vaughan's stomach dropped. There had to be another way to help her. "Will you stay?"

"Of course, Your Grace."

"Thank you." His shoulders slumped with relief. "Once the weather has cleared, I will have a footman sent to collect a change of clothes for you, if that is amenable."

Dr. Edmund bowed. "That would be most appreciated. Never fear, I shall remain here until the duchess is through the worst of the fever. Now, let's see what we can do to make her comfortable."

VAUGHAN COULDN'T TAKE HIS EYES OFF HIS WIFE. HE'D BEEN afraid to so much as doze since Dr. Edmund had retired to bed for the night. Poor Emma did not look peaceful in sleep. Her face was scrunched up, and her forehead was damp. She had yet to wake, but nor had she taken a turn for the worse.

He reached for a fresh cloth and dunked it into the bowl of cold water on the nightstand beside her bed, then wrung the water out. He folded the damp cloth and pressed it to her forehead. She murmured something, but her eyes never opened.

The back of his neck prickled, and his heart skipped a beat as fear coursed through him. What if she never recovered?

No, he couldn't let himself think like that. She would heal.

And then she'd give him a verbal bollocking for allowing this to happen.

When the cloth grew warm, he tossed it aside and wet another, placing it on her forehead to keep her cool.

"What else can I tell you?" he mused.

Her silence and stillness had unnerved him, so he'd been sharing stories from his youth. He'd never have told her any of this if she'd been conscious, but he didn't seem to have the same problem when he knew she wouldn't remember any of it.

"Since I didn't have many friends, I spent a lot of time with the horses. In hindsight, I probably caused trouble for the stable master by getting in the way and slowing down their work, but he was always welcoming. He answered all of my questions patiently, and when one of our mares foaled, he convinced my father to let me keep the foal."

He lifted the cloth and touched her skin. She was still warm, so he replaced the cloth with another one.

"I spent hours with that horse. At first, I would help care for him, and eventually I was allowed to take him for walks on the estate. We had such great adventures." He smiled to himself. "I still have him now. In fact, he was the horse you rode with me on the way back from the folly. I'll have to introduce you properly some time."

He stroked her hair back from her face, then caught himself and stopped.

No.

He could care for his wife. That was the gentlemanly thing to do. But he shouldn't be affectionate with her. That was inviting trouble.

"You know that I'm friends with Longley," he said. "We met as boys at Eton. I was shy, but we arrived at the same time on our first day, and he took me under his wing. He didn't mind that I didn't talk much. When I asked him about it, he laughed and said that it meant he got to talk more about himself, which was his favorite hobby."

He stretched, hoping to ease the kinks in his back. His spine popped and cracked, but his shoulders were still tense from sitting for so long, and his legs were twitching with the need to move.

He stood and paced the length of the room several times, trying to burn off his excess energy. When he sat again, he removed the cloth from her forehead. She was no longer quite so sweaty, and he didn't want to chill her.

"Longley and the horse, Trident, were the best parts of my life, growing up. Don't tell Longley that, though, or I'll never hear the end of it. My parents were... shall we say, absent?"

Technically, his father had been physically present more often than not, but mentally and emotionally, he was far beyond Vaughan's reach. He'd been obsessed with his wife. Buying her the perfect gifts, showering her with jewels, and knowing where she was at every moment.

Not that he actually did anything about it if she was with another man. He just seemed to enjoy torturing himself with the information.

"What am I going to do about you?" Vaughan mused. "I don't want to hurt you. I did make it clear at the beginning that I wasn't looking for love."

She shivered, and for a moment, he thought she'd heard him. But then she shivered again, a full-body shudder that rolled through her so violently, he feared she was suffering a seizure.

"It's all right," he murmured, drawing the bedspread up to her shoulders. "You're going to be fine."

She'd damn well better be. He'd gone to the effort of getting a wife and caring for her through her sickness. She couldn't give up now. He reached beneath the blankets and clasped her clammy hand in his, and at some point, he fell asleep.

A knock at the door woke him.

"Your Grace," Dr. Edmund called.

"Come in," Vaughan replied, blinking himself back to full consciousness.

The doctor strode inside, his gaze already seeking out Emma. As he drew closer, he scrutinized her from head to toe, then he grabbed her wrist and took her pulse.

"I know it doesn't seem like it, but she's doing as well as can be expected," he said. "Another day or two, and the fever should be gone."

Vaughan slumped. God, he hoped so. He was tired. Sleeping on the chair beside her bed had left him quite unrested, but he'd never have been able to abandon her in order to get a proper night's sleep. He couldn't let her down like that when he was already disappointing her in other ways.

The doctor left, and Vaughan continued his vigil for another long day. His only company was Daisy, who brought him meals.

When there was no change by nightfall, he requested his evening meal be served in the duchess's bedchamber and he didn't take his eyes off her while he ate.

Eventually, he moved to the chaise and huddled beneath a blanket in an effort to get some sleep—even a little bit would help. But almost as soon as he'd left her side, Emma began to thrash.

He rushed to her, moving the candle on the nightstand closer. Her forehead was damp, and the bedclothes around her were saturated with sweat.

She whimpered and threw her head back. Vaughan reached for her, but then stopped himself. He didn't know whether it would be best to try to wake her or to let her sleep. He sent for the doctor.

Dr. Edmund appeared in his nightshirt. He frowned when he saw Emma, which didn't bode well. He checked her over and shook his head.

"I'm afraid all we can do is wait to see if the fever breaks," he said.

Vaughan's jaw clenched. He hadn't missed the fact that Dr. Edmund had said "if." Previously, it had been "when."

"Is she getting worse?" he demanded.

The doctor shrugged. "As I've said, it's difficult to tell. The fact that she's taken a turn like this could mean she's getting through the worst of it and expelling the fever from her system, or…."

"Or?" Vaughan prompted grimly.

"Or it could mean that the fever has got its claws into her," Dr. Edmund admitted.

Vaughan felt rooted to the spot. He stared at the other man, his stomach rock hard.

"No. She'll be all right." He flopped onto the chair beside her, his heart racing frantically. "Do you hear that, Emma? You *will* be all right."

Wisely, the doctor left.

Vaughan couldn't look away from the pale countenance of his wife. A voice in the back of his mind whispered that if he did so, he might lose her.

The hairs on the backs of his arms lifted as the knowledge slammed into him that, in this moment, he reminded himself of his father. Twisted up over a woman. Riddled with terror because of her. Unable to face the possibility of losing her.

Oh, dear God. This could not continue.

EMMA DREAMED OF A WARM, RUMBLING VOICE, A FIRM HAND IN hers, and gray eyes that were soft with affection. She imagined lying in a comforting embrace while a man whispered words of love.

Unfortunately, when she woke, she was alone.

She blinked to clear the sleep from her eyes, then stretched her arms over her head. Her stomach grumbled, complaining that it hadn't been filled for some time, and she rubbed it absently.

She tried to lift herself onto her elbows, but her arms were weak, and all she managed to do was prop herself up on her pillows. She looked around the dim room. Everything was exactly where it ought to be. The chaise, the desk, and the massive portrait of some ancestor whose name she didn't know.

There was no sign that anyone else had been here.

She sighed. It was a lovely dream, she supposed. But perhaps no more than that.

Fingers curved around the frame of the door to the hall, which was ajar, and then Daisy's face appeared around it. Her eyes were weary with dark smudges beneath them, but she brightened as soon as she spotted Emma.

Daisy stated the obvious. "You're awake."

"I am," Emma rasped, her throat dry. "Was I ill?"

She vaguely recalled being too hot and too cold all at once.

"You had a fever," Daisy said, walking to the bedside. "I thought you'd caught your death in that godforsaken storm."

"Oh, yes." She remembered the storm, and rolling her ankle while out in it. Then the duke helping her back, and seeing the doctor.

Learning that Vaughan intended to leave. Their argument. Her insides clenched, and her heart sank.

Daisy exhaled long and slow. "You have no idea how glad I am to see you up."

"How long has it been?"

"Three days since the storm," Daisy replied. "You had us all worried."

Was it Emma's imagination, or were tears sparkling in Daisy's eyes?

"Don't do it again," Daisy said.

Emma relaxed against the pillow. "I'll try not to, but I make no promises."

Daisy came closer, opening her arms as though she might hug Emma, but then she stopped, her nose wrinkling.

"Let's not do that," she said. "You haven't bathed, and you've sweated a lot."

Emma gasped. "Are you saying I smell?"

"Well... I'll refrain from actually saying it, if it makes you feel better." Daisy's expression was mischievous. "I'll get you a drink. You must be thirsty."

"Yes, please." Her mouth felt like it had been filled with cotton wool, and even swallowing was difficult.

Daisy departed and returned a moment later with a glass of water. She set it on the nightstand and helped Emma into a more upright position before guiding the glass to her lips. Emma drank, and the cool liquid both soothed and stung the inside of her mouth. Once the glass was drained, Daisy patted her lips dry with a cloth.

"Are you hungry?" Daisy asked.

"Starving," Emma admitted. "But I don't know how much I'll actually be able to eat."

Despite another rumble reminding her of how empty it was, her stomach was also unsettled. She wouldn't be surprised if eating made her nauseous.

"I'll see what Mr. Travers has for you." Daisy took the glass and left Emma alone with her thoughts again.

She lowered herself back into the bed and wriggled over so she wasn't lying in the same damp patch she'd woken up in. She really would like to bathe. Perhaps Daisy would help her after she'd eaten.

She gazed at the ceiling, weariness settling into her bones, until the scent of beef wafted into the bedchamber. She sat, checking the tray Daisy carried to see what she'd brought.

"There's beef broth," the maid said, nodding toward the bowl in the center of the tray. "Some bread to go with it. And, because I talked him into it, a nice piece of apple pie for after."

Emma's heart warmed, and some of the disappointment of waking alone faded. "Daisy, you are a gem."

Daisy grinned. "Everyone insists broth is the proper thing for recovery, but personally, I always feel better after eating pie."

"I wholeheartedly agree."

Daisy positioned the tray on Emma's lap, then pulled a chair alongside the bed and sat while Emma ate. She made her way through most of the broth and bread without casting up her accounts, so she decided to try the pie.

Tart, sweet, and with a deliciously spicy undertone.

"Send my compliments to Mr. Travers," she said. "The pie is wonderful."

"I know. I had some earlier."

Emma was glad to hear it. She knew some aristocratic families did not permit the servants to eat the same fare as they did, but she was of the opinion that servants worked far harder than she did and ought to eat just as well.

She'd asked Mrs. Travers what the protocol was soon after she'd arrived, and she had been relieved that things were already run as she liked, so she wouldn't have to have words with the duke about it.

Speaking of the duke….

"Is my husband at home?" Emma asked.

Daisy pursed her lips. "His Grace left the house earlier."

Emma's stomach plummeted. So much for her sweet dreams of an attentive man who'd hovered over her and treated her like she was precious. Instead, he was gallivanting around the countryside without a care in the world.

"He's gone?" Her voice was hollow.

"Yes, Your Grace."

She must have imagined the whole thing. If so, what a horrible trick for her mind to play. To give her a thread of hope to cling to after learning how he intended to leave her.

Did he even care she'd been ill at all?

No, that wasn't fair. Vaughan wasn't unkind. No matter how upset she'd been to discover that he intended to leave her, she shouldn't make assumptions that were probably untrue.

"Did he say when he would be back?" Her heart rate picked up. He wouldn't have left for London. Not when she was unwell. Would he?

"I'm afraid not, but I don't imagine it will be late." Daisy smiled encouragingly. "He's a sensible man, the duke."

"Hmm." Emma couldn't think what else to say.

"Although not entirely sensible," Daisy mused. "He was quite temperamental when it came to your health."

Emma cocked her head, surprised. "Pardon me?"

"Oh, yes," Daisy said. "He didn't move from your bedside until this morning. He sat by you day and night until the fever broke."

Emma's heart took flight. She hadn't imagined it. He *did* care. At least a little.

CHAPTER 19

Norfolk,
December, 1819

EMMA TURNED THE PAGE, ENJOYING THE WARMTH OF THE SUN on her back while she lounged on a sofa in the library, reading *Mansfield Park*. She reached for her teacup and drank, completely absorbed by the story of Fanny Price.

"Your Grace."

She glanced up, surprised by the interruption. She hadn't heard Mr. Yeats enter.

"What is it?" she asked.

Mr. Yeats crinkled his nose. "A Mr. and Mrs. Mayhew are here and requesting to see you."

Emma gaped at him. "I beg your pardon."

"Mr. and Mrs. Mayhew," he repeated. "A London gentleman, by the sounds of him, and a lady about your age with fair hair."

Emma shook her head. That didn't make any sense. Violet and Mr. Mayhew were on their way to Essex. Violet had told her as much. Yet, she couldn't fault Mr. Yeats's description. Something must have happened to bring them here.

"Thank you for informing me. Please show them to the gold drawing room. I will be with them soon."

Mr. Yeats bowed and departed. Meanwhile, Emma closed her book and rose to her feet, her stomach churning with a horrible combination of dread and anticipation. She loved her sister, but she'd also liked the idea of there being a long carriage journey between them.

She set the book down to return to later, checked her dress to make sure she wouldn't embarrass herself by appearing less than impeccably turned out, and slowly made her way to the door, her ankle still slightly tender. Secretly, she dreaded the time it would be fully healed, because then Vaughan would leave.

She reached the drawing room more quickly than she'd like, and hovered outside for a moment before stepping into the doorway. Violet and Mr. Mayhew stood in front of the white marble fireplace. Violet's chin was tilted up, and their closeness spoke of intimacy.

This should not have taken Emma by surprise, but somehow, she'd forgotten that her sister's marriage wasn't the same as hers, where she was required to keep a polite distance from Vaughan during the day.

Violet was in love.

Judging by his tender expression, Mr. Mayhew was too. Or, at the very least, he was smitten. Just like every other man who had ever met Violet.

"Emma!" Violet exclaimed, turning toward her. Her eyes lit up, and a genuine smile crossed her face.

Emma immediately felt bad for resenting her.

"It's so lovely to see you," Violet said as she sashayed to Emma and took her hands, giving them a squeeze. Emma instinctively squeezed back.

"What are you doing here?" Emma asked. "I thought you were bound for Viscount Mayhew's estate."

Violet lifted one slender shoulder and dropped it. "We decided we would pay you a call on our way."

For having spent a lot of time on the road, Violet looked remarkably fresh.

Emma forced herself to smile back, despite her concern at how the visit might play out. "You didn't write to tell me you were coming."

Violet giggled. "Of course not. I knew there would be room for us here. We're family, and this estate is…." She looked around, her eyes widening. "Absolutely enormous."

Emma released Violet's hands and turned to her other guest. "Mr. Mayhew. How good to see you again."

Given that she had been interested in this man at one time, she expected to experience a stab of loss at encountering him again. Fortunately, when her gaze swept over his twinkling brown eyes and handsome face, it never came.

"Lady Emma." He raised her gloved hand to his lips, brushing a kiss over the back of it, and then sketched a deep bow. "Or should I say, Duchess?"

He exchanged a glance with Violet, amusement gleaming in both of their eyes.

"You played those cards close to your chest," Violet said.

Emma didn't reply, because really, what was there to say?

"Do you intend to stay long?" she asked.

"Perhaps a couple of days," Violet said. "It would be lovely to have a break from travel."

"Of course." However she might feel about them at the moment, Emma would never turn her family away. "Would you like a tour of the house? I'm sure you need to stretch your legs after being cooped up for so long."

"That would be delightful," Violet said. "I'd love to see more of Ashford Hall."

Emma rang for Mrs. Travers and asked her to prepare a room for the Mayhews and to inform the duke of their arrival, then she led her guests through the lower level of the house. Violet's eyes were the size of saucers as they entered the ballroom. Emma didn't blame her. It was finer than any London ballroom she'd ever seen.

"And to think, I could have been the mistress of all of this," Violet mused. Beside her, Mr. Mayhew stiffened. She turned toward him, wearing a mischievous smile. "Never fear, darling. I'd rather have you than a gilded life."

Mr. Mayhew visibly melted. "You have a poet's soul, my lady."

Emma bit her lip to prevent herself from asking how this was the same sister who'd insisted not more than two months ago that she'd be happy with a title and plenty of wealth. Had Violet been hiding a romantic streak all that time, or had she allowed herself to be carried away by passion?

Having experienced passion for herself, Emma could understand that, but she still struggled to reconcile the devoted wife in front of her to the mercenary debutante she'd once been.

That said, the thoughtlessness of making comments such as how she could have chosen Emma's current life for herself proved that her sister was still the same person in many regards. It had probably never occurred to her that in doing so, she'd reminded Emma that she was only Vaughan's second choice of bride.

"Let's explore upstairs," Emma said, unwilling to watch them make calf eyes at each other. She led the way, maintaining the briskest pace she could without hurting her ankle further. She didn't want to encourage conversation or any romantic dallying in the mansion's many nooks.

She tried not to think about how Vaughan would react to Violet's presence. Would seeing her make him regret his marriage? After all, it wasn't Emma he'd originally wanted.

Once they'd finished their tour, Emma showed Mr. Mayhew out the back door so he could explore the grounds. Meanwhile, she and Violet retired to the drawing room. She requested tea from Mrs. Travers but not cakes because she knew Violet would have something to say if she learned how often Emma chose to indulge her sweet tooth.

Emma poured tea for Violet and then herself, adding sugar to her own and refusing to look at Violet while she did so. She only raised her eyes once she was stirring the tea and the window for her sister to make a comment had mostly passed.

Violet relaxed on the chaise, blowing on the surface of her drink, her lips curved contentedly. She'd stopped surveying their surroundings, which hopefully meant she wouldn't make any further comments about how Ashford Hall—and Vaughan—could have been hers.

"You didn't sound like yourself in your letter," Violet said. "I wanted to look in on you."

Emma averted her eyes as guilt lanced through her. Here she'd been thinking uncharitable thoughts, and meanwhile Violet was only here because she was worried about Emma.

Her chest tightened. Why did she always revert to imagining the worst possible scenarios when it came to her sister?

"That was kind of you," Emma said, meaning it. "Honestly, I'm still coming to terms with the situation."

Violet frowned. "You mean your marriage to the duke?"

"Yes. It hasn't been the easiest transition, although I shouldn't complain. Ashford and his staff have made every effort to accommodate me."

Her frown deepened. "Why are you finding it difficult? I always thought once you found your love, everything would fall into place."

Emma chewed her tongue, wondering how much to say. Then again, nothing she said would be a surprise to anyone other than Violet.

"I don't love him." She sipped her tea, grateful for the hint

211

of sweetness to fortify her. "I think I could, in time. But that's not why I married him."

"Then why did you?" Violet looked confused. "You were always so adamant that you would marry for love."

Emma looked at her steadily, waiting for realization to dawn on her.

"Because of our broken engagement?" Violet's confusion didn't lift. "But why? He's a duke. Nobody would have held it against him."

"But they held it against us," Emma said. "The ton turned on us. Mother feared we might be cast out entirely."

"So, then what?" Violet asked. "Mother suggested you marry the duke in my place, as if we are interchangeable?"

Emma shrugged. That was about the sum of it.

"And you went along with it?" She sounded bewildered. "Why would you do that?"

"If we were cast out, I wouldn't have had many other options," Emma said. "Nor would Sophie."

"Oh, Emma." Violet's face fell as she finally realized what she'd done when she'd run off with her now-husband. "I am sorry. I never meant for this to happen."

Emma smoothed her skirts. "I know."

Violet may be self-centered, and remarkably oblivious at times, but she wasn't a bad person.

Violet reached over and took Emma's hand. "Are you terribly unhappy?"

"No. I'm just taking a while to find my place in this new life." She drank more of her tea with her free hand, then set it down as the cup began to tremble in her grasp. "This isn't your fault."

Violet snorted.

"Well, not completely," Emma corrected. "I agreed to this solution, and the duke gives me anything I ask for."

Except for his time and affection, but Violet didn't need to know that.

There was a knock at the door, and then it swung open to reveal a pair of men framed in the doorway.

Mr. Mayhew beamed. "Look who I found while I was exploring the grounds."

Vaughan appeared to wish he were anywhere else. Emma winced internally. The poor man. Not only had he been jilted, but he was now confronted with the reality of their marital bliss.

"Good afternoon, Your Grace," Violet said, sweeping into a curtsy.

Vaughan nodded. "Lady Violet. A pleasure to see you."

The words stuck on his tongue as if he didn't really want to say them. Thankfully, before anyone could speak again, the door opened a second time, and Mrs. Travers bustled in.

"I have prepared a bedchamber for Mr. and Mrs. Mayhew," she said.

"Perfect." Relief washed through Emma. "Will you please show them to the room?"

≈

As soon as Mr. Mayhew and the former Lady Violet Carlisle followed Mrs. Travers into the corridor, some of the tension that had thrummed through Vaughan ever since he'd encountered Mr. Mayhew seeped away.

He tilted his head to Emma in acknowledgement and went to his office, only realizing after he entered that Emma was right behind him. He poured himself a brandy and was about to take it to his desk when Emma spoke.

"May I have one too?"

He hesitated, having not expected the request. He put his glass down and poured another, then passed it to her. She sipped and, surprising him once again, didn't so much as wrinkle her nose with distaste.

213

"I must apologize for my sister turning up unannounced," Emma said.

Something in her tone caught his attention, and he studied her, realizing later than he ought to that she was obviously distressed. Her complexion was paler than usual, and she was downcast. Did Violet usually have this effect on her?

"It isn't your fault," he assured her. "Unless you invited them here."

She scoffed. "Of course not."

His eyebrows flew up at her tone.

"You were betrothed," she said pointedly. "Do you think I would invite my husband's former betrothed to visit so soon after our wedding—even if she is my sister?"

Vaughan supposed not. He could imagine how it might be awkward for both of them.

"I'll grant you that it seems unlikely," he said.

He sipped his brandy and studied her. He needed to distance himself from her, that wasn't up for debate, and he'd intended to make it clear sooner rather than later that he'd be leaving now that she was recovered. It wasn't the time for that conversation, though. Not when she was already upset.

"Is there another reason that you don't seem pleased by her visit?" he asked.

Emma rubbed her chest absently. "Let's just say that I have complicated feelings for Violet. I love her, but sometimes I want to shake her a little."

He took another drink to hide his smile. "That is fair. I think, if I had a sibling, I might sometimes want to shake them too."

She snorted a laugh, then covered her mouth, her eyes wide with horror. "Please ignore that," she said. "So, you don't believe it makes me a bad person?"

"Honestly?" he asked.

She swirled her brandy but didn't drink it. "Of course."

"I think you're a very good person." He hoped she didn't take that as encouragement to romantically pursue him, but it wouldn't have felt right not to say it. It was true, after all. She'd risen to the occasion of protecting her family. Not everyone would do that.

Affection blazed in her deep blue eyes. Blast.

"What can I do to help you endure this visit?" he added hurriedly before she could respond in a way he might not like.

"It would salve my pride if it looked like we can at least tolerate each other," she said. "You have been avoiding me. Again."

Damn it. Perhaps there was no escaping the topic he'd been delaying addressing since she'd awoken from her fever.

"I will try to do better until they depart," he told her. His gut roiled with nerves, but he blurted out the next part before he could second-guess himself. "I will likely leave soon after."

Emma narrowed her eyes. "May I come with you?" she asked. "It would be nice to see my family again."

His stomach sank. He hadn't expected her to ask. Not after their earlier disagreement.

Now he felt like a cad.

"There's a chance you're with child," he said. "Until we know for certain, I don't want to risk you traveling."

While it was partly the truth, it also partly wasn't, and judging from Emma's expression, she knew that. She didn't look happy.

CHAPTER 20

EMMA INHALED THE SCENT OF WET GRASS AS SHE WANDERED IN the garden behind Ashford House. Despite the overcast sky, the smell of grass always reminded her of summer days spent outside at her parent's country home.

She rounded a hedge and stopped in her tracks. Ahead of her, beside the rose garden, which was currently full of bare, thorny plants, were Violet and her husband.

Mr. Mayhew's back was to Emma, and his hands rested on Violet's hips. Her face was tilted toward him, her lips parted and smiling.

Emma ducked behind the hedge just as Mr. Mayhew lowered his head toward Violet. She could only assume a kiss was to follow.

She crouched behind the hedge, unsure what to do. If she turned and walked away, they might hear her. If she carried on as she'd intended, they would definitely see her. She didn't want to interrupt a private moment, especially not when she felt wrong for having witnessed it.

Her heart gave a dull throb.

How she wished she and Vaughan could have the type of union where she might kiss him in the garden in the middle of the day. Instead, their physical intimacy was limited to nights in the bedchamber, and even then, he hadn't come to her since before she'd been ill.

A nasty voice in the back of her mind said that it wasn't fair for Violet to have the kind of marriage Emma had always wanted when she'd never before expressed interest in love. Meanwhile, Emma had a man she could love, given time, but who was determined to keep her at a distance.

"Emma, you can come out now!"

Emma flinched. Drat. While she'd been stewing, it seemed that Violet had noticed her. She emerged from behind the hedge sheepishly, relieved to find that Mr. Mayhew was gone.

"I'm so sorry." Emma's cheeks were hot as she walked to her sister. "I didn't mean to intrude."

"Nonsense." Violet beamed. "I hope we didn't make you uncomfortable."

"Not at all," Emma lied. After all, it wasn't their affection that had bothered her, exactly. More like the lack of it in her own life. And that was very much a private issue.

Violet held her arms out and spun in a circle, her face tipped up to the gray sky as if the sun shone down on her. "I'm just so happy to be in love."

Envy flared in Emma's chest, but she quickly squashed it. She'd certainly experienced envy plenty of times before when it came to Violet, but it was such an ugly emotion. She ought not to indulge in it.

Violet dropped her arms to her sides and met Emma's gaze. "I can't believe I used to scorn the idea of a love match. Thank you for always being so certain that love was what you wanted. Your attitude made me realize that love was an option."

Emma didn't know what to say to that, so instead she focused on the reason she'd come looking for Violet in the first place.

"The carriage is ready for our trip to Beecham," she said.

"Wonderful." Violet looped their arms together. "I'm looking forward to seeing what they have to offer."

Emma silently questioned whether Violet's hopes might soon be dashed. Beecham was a charming town, but it was only small. There were a handful of shops at most. Not what Violet was used to in London. But then, she had recently spent a lot of time traveling, so perhaps she knew what to expect.

They strolled through the house together, moving slowly so as not to strain Emma's ankle. Emma waited in the foyer while Violet fetched her pelisse, and then they left in the waiting carriage. Daisy had offered to go with them, but Emma declined. She knew her maid didn't like shopping with Violet. Her sister tended to buy far too much and expect others to carry it.

"It's a nice part of the country," Violet said, looking out the window. "Quite scenic."

"It is." Personally, Emma would have no difficulty spending long periods of time here. "Will you be all right in the country until the beginning of next season?"

Violet turned to face Emma, wincing. "I'd rather not, but I will simply have to exercise forbearance. Lord Mayhew has made it clear that he will not countenance us returning to London sooner. If we were to flout his order, we would not be welcome in Mayhew House."

Emma experienced a pang of sympathy. That must be difficult for Violet, who'd always preferred the city.

"I hope the time passes quickly," she said.

"From your mouth to God's ears." Violet tugged on one of the curls surrounding her face. "I don't imagine you will have the same problem. You must be ecstatic to be living in the country."

"I do rather like it," Emma admitted. "I like my new home, but I will miss our family."

She intentionally did not mention also missing Vaughan. Nobody—least of all Violet—needed to know that her husband intended to leave her behind. The longer before Violet heard of his impending defection, the better.

The carriage trundled into Beecham, and Emma peered out the window, watching as they passed quaint houses on the roadside. A few minutes after they came within the village boundaries, the carriage stopped outside a block of shops on their high street.

"There's not a lot of it, is there?" Violet remarked.

"But it is charming," Emma said loyally. This was going to be her new home, after all.

A footman opened the carriage door and helped Violet down. Emma followed. No sooner had she stepped onto the pavement than a shrill voice called for her.

"Duchess!"

She spun around and barely swallowed a groan. Miss Snowe was making her way out of the nearest shop, her maid walking behind her, laden with paper bags.

"How lovely to see you, Miss Snowe," Emma said, wishing she could get back into the carriage and leave. Beside her, Violet hovered, obviously waiting for an introduction.

Miss Snowe turned to Violet, and her eyebrows arched higher.

"Miss Snowe, please allow me to introduce my sister, Mrs. Mayhew. Violet, this is Miss Snowe of the local gentry."

They exchanged pleasantries, each watching the other with interest. Emma supposed that Miss Snowe knew exactly who Violet was, given the gossip she'd mentioned when she and her mother had visited Ashford Hall.

Emma wasn't sure if the women would be friends or foes, but when Violet flashed her dimples, she suspected it would be the former.

"I adore your dress," Violet said. "Did you get it locally?"

"Lord, no." Miss Snowe waved her hand dismissively. "I ordered it when I was last in London."

"Do you go there often?" Violet asked.

"As often as I can," Miss Snowe said. "That being said, the milliner here is adequate for anything basic. I was about to visit. Would you like to join me?"

"Oh, yes, please."

Just like that, Emma was stuck with Miss Snowe. Of course, she could have objected, but that would have been impolite, and given what she'd learned of the Snowes' position in local society, everyone would soon have heard of the duchess who thought herself above them.

"This way." Miss Snowe gave Emma a tight-lipped smile and proceeded to ignore her as she led Violet to the Beecham Milliner two doors down.

The shop had broad windows that displayed a range of fabrics. Emma paused to look through the window before entering. The fabrics arranged in the window were predominantly cotton and linen with little in the way of silk or velvet, but that was to be expected, considering the milliner's local clientele.

Emma doubted there was much reason to wear silk in rural Norfolk.

A bell tinkled as she crossed over the threshold, and a plump woman around her mother's age greeted them. When she discovered Emma's identity, she practically fell over herself to assist them, and Emma bought a great many ribbons, and a pretty bonnet, even though she didn't really need any of it.

She wanted to make a favorable impression.

Miss Snowe and Violet thankfully seemed content to discuss fashion without much input from Emma. Violet purchased a hair ribbon but nothing else, explaining that it would be too difficult to ship an order to her new residence. Miss Snowe ordered a cotton day dress.

By the time they were finished, Emma was parched.

"Is that a tea room?" she asked, squinting at the building across the road.

"It is," Miss Snow said. "The proprietress, Mrs. Duncan, makes very nice tea."

"Shall we stop for a cup?" Emma asked.

When the others agreed, they made their way across the road and into the narrow two-storey building.

Emma inhaled the mouthwatering aroma of freshly baked scones as soon as they set foot inside. A moment later, her stomach grumbled. Violet shot a look at her, but Emma shrugged. She'd only had a light luncheon, so of course she was hungry.

"Miss Snowe," a woman said, her nose flaring slightly as if she'd encountered an unpleasant odor. She dipped into a curtsy. "A pleasure, as always. Who are your friends?"

"The Duchess of Ashford," Miss Snowe said, gesturing to Emma. "And her sister, Mrs. Mayhew."

The woman's eyes widened, and she swept into another, deeper curtsy.

"Your Grace," she breathed, keeping her eyes down respectfully.

"This is Mrs. Smith, the proprietress," Miss Snowe said.

"It's lovely to meet you," Emma said, her tone warm. She got the impression she would like Mrs. Smith.

Mrs. Smith straightened and nodded at Violet. "Mrs. Mayhew."

"We would like some tea," Miss Snowe said, lifting her chin haughtily.

"I'll brew it momentarily," Mrs. Smith said. "Is there anything else?"

"Could I trouble you for one of whatever is responsible for that wonderful smell?" Emma asked.

Mrs. Smith brightened. "A scone—would you like jam and clotted cream with it?"

Emma's stomach growled again. "Yes, please."

While Mrs. Smith prepared their tea and Emma's scone, the three women sat at a table near the window. Miss Snowe's maid hovered nearby, the poor girl.

Some light filtered inside, but the tea room was dim, and the maroon ceiling and maroon-and-white wallpaper didn't lighten it at all.

Violet looked amused. "You know, I could have been the one getting fawned over."

"I had heard that," Miss Snowe said.

Emma thought she might follow it up with a sly remark, considering she'd used that fact in an attempt to embarrass Emma during their previous encounter.

"Really?" Violet sounded surprised. "Does gossip from London travel this far?"

"It's not so far, really," Miss Snowe replied. "It's not as if we're in Northumbria."

Violet inclined her head. "True."

"But I know something I doubt you do." Miss Snowe sent a sidelong look at Emma before refocusing on Violet.

"Oh?" Violet leaned toward her. "What's that?"

"I, too, almost married the duke."

She looked so smug that Emma wished she could strip the expression from her face. Emma seriously doubted that Vaughan had ever considered marrying Miss Snowe, but even if he had, it was most impolite of her to bring it up in Emma's presence.

Although that seemed rather the point.

For some reason—perhaps because Emma had what she wanted—Miss Snowe was determined to upset her.

"Were you really?" Violet demanded, her mouth forming an "o" of surprise.

Miss Snowe nodded and glanced at Emma with a cattish smile.

Violet, apparently not realizing what she was up to, said, "Tell me more."

～

VAUGHAN WAS RELIEVED WHEN, AFTER DINNER, HE WAS ABLE TO retire to his office. He'd offered to share a drink with Mr. Mayhew, but the other man had been more interested in working on a poem he was writing. That suited Vaughan just fine.

Dinner had been an uncomfortable affair, the Mayhews altogether too cheery, Emma unusually quiet, and Vaughan not in the mood to talk.

He opened his desk drawer and withdrew a stack of letters from within—primarily correspondence from his solicitor and estate manager. He unsealed the one on top and was halfway through reading it when there was a knock on his door.

"Come in," he called, expecting it to be Emma.

However, it was Violet who stepped into his office.

His fingers tightened around the pen he'd been using to keep his place as he skimmed along the text. His jaw clenched, and he felt the sudden need to leave.

He had no feelings for Violet—he never had—but given their previous betrothal, it was improper for her to be alone with him, especially when he knew his wife had mixed emotions about her already. Nothing good could come of this encounter.

Violet wasn't particularly intuitive, though, so she padded to the guest chair on stockinged feet and sat.

"I would like to apologize properly for jilting you," she said, her expression uncharacteristically solemn. "I should have done so before now, and I want you to know that I really am sorry."

Oh, God.

Vaughan glanced up at the ceiling and wished he could snap his fingers and avoid this conversation.

"It's already forgotten," he said, hoping she would drop the subject.

"No, it's not." Her chin took on a stubborn slant, reminding him of Emma when she was being obstinate. "I never meant to hurt you. Please believe that. I thought Emma's notion of a love match was fanciful, and I didn't intend to pursue one of my own."

Ah, so there it was. Direct confirmation that Emma wanted love. For some reason, it hurt to know for certain that he'd gotten in the way of her achieving it.

"Then why did you?" he asked.

Her lips twisted wryly. "I met my husband. Once I worked out what I felt for him, it could not be denied, and I knew I couldn't marry anyone else."

Vaughan twirled the pen between his fingers, wondering —for the hundredth time—how he'd so badly misjudged Violet when he'd chosen her to be his future duchess. He felt like his bridal search had been doomed from the moment he'd set his eyes on her.

"Why not become betrothed to Mayhew right away?" He didn't understand her logic. "Why accept my proposal if you knew you had feelings for another man?"

Violet shrugged. "As I said, I didn't immediately realize what I was experiencing. When you proposed, it was everything I'd ever said I wanted, and my mind was in a muddle, so I instinctively accepted. I regret that now. If I'd turned you down, it would have been a scandal, but nothing of this scale, and I wouldn't have needed to elope."

She reached across the desk and placed her hand on his unoccupied one. He froze, shocked by the contact.

"I hope you have found what you wanted, even if it isn't with the sister you initially intended to wed," she said.

A shadow flickered in the hall, catching Vaughan's attention before it returned to Violet. He snatched his hand away, placing it on his lap where she could not reach it.

"I appreciate your apology, and I believe you had good intentions when you came in here."

Probably.

"But you are dishonoring both the duchess and your husband by being alone with me. Please do not seek me out alone again during your stay with us."

Violet's mouth dropped open. "E-Excuse me," she sputtered.

"I believe you heard me perfectly." He stood, and gestured toward the door. "Please return to your husband."

Violet's mouth snapped shut. She rose with a huff and stalked out of the office. Vaughan watched her go. He'd dodged a bullet with that one. She wasn't half the woman Emma was.

CHAPTER 21

EMMA WOKE UP ALONE.

Nothing about that was unusual. However, her chest ached with an overwhelming sense of loneliness.

Despite all appearances to the contrary, she'd felt as if she'd been making progress on her closeness with Vaughan. To be sure, he hadn't made love to her for a while, but she suspected that was only because she'd been ill.

Now she was certain it was more than that.

Last night, she'd been going to speak with him in his office when she heard voices inside and paused. She'd peeked around the door frame and caught a glimpse of Vaughan and Violet holding hands across the desk like long lost lovers, and then she'd fled.

The sight had made her insides hollow. She'd felt sick and empty all at once. She hadn't been able to face either of them after that, so she was relieved it was the end of the night and she could go to bed without being disturbed.

Unfortunately, this morning, reality came crashing back. Or at least, it would if she'd let it, but she had a plan to delay the inevitable for a while longer. She reached for the bell and summoned Daisy.

"Good morning, Your Grace," Daisy said as she breezed into the bedchamber. She stopped in her tracks on the way to the windows to pull the curtains, her head swiveling as she stared at Emma.

"You look terrible," she exclaimed.

"I feel it," Emma said. "Would you be able to bring me a tray of breakfast and tell our guests and the duke that I am unwell?"

Daisy continued to the window and pulled the curtains open, allowing weak sunlight to stream into the room.

"Of course," she said, approaching the bed. "What's wrong? Is it a headache? Do you think you might cast up your accounts?"

"A little of both." At this point, it wasn't even a lie.

"Should I call for Dr. Edmund?" Daisy sounded worried, and Emma hung her head, a little ashamed. Perhaps it hadn't been the best plan to feign illness so soon after her fever, but she couldn't think of any other way to evade both her sister and her husband.

"No, thank you. I'm sure it's nothing serious. I just need to rest."

Daisy didn't look convinced, but she left to spread the news and fetch breakfast.

Emma closed her eyes. The image of Violet and Vaughan illuminated by the candlelight, their hands clasped, sprang straight to her mind. She cursed. This wasn't a good time to have been born with a vivid imagination.

Her heart throbbed. If someone had taken a knife to it, she didn't think the organ would hurt this much.

Obviously, she cared more deeply for her husband than she'd thought. She'd known she admired him, but this went further than that. In hindsight, she should have realized it would. How was she to resist a man so thoughtful and intelligent?

Especially when he'd sat faithfully by her side during her illness?

She just needed to get into her head what she should have known all along. What she *had* known all along but did her best to ignore.

She wasn't the Carlisle sister Vaughan wanted. She was just his second choice.

Her cheeks were damp, and when she raised her hand to them, she realized she was crying. She rolled onto her side and drew her knees to her chest, wrapping her arms around them in a comforting embrace.

A sob wracked her body, and then another. When she heard footsteps in the hall, she sniffled, wiped her eyes, and forced herself to put on a good face. Never mind that Daisy would be able to see she'd been crying. She wouldn't push for reasons.

Daisy entered briskly and carried a tray to the bed. Emma sat up, and Daisy passed her the tray, which Emma placed on her lap.

"Thank you," Emma said.

"Is there anything else you need?" Daisy asked, worry marring her brow.

"Not for now."

Daisy excused herself.

Emma poured a small cup of tea and sat the teapot and the teacup on the nightstand. She glanced at the tray, which held a plate of buttered toast with a dollop of jam on the side. She spread the jam on the toast and took a bite.

The toast was dry as dust in her mouth, and she had to chew for ages before she was able to swallow. Disappointed, she pushed it aside and sipped her tea to wash it down.

When she'd emptied the teapot, she rang for Daisy to collect the tray, and then she found the copy of *Mansfield Park* she'd been reading and picked up where she'd left off.

Soon after, there was a knock at the door. Expecting it to

be Daisy, she called out for her to enter, only to bolt upright when it was Vaughan who appeared at the end of her bed.

"What's wrong?" he asked, gazing down at her.

She opened her mouth, then closed it, caught off guard.

"I don't feel well," she said when she came to her senses.

He frowned. "So Daisy said. Specifically, what seems to be the matter?"

"Um." She blinked up at him. She hadn't expected to have to answer that question, so she didn't have a good response prepared.

"Do you think you might be with child?" he asked. "I've heard women often feel ill during their confinement."

She fought the urge to bury her face in her hands and groan. Lord, why had she not considered he might think that? She didn't want to get his hopes up for no reason.

"It's too soon to know for sure," she said.

"Hmm." His lips pressed together. "Are you nauseous?"

"A little." She glanced at the door as if it might offer up suggestions on how she could escape this conversation.

He rounded the bed and touched her forehead. "You aren't as hot as you were when you had the fever."

She flushed, feeling guiltier by the moment.

He tutted. "I hope it hasn't returned. The doctor was sure you were in the clear."

"I don't think it's that," she said. "Most likely I'm overtired."

His eyes narrowed. "Have you not been resting enough? Is it your sister's visit that has made you overwrought?"

At the mention of Violet, Emma's tears returned with a vengeance.

She felt like an observer in her own body as Vaughan turned ashen, obviously uncertain how to react. Gently, he sat on the edge of the bed and patted her upper back. He murmured words that were supposed to be soothing, but his kindness only deepened her pain.

He was such a good man underneath his stiff surface, and she wanted him so badly. How unfortunate that he did not feel the same way toward her.

"I'm sorry," she sobbed.

"Whatever for?" He sounded baffled.

She sniffed, tears streaking down her face uncontrollably. "I'm sorry I'm not Violet."

He cocked his head and looked at her as if she were a foreign species.

"I saw you together," she explained miserably. "Do you love her?"

OF ALL THE RIDICULOUS IDEAS...

Despite the awfulness of the situation, Vaughan burst into laughter. Apparently, that was not the appropriate response, because Emma turned away.

"No, don't be that way." He took her chin between his thumb and forefinger and turned her back to face him.

Her lower lip trembled. "I don't understand."

She wasn't the only one.

"Neither do I," he said. "I don't understand how, after everything she's put us through, you could possibly think I have feelings for Violet."

It was ludicrous.

Yet, Emma's cheeks were soaked, her eyes puffy, and it was obvious now that she was upset rather than unwell.

"She has a way of drawing people in," Emma said as if it were obvious. "She's magnetic. It's always been that way."

Vaughan's throat ached at the thought of how difficult it must have been for Emma to grow up with a twin who was, ostensibly, prettier, more popular, and more congenial than she. Slowly, he moved nearer to her. It was the first time they'd been so close without sex to distract them.

He drew in a deep breath. "Would you like to know why I courted Violet?"

Emma looked as though she'd rather discuss anything else, but she nodded. He was glad for that. What he had to say would surely help her even if she was hesitant to listen.

"I never wanted a wife," he said. "But my cousin, Reginald, is in line to inherit after me, and he's a terrible bully. He was awful to me as a child, and I don't want the dukedom going to him or his offspring. Hence, the need for a duchess to sire an heir."

"I understand the desire for an heir," Emma said.

He'd thought she would—even though she couldn't fully comprehend his dislike of Reginald. Most aristocrats wanted to keep their title in their direct line.

"I decided to look for a bride who wouldn't want anything from me other than a title and a life of comfort," he said.

Emma's forehead scrunched, and her lips parted, but she didn't interrupt.

"On the surface, Violet seemed perfect for that. I thought she would be an easy wife who would be content to have my heir without making demands on my time or attention."

Emma's lips curled slightly, as if she was amused against her better judgment. "Violet is not what one would consider low maintenance."

Vaughan shrugged. "Money, I'm happy to give."

It was his heart he wasn't willing to share.

"What about compliments?" Emma asked. "Violet has always needed those."

"Not so difficult." Not compared to risking something deeper. "It helped that she was popular among society. As you may have noticed, I'm not always adept at social niceties, and I believed she would be able to ease my way at social gatherings."

"She would be good at that," Emma said, her face not giving away how she felt about it.

Vaughan rested his hand on Emma's blanket-covered leg. "Violet would have been convenient, and she wouldn't have tempted me to want more than I should."

At this, Emma stiffened. Her gaze locked on his, questioning.

He mentally fortified himself. He'd never shown so much of himself to another person, but in order to help her overcome whatever insecurities she was harboring, it must be done.

"You, on the other hand, are a most inconvenient wife," he told her, never letting his eyes leave hers. "You make me want things I can't have."

EMMA'S HEART WAS ABOUT TO BEAT OUT OF HER CHEST. SHE gripped the blankets because the alternative was to grab him.

"Are you saying… that you're attracted to me?" she asked, impressed with herself for being brazen enough to voice the question.

She'd never quite been sure where she stood with Vaughan in that regard. He seemed to find her pleasing in bed, but he wasn't very vocal outside of that.

"I'm surprised it's not obvious," he said, "considering that I intended to leave Ashford Hall several days ago and haven't yet been able to bring myself to do it."

Somehow, Emma felt simultaneously sick at the thought of his departure and thrilled by the possibility that he was as enchanted by her as she was by him.

"That, and the fact that I sat by your side like a faithful dog while you were ill with the fever," he added, his expression wry.

Unable to hold back for any longer, Emma reached for his hand. He didn't physically pull away, but she sensed his emotional withdrawal like the crack of a whip. Her stomach dropped.

"I don't understand. If we're mutually attracted to each other, and I assure you, I am also attracted to you"—her cheeks heated at the admission—"then why can't we indulge in the attraction and see where it leads?"

Now Vaughan did extract his hand from hers. He shifted to the side, creating a space between them that usually wouldn't have been significant, but to Emma at this moment, it seemed like an uncrossable void.

"I never wanted a love match." His voice was gentle. "I *don't* want one."

She flinched. Was he saying that their attraction didn't change anything? That he was prepared to just ignore it? If so, was that simply out of habit? Perhaps he could be persuaded to try.

"Why?" she asked. "Why are you so against love matches?"

He set his mouth in a grim line. For a moment, she didn't think he would answer, but when he did, she was left even more confused.

"My father married my mother for love." His voice held a bitterness that she'd never heard from him before.

"Oh." Was that somehow a bad thing? Had his mother been beneath the duke socially and it had caused problems?

"He adored her." Vaughan shook his head, gazing into space. "He worshiped the ground she walked on, and in return, she made him miserable."

Her gut hardened. Somehow, she knew this wasn't a happy story.

"How so?"

"She cuckolded him over and over again. I became aware of it when I was young. I witnessed her with another man."

"Oh, Vaughan. I'm so sorry." It wasn't enough, but she

didn't know how to comfort him. No young boy should be forced to live with that knowledge.

"I don't think she even tried to be discreet," he said. "Everyone knew, and my father became unmanageable because of it. He obsessed over her. Kept a close eye on her. But it never mattered. Even if he'd caught her red-handed, he'd have forgiven her because she knew just how to play him."

It was a shame the former duchess was dead. Emma would have liked to have stern words with her.

"She made him weak," Vaughan said. "And it didn't only affect him. Boys at school taunted me about it, and Reginald was the worst. I tried speaking to Father, but he only cared about his own feelings."

"I'm so sorry." The duke should have protected his son.

"Even when she died in a carriage accident with one of her paramours, he didn't stop loving her. He withered away and died soon after. With her gone, I think he stopped caring whether he continued breathing, so one day he just didn't."

Emma's insides were a tangled web of sympathy and horror. She could understand now why the idea of a love match was so repugnant to Vaughan. His parents had set a terrible example, and on top of that, it sounded as if neither his mother nor his father had been as present for him as they should have been.

"That isn't proper love," she said firmly, twining her fingers in the blankets again so she wouldn't reach for his hand. "A real love match isn't one-sided. From what you've said, I assume that your mother used your father's love to machinate against him, and whether intentionally or not, to hurt him. That isn't right, and I'm sorry for it."

Vaughan didn't react. If not for the movement of his throat as he swallowed, she might have thought he hadn't heard her.

"Neither of them cared for you as they should have either."

They'd failed as parents, in Emma's opinion. Her own parents had never coddled her, but at least she'd known they cared on some level.

"It wasn't...," Vaughan trailed off.

Emma clenched her fists. She really wanted to hold him.

"Love doesn't have to be that way," she said, willing him to understand. "It can be beautiful if both people are equally invested."

He turned to face her. "As it stands, I think you would be more invested than I, Emma. And while I don't wish to be in my father's position, nor do I wish to play the role my mother did. I won't misuse you that way."

"Then don't." Emma growled in frustration. "Do you believe me to be coercive?"

He hesitated, then said, "No."

"Good. I don't consider you to be that way either. In which case, there's no reason we can't try. If it could make us happy, isn't it worth taking a chance?"

She wanted it more than anything, and she was so close to helping Vaughan break through his self-imposed barriers that she could almost taste it.

But then he shook his head.

"I'm sorry, Emma. I don't say this to hurt you, but you have to realize that you will never get the love you so desperately want from me."

CHAPTER 22

VAUGHAN FELT AS THOUGH HE'D BEEN TURNED INSIDE OUT, HIS organs on display for the world to see. He rose from the bed, trying not to look at Emma, whose expression a moment ago had devastated him.

He'd tried to tell her earlier. He'd made his boundaries clear.

But still, she was hurt.

He wanted to fix it, but he'd come to her room to help her in the first place, and he'd only made things worse. He had no doubt he was capable of doing the same thing all over again.

"I'll make sure Violet doesn't bother you," he said gruffly, and then he left. He closed the bedroom door behind himself, relieved she didn't call out after him.

He strode down the hall, encountering one of the maids coming out of the bedchamber Violet and her husband were occupying.

"Beth," he said.

She turned to him.

"Can you please inform Mrs. Mayhew that her sister is sleeping and isn't to be disturbed?"

She curtsied. "I'll do that right away, Your Grace."

She hurried away from him down the corridor. Hmm. Presumably that meant Violet and Mr. Mayhew were not in the bedchamber. Hopefully he didn't come across either of them. They'd shared polite chitchat over breakfast this morning, but he was still irritated with Violet for coming to his office yesterday.

Especially now that he knew Emma had seen them.

Vaughan glanced out of a window. On the horizon, trees blew in the wind, and the sky was gray. Perhaps not the best riding weather. Instead, he made his way to the library to his other great escape: books.

As he entered, he noticed the scratching of a pen on paper and froze.

Unfortunately, Mr. Mayhew, who was seated at a desk facing the door, had already seen him. He nodded in greeting. Vaughan nodded in return. Perhaps he could get away without engaging. Right now, he really wanted to be alone with a book.

He surveyed the shelves until he found one he hadn't read, took it down, and carried it to a comfortable armchair in front of the empty fireplace. He glanced at it, wondering whether he should call for it to be lit. The temperature was plummeting outside. Perhaps soon.

He sat and adjusted his position, then opened the book to the first page.

"Aren't you going to enquire about what I'm working on?" Mr. Mayhew asked before Vaughan had even read the first sentence.

Vaughan raised his head, a furrow forming between his eyebrows. "You looked busy. I didn't want to interrupt."

Mr. Mayhew flourished his pen. "I am writing a poem."

"I hope it's coming along well." Vaughan enjoyed poetry, but not the flowery stuff he knew Mayhew preferred.

"I'm at a bit of an impasse, actually."

"Ah." Hence their current discourse.

"I'm writing about love, and it's made me think. You and I are brothers of a kind now."

Vaughan sighed. He should have turned and left the room as soon as he'd seen Mayhew. He wasn't in the mood for conversation.

"We are?" he asked.

"Of course." Mayhew looked surprised by the question. "Having married a pair of sisters. Twins, no less."

"Then we are brothers-in-law." Not nearly the same thing, but perhaps Mayhew just wanted to be able to claim to be related to a duke.

"So we are." Mr. Mayhew seemed delighted by this. "I dare say, I must apologize for the whole jilting episode. I couldn't allow you to marry Violet. I had to snatch her up for myself. You understand, I'm sure. She's a jewel."

Vaughan stared at the man in utter disbelief. Where on earth had he found the nerve to say such a thing?

One did not speak of their host's jilting. They brushed it under the carpet and hoped no one ever raised the subject again.

Mr. Mayhew chuckled, but it was strained. "All's well that ends well, eh?"

Vaughan cocked one of his eyebrows.

"Emma may be a pale imitation of Violet, but she's still better than many of the other misses on the marriage mart," he continued, digging himself into a deeper hole. "You could have done worse."

The man had a death wish.

Vaughan could think of no other reason for his actions. Fury thrummed in his veins as he set the book down calmly on the arm of the chair, rose to his feet, and crossed the room. When he stood above Mr. Mayhew, he glared down at him with all of the dislike he'd tried to hide thus far.

"My wife is not a pale imitation of anyone." His voice was

low and dangerous. "Especially not a self-centered creature like Violet. The duchess is beautiful, clever, and compassionate, and if you or Lady Violet dare to disrespect her in her own home again, I will pack you into a carriage and send you away myself."

Mr. Mayhew stared up at him, wide-eyed.

Before he could say or do anything he might regret, Vaughan stormed out of the library. He stalked through the house, out into the bracing wind, and over to the stables.

"S-Sir?" a stable boy stammered after getting a look at his face.

"I'm taking Trident out," Vaughan said.

While Vaughan went to the door of Trident's stall, the boy brought his saddle over. Vaughan opened the stall, entered, and rubbed the horse's neck, already feeling his blood pressure drop. He saddled Trident, walked him outside, mounted, and turned to face the boy, who was hovering in the doorway.

"I won't be long," he called.

Much as he needed the escape of riding, staying out when the weather was turning would be a fool's move.

He broke into a trot, then a canter. The wind whipped at his clothes as he urged Trident faster. The horse's strides grew longer, and together they streaked down the road and across a field.

Vaughan could hear nothing but the wind and hooves and see nothing but his land sprawling in every direction. His fingers were numb with cold, but he barely noticed, focusing instead on the rolling gait beneath him.

His breathing calmed as the familiar actions soothed him. Eventually, he slowed, and when he did, he spotted something nearby.

The folly.

Goddamn. Even now, he couldn't outrun thoughts or memories of his wife.

He turned and guided Trident home.

Hours later, after a subdued dinner during which no one spoke except to exchange banalities, Vaughan stood in front of the door between his chamber and Emma's.

He knew he shouldn't disturb her. He'd be leaving as soon as the Mayhews did, and it wasn't fair to Emma for him to send her confusing messages.

Yet he couldn't help himself. He knocked on the door and turned the handle. Vaughan entered Emma's room, his gaze immediately drawn to where she sat near the foot of the bed as her maid brushed her hair so that it shone like gold and fell around her shoulders in silken strands.

His breath caught. God, she was stunning. How had he gotten so fortunate as to have this beautiful creature as his wife?

She wasn't looking at him, but she must have heard his arrival, because she said, "Daisy, you may leave."

Daisy shot a curious glance at Vaughan, then handed Emma the hairbrush, curtsied, and hurried out, closing the hall door behind herself.

Emma held the brush up. "Would you care to do the honors, Your Grace?"

Vaughan's legs carried him to her of their own accord. He took the brush and stood behind her. Gently, he ran the brush from the top of her head and down the glossy length of her hair to the ends. He'd never brushed a woman's hair before, and he moved carefully, afraid he might snag it and hurt her.

After a few strokes, he became more comfortable with the motions, and the tension drained from his shoulders. He allowed himself to enjoy the whisper-soft caress of her hair against his skin. She hummed in contentment, and the sound went straight to his cock.

He cleared his throat. "You have lovely hair."

"Thank you."

He could not see her face, but she sounded pleased.

"I worry I do not tell you enough how beautiful you are," he said. "You captivate me."

She let out a sigh, but it was not an unhappy one.

"I cannot offer you love," he said, continuing the rhythmic movements. "I'm afraid that hasn't changed. But I can offer you pleasure until I depart."

He waited anxiously for her response. She seemed to have enjoyed his attentions previously, but he hadn't come to her in far too long, and given their conversation earlier today, he feared she would not welcome him.

Finally, she said, "If that is all that you can offer me tonight, then I accept it."

He closed his eyes, relieved beyond reason. "Thank you."

"I think my hair has been brushed enough now."

He passed her the brush, and she rose slowly and placed it on the dresser, then turned to face him. Her cheeks were pink, and her eyes darkened as she came toward him. He was eager to see what she would do. So far, he had been the pursuer in all of their encounters.

She took hold of his waist and stretched up onto her toes, parting her lips in a clear invitation. With a groan, he lowered his head and took her mouth. She tasted faintly of tea. She must have had some before retiring to her room.

When she pressed closer, he cupped her bottom and cradled her against his erection. She rolled her hips, and he tore his mouth from hers and brushed his lips down the side of her neck, inhaling vanilla and woman.

He cupped her breast, rubbing his thumb over the fabric of her dress. He needed to get his hands on her properly.

"Take the dress off," he growled.

She pulled away from him and caught her lower lip between her teeth. "I'll need your help to undo the buttons. Daisy usually does that before she leaves."

"Right. Of course."

She presented her back to him. His fingers tripped over the buttons as he rushed to unfasten them. Damn his fumbling fingers. They were too big for such delicate work. Eventually, he managed to undo enough of them to get her free. She raised her arms, and he lifted the dress over her head and set it over the chair.

His smile grew wicked at the sight that greeted him. His wife in her petticoats and undergarments. Possessiveness surged through him. No one else had ever seen her this way, and in that moment, he wished with all his heart that he could say no one ever would.

Once she was nude, he undid the tie of his own robe. He'd undressed before he'd come to her. He stood motionless and watched as Emma's hungry gaze darted across his chest, down his abdomen, and paused when it landed on the thick shaft of his cock. Her tongue flashed out and wet her lips.

Good God, was she trying to kill him?

"May I…." She hesitated.

"What, sweetheart?" he asked. When it came to this, he would gladly give her anything she wanted.

She rubbed her lips together and lifted her eyes as high as his chest but didn't meet his gaze.

"You… put your mouth on me," she said.

Oh, Christ.

"I did."

Her blush deepened, and spread down her neck. "It felt divine. Would you like it if I put my mouth on you?"

His cock twitched, very much on board with this idea.

"Yes, but I don't want you to think you must," he said earnestly. "I experience pleasure every time I'm with you regardless of where your mouth goes."

She raised her chin, her expression determined. "I want to."

Fine, then. Far be it for him to refuse.

"Where would you like me?" he asked.

She glanced at him, and then around the room. "Can you lie on the bed?"

He did so, scooting up so his legs didn't hang off the end. Emma crawled over him, straddling his legs. She stared down at him for a long moment, her head cocked as she worked out the logistics. When she'd thought it through, she took some of her weight on one arm and used the other to grip him.

He fought not to buck his hips. He didn't want to startle her. She ran her hand along his length, her thumb gliding up and over the throbbing head. He swallowed a moan. Her touch was too soft and unsure, but seeing her hand on him and the curiosity shining in her eyes more than made up for it.

She dipped her head and pressed a kiss to the tip of his cock. A dribble of fluid beaded there, and she eyed it with interest.

"What's this?"

"My seed," he explained. "It means I want you."

A satisfied smile curled her lips, and her tongue flicked out and lapped it up so fast that he didn't have time to react. Pleasure sizzled through him.

"Hmm." She licked him from root to top, slow and torturous.

He exhaled on a shudder.

"Do you like that?" she asked, licking him again, as if he were her favorite confection.

"Yes," he rasped.

Her brow furrowed with concentration, and she continued to lick him with a combination of leisurely and quick lashes of her tongue. It was never enough, but it set his every last nerve on edge.

She paused, looking thoughtful.

"What—?"

He didn't get to finish the question because at that

243

moment, she sucked his entire length into her mouth. Her throat convulsed around him—it felt so damn good—but she drew back, her eyes watering.

"Not so much at once," he said. "Just a little. Whatever you can take."

She nodded, and enclosed his cockhead with her warm, wet mouth. She teased him with her tongue and hollowed her cheeks, sucking slightly.

"That's perfect," he rasped. "You're doing so well."

She sunk another inch, and curled her tongue around him. He clenched his fists in the bedspread.

Don't release. You can withhold it.

His fingers tangled in her hair, and he guided her off his cock. Her eyes clouded with confusion.

"I need you," he said, grabbing her by the hips and rolling her beneath him.

He delved between her legs with one of his fingers, cursing at the slick glide. The little minx had gotten aroused from having him in her mouth. She really was a gift from the heavens.

He kissed her as he slid one finger into her. Her breath hitched as he pressed a second one inside her, but then she softened and hummed against his mouth.

"You are incredible," he murmured, his lips brushing hers with each word. "Like you were made for me."

Except for that whole love concept.

But they'd tabled that for now, and he tried to ignore a brief prickle of guilt.

"I want you," she whispered, writhing against his hand. "It's been too long. I waited for you every night."

"I'm sorry to have left you unsatisfied." It wouldn't happen again. At least, not while they remained here together.

He positioned his cock at her entrance and pushed in. She

wrapped her lower legs around his, bringing them into alignment and giving him leverage to get deeper.

They moved together, her hot channel engulfing him over and over again, robbing him of his sanity. Their lips met and clung. He speared his tongue into her mouth, and hers stroked against it, like velvet on velvet.

She whimpered and cried out. From the way she clutched at his shoulders, he knew she was close to the edge. He gritted his teeth, determined not to spill before he brought her bliss.

And then she threw her head back, shuddering and babbling as she came. Her body clasped him tighter, like she was milking him, and he let go, filling her as he thrust as deep as he could get, wanting to be one with her. His balls emptied, and he buried his face in the side of her neck and groaned.

CHAPTER 23

EMMA LAY PINNED BENEATH VAUGHAN, EVERY INCH OF HER buzzing with pleasure. Another tremor rippled through her, and she shivered.

Vaughan lifted himself up enough to kiss her forehead and then rolled off her. She expected him to make his escape now that they were finished, but to her surprise, he wrapped one of his arms around her and drew her close. She rested her head over his chest and snuggled in.

She listened to the beat of his heart—steady, if a little fast —and waited for him to speak. It took several moments before she dared to disturb the moment by looking up at him.

He was asleep.

She hesitated, uncertain of what to do. Experience had taught her that he didn't like to sleep with her, but he wouldn't have held her close if he intended to leave, would he?

She studied his sleeping face, which so much more relaxed than when he was conscious. That was hardly surprising, though. The man carried a lot of worry on his shoulders. He was responsible for many others, including her. When did he get a reprieve?

Affection swelled in her chest as she kissed him lightly. He didn't stir. She bit her lip. She wouldn't normally have minded the rush of bliss that came with such tender feelings toward another person normally, but if she allowed herself to indulge in them this time, they would only cause her to get more attached to Vaughan.

A man who'd already said he wouldn't love her.

Not couldn't. Wouldn't. Because he actively chose not to.

That hurt—even though she understood his reasoning. She just wished he could see that she wasn't like his mother. She wouldn't use love to control him. She'd use it to build him up.

Her mind whirred, hundreds of thoughts buzzing through it. If only she could shut them off and enjoy the moment, but instead she was confronted by possibilities.

What if she could persuade him to give love a chance?

What if she earned the love of this wonderful man?

But what if she fell in love with him, and he didn't feel the same?

What if he broke her heart?

She closed her eyes. She had a decision to make. She could continue to pursue a romantic connection with Vaughan and hope that eventually he'd see that it didn't have to turn out like his parents' marriage, or she could give up on that and do what she could to protect her already dented heart.

She wasn't inclined to admit defeat. Especially not when she cared for him and believed he returned the sentiment. But if she continued her campaign to win his affection, she'd likely only cause herself pain.

Vaughan's conviction hadn't wavered during their time together. She had no reason to believe it would do so in the future.

It was fanciful of her to hope it would.

His heartbeat slowed as he slept. Its regular thud and the warmth of his chest beneath her cheek made her want to throw caution to the wind and pray for a good outcome.

But perhaps she should embrace the distance he was doing his best to put between them. At least until she figured out how to shield herself from hurt. There might be a way she could woo him, but she was too raw at the moment, and another rejection would challenge her ability to recover.

She opened her eyes, blinking as they readjusted to the dim light cast by the candles. She eased away from Vaughan. As he murmured and rolled onto his side, she slipped from the bed. Her mind was too busy to sleep. She'd have to get a book from the library to distract herself.

She dressed in her nightgown and wrapper, and lit a candle, then she padded out of the room on bare feet, using the candle to light her path.

"Emma," a soft voice said.

She glanced up, her hand flying to her chest. Violet stood in the hall outside the bedchamber they were using. She carried a candle in its holder that lit the underside of her face, making her appear ghoulish.

"You startled me," Emma said.

"I'm sorry." Violet studied her and then smiled. "I'm glad you look better."

Emma winced internally. She ought not to have lied about being ill in order to get out of seeing people. She should have known that Violet and Vaughan would not be having a rendezvous behind her back. Her sister may be selfish, but she wasn't intentionally cruel.

Violet smirked. "Perhaps it is because you have been well loved."

Emma gaped at her. "Excuse me?"

Even if it were true, she'd never have expected Violet to say as much.

"Do not sound so shocked, sister dearest," Violet said. "You are up and about late at night, your cheeks are flushed, your eyes are sparkling, and it's become quite clear that the duke adores you, so what else am I to think?"

Emma scoffed, keeping her voice low so as not to wake either of their husbands. "The duke does not adore me. Perhaps he is attracted to me, but that is all."

Violet shook her head, her lips twisted wryly. "Nonsense. He has chastened both me and Mr. Mayhew quite fiercely in defense of you. The man is smitten."

A burst of hope filled Emma's chest, but she slammed a lid over it. She couldn't afford to become hopeful, only to have Vaughan remind her of what they were…and weren't.

"Ashford does not love me," she said even though it pained her to do so. "He never will. He didn't even want me at first."

Violet's smile faded. "You really believe that."

"It's the truth."

Violet pressed her lips together and nodded. "In that case, I'm sorry for upsetting you. I only meant to tease."

Emma relaxed a little. "I know."

Violet turned toward the bedchamber door, then hesitated. "If you ever wish for time away from the duke, you are always welcome to visit us. Whenever you like. Even if you want to come with us when we leave here."

The crushing grip on Emma's heart lessened.

"Thank you. That's very kind of you."

Especially considering Violet had no idea how her father-in-law would react to her having extended the invitation.

Emma bit her lip. She wanted to tell Violet that it would never happen—surely it would be awkward—but perhaps putting physical space between herself and Vaughan was what she needed to gain perspective.

"I will consider it," Emma said.

THE DAYS FOLLOWING THE NIGHT THAT VAUGHAN HAD FALLEN asleep in Emma's bed were strange. Everyone at Ashford Hall was oddly formal with one another, and when Vaughan visited Emma that evening, he found her already in bed and pretending to be asleep.

She couldn't truly have been sleeping, because he'd created enough ruckus to wake anyone. Still, he'd decided to take the hint, and he'd stayed away. Now, with his departure from the hall only hours away, his heart was heavy.

He poured himself a cup of tea and carried it to the dining table, then returned to the side table to fill his plate. The aroma of eggs and freshly baked bread made his stomach grumble. He stacked toast on his plate, then covered it with egg and added a strip of bacon to the side.

He joined the others, who had already been seated. Emma was to his left, spreading jam on a slice of bread. Violet and Mr. Mayhew were to his right. Violet had served herself only fruit, while Mr. Mayhew was clearly enjoying everything on offer.

"We leave today," Violet announced unnecessarily. Everyone knew the Mayhews were due to depart after breaking their fast.

However, as he noticed Violet and Emma exchange a glance, he wondered whether he might be missing something.

"You're packed?" Emma asked.

"We are," Violet said. "We are due to depart in an hour."

Again, why repeat something everyone knew?

But Emma nodded, a flash of emotion crossing her face.

"Have you finished your morning ablutions?" Violet asked Emma.

Vaughan frowned as he cut his eggs and toast into bite-size pieces, bewildered by the abrupt change of topic.

"Almost," Emma said. "I have only a couple more tasks to complete."

"I have not seen Daisy this morning," Violet said, confusing Vaughan even more. Violet never enquired after the servants. Never.

"She's addressing a personal matter," Emma replied. "I'm sure she will be done soon, though."

Vaughan speared another piece of toast and glanced at Mr. Mayhew, wondering if he was as baffled by this conversation as he was, but the man seemed unaware of anything other than the giant mound of bacon he was intent on decimating.

"Good," Violet said. "I do like it when everything is timely."

Emma's cutlery clinked as she set her knife aside and took a bite of her toast. "You needn't worry about that."

They continued the discussion for a while longer. Vaughan focused on eating and didn't attempt to contribute because he had no idea what in the hell they were talking about. When the meal was finished, he stood.

"Duchess, may I speak with you?" he asked as Emma rose.

"Of course, Your Grace."

He headed straight into his office, where he stood, framed by the window.

"What is it?" Emma asked as she came in behind him.

He gazed through the window, over the green hills, and toward the blue horizon. It was a good day to travel. Perhaps he'd ride Trident some of the way.

"You and Violet are up to something," he said, turning to face his wife. "What?"

Emma hesitated. "What makes you think we are?"

"You are behaving strangely."

She grimaced and perched on the chair in front of his desk. "All right. I intended to discuss this with you now anyway."

That sounded ominous.

"Discuss what?" he prompted.

She looked down at her hands, then back at him. "Generally speaking, have you enjoyed our interactions since we've been married?"

A kernel of dread formed in the pit of Vaughan's stomach. Where was this going?

"Yes," he said. "You know I am attracted to you and that I like you as a person."

She pressed her lips together, turning them white for several seconds before she huffed out a breath. "Then won't you at least consider the possibility of seeing whether love might grow between us? Or at least cohabitating with me on a trial basis?"

The dread in his gut dissipated, but frustration quickly took its place. There was no reason for this subject to be raised again.

"I've made my feelings on the matter clear," he said. "I've never wavered. If you expect me to change, that is an error on your part."

He strode to his desk and began adjusting several ledgers stacked on the corner so he wouldn't have to see how she reacted to his words. He didn't want to witness her pain.

"Do you still intend to leave soon after Violet and her husband do?" Her voice was crisp. She didn't seem deflated by his rejection. At least, not that he could tell without looking at her.

"Yes," he replied, just as crisply.

"And I may not accompany you?" There was a thin thread of hope in her voice.

"No." He snapped that thread, hating himself for it even as he did.

"Hmm." Her tone grew thoughtful. "Is that because I may be increasing, or is it because you simply don't wish me to?"

At that, he glanced over. Her chin was raised defiantly, and those dark eyes of hers gleamed. Admiration rose within him at the silent challenge. Emma was a strong woman. Anyone who considered her sister superior was a fool.

"The possibility you may be carrying a baby factors into it," he said truthfully. "But I believe that keeping our distance from each other will allow us to get some much-needed perspective. That's the most important thing."

"I understand." She looked disappointed. "I would like to point out that we do not know for certain whether I'm increasing, and even if I am, many women travel this early in their confinement without issue."

Vaughan inclined his head in acknowledgement. "As I said, that is only part of the equation."

"I'm glad to hear that."

His eyes narrowed. Her expression was far too innocent. She was playing at something.

She drew her shoulders back. "There is no reason for me to stay at Ashford Hall if you are not here."

"It's your home." He didn't like where this was going.

"I am going to accompany the Mayhews to their estate," she said.

"But you might be pregnant," he protested.

"And I might not be," she said. "I have already discussed this with them, and we will travel slowly, taking plenty of time for rest. There is no reason to worry."

There was every damned reason to worry. His wife was trying to leave him. It hurt more than he would have expected. Was this how she felt every time he rebuffed her? If so, he felt like even more of a cad.

"What about when you return?" he asked. "You expect me to believe you will be safe on your own?"

"Daisy is coming with me, and we will take a footman if need be."

She had an answer for everything, and the stubborn tilt of her chin told him that nothing he said would move her.

His heart sank.

CHAPTER 24

Norfolk,
January, 1820

EMMA FELT HOLLOW AS SHE CLOSED THE LAST OF HER BAGS AND handed it to the waiting footman. She'd emerged from her confrontation with Vaughan as the victor, but she didn't feel like she'd won anything.

She'd hoped that Ashford Hall might become her home, and maybe it still would, but at the moment, it felt very final, as if she were shutting a door behind herself. Her mood was so melancholy, she'd even been tempted to wear lavender—a color of mourning—but had decided that would be overly dramatic.

Instead, she'd opted for a simple dress that would be comfortable while traveling, and she'd packed several books into a valise she intended to take with her in the carriage.

The footman carried her bag away, leaving Emma with nothing more to do than bid farewell to her husband.

Her throat prickled as she made her way to his office. He sat behind his desk, staring blankly into space. If she didn't know better, she'd think him sad to see the back of her.

"I'm leaving now," she said.

He blinked, seeming to come back to himself. "Won't you reconsider?"

"I'm afraid not." If she did, she'd only end up aching inside when he left.

A brief flicker of emotion passed across his face. It could have been pain, but it disappeared so quickly she couldn't be sure.

"Then let me walk you out," he said.

He came around from behind the desk and took hold of her elbow. Emma's breath caught, and she hoped he hadn't noticed. His warmth radiated between them, giving her the impression that her body was pressed alongside his even when there was a respectable space between them.

She breathed in and out, willing herself not to get emotional or melt into a puddle as she tended to do when he was close. If she weakened, she might throw herself into his arms and beg him to take her with him instead. That could not be allowed. She had her dignity.

Mrs. Travers opened the front door and held it for them. Emma said goodbye as she walked past the housekeeper. She knew that the hall would be in capable hands with Mrs. Travers in residence.

Vaughan walked her to the carriage. Violet, Mr. Mayhew, and Daisy were already seated inside.

"Please travel safely," he said, helping her onto the step.

"I will."

He hesitated, then added, "Write to me when you arrive. I want to know that you are well."

She nodded and stepped inside the carriage. A footman closed the door behind her, and she sat on a bench beside Daisy, who passed her the copy of *Mansfield Park* she'd been reading.

Emma held the book tightly and gazed out the window as the coachman prepared the carriage, and then they began to inch forward. Vaughan stood in front of Ashford Hall, his hands at his sides and his eyes straight ahead.

As they drew away, Emma raised her hand and waved at him. He did not wave back, although the slight tilt of his head could have been a nod of acknowledgement.

To Emma's absolute horror, as soon as he was out of sight, she burst into tears.

Across the carriage, Mr. Mayhew stared at her, aghast.

"Oh, dear," Violet murmured.

"There, now," Daisy said, patting her shoulder.

The comfort didn't help. Emma only cried harder.

This had never been what she'd pictured as her life. She'd wanted a house full of laughter and happy children. She'd longed to share secret smiles with her husband and lie down with him at the end of the day.

She'd never wanted this.

She had a husband. Even one who was kind and thoughtful. She had a grand house, the likes of which she'd never dreamed of. But that bright future she'd envisioned?

It was ashes.

"I'm so sorry," Violet said, reaching out as if to take Emma's hand, only to drop her own when she realized the distance between them was too great. "Is there anything I can do?"

Daisy slung her arm around Emma's shoulders, and despite their audience, Emma leaned against her maid.

"Let your feelings out," Daisy urged. "It does you no good to bottle everything inside."

Even through her damp eyelashes, Emma could see enough of Mr. Mayhew's expression to realize he wished she *would* keep her feelings bottled up. There was no stopping them, though. As soon as they were uncorked, they'd become impossible to contain.

Eventually, she ran out of tears. Daisy mopped her cheeks, and Emma thanked her profusely and then buried her face in a book, too embarrassed by her behavior to engage with the others.

Night had fallen by the time they reached the Mayhew estate and turned onto the path that would lead them to the dowager house, where Violet and Mr. Mayhew were to reside.

Lord Mayhew and several servants met them in front of the reasonably sized brownstone house with a slate roof and ivy growing up the wall.

"This is to be our home," Mr. Mayhew said to Violet as they disembarked.

"It's lovely," Violet said.

It was. It wasn't nearly the same scale as Ashford Hall—in fact, it would fit inside the hall several times over—but it had a charming garden and an unassuming exterior. If Emma had been brought to this house by her husband, she'd have been pleased, and while she knew Violet had once harbored larger aspirations, to her credit, she seemed to like it.

Lord Mayhew greeted his son with a handshake and then gave Violet a slight bow and Emma a deeper one.

"Welcome home," he said. "Your Grace, a guest bedroom has been prepared for you."

"Thank you," Emma said.

"Good evening, Mr. and Mrs. Mayhew." He arched his thick eyebrows as if that address was going to take some getting used to.

Lord Mayhew introduced them to the servants, including the housekeeper, Mrs. McPhee, two maids, a cook, and a footman. Once introductions were completed, he took his leave and returned to the main residence.

Mrs. McPhee addressed Daisy as he departed. "There is space for you in the servants' quarters. I'll show you where to go once I have escorted Her Grace and Mr. and Mrs. Mayhew to their quarters."

"You may show her there directly," Mr. Mayhew said,

raising multiple eyebrows. He drew Violet into his arms. "Let me give you the tour myself, my beloved."

Emma cleared her throat. Perhaps she hadn't thought through the implications of returning home with newlyweds.

"Mrs. McPhee, if you show me to my chamber, I will retire for the night. I'm exhausted."

Violet pulled away from her husband. "Oh, Emma, you must accompany us on the tour."

"Tomorrow," Emma said firmly.

Violet pouted but didn't press the matter.

"This way, Your Grace." Mrs. McPhee guided her inside and led her up a staircase. The bedrooms were on the second floor, and Mrs. McPhee took her to one that overlooked the garden at the rear of the house.

Once the housekeeper had explained everything necessary, Emma closed the door behind her. She collapsed onto the bed and stared at the ceiling. She'd been so sure this morning that she was making the best possible decision, but now she had to wonder.

Had she ruined any chance she might have had at convincing Vaughan to open his heart to her? And why did she already miss him?

She shook her head. She shouldn't get caught up in maudlin thoughts. She was sure that Vaughan wasn't missing her, and at least nothing here reminded her of him.

Somehow, that only worsened the hollow ache in her chest.

❧

VAUGHAN TOSSED BACK A MOUTHFUL OF BRANDY AND PLUNKED the glass onto the table.

"Another, please," he said loudly enough to be heard over

the cacophony of voices typical of a busy evening in the Regent.

A server appeared at his elbow and reached over to pour more brandy into the empty glass. Vaughan thanked him, grabbed it, and sipped this time. He was already well on his way to being soused, so there was no reason to rush anything.

His head spun as he inhaled cigar smoke, and he sputtered.

Longley eyed him disapprovingly. "This isn't like you."

"What isn't?" Vaughan asked, although he knew exactly what his friend meant.

Longley folded his arms over his chest. "Why are you here instead of in Norfolk with your lovely new wife?"

An image of Emma's face as she'd driven away flashed through Vaughan's mind. Her eyes had been downcast, but her shoulders were straight. She was so strong, his duchess.

And now, she no longer shared a home with him—a thought that made him oddly morose.

"What's wrong?" Longley asked, apparently seeing something in his expression to cause concern.

Vaughan sipped his drink again, barely even noticing the burn.

"Emma is visiting with Lady Violet at the Mayhews' Essex estate," he said. "Meanwhile, I am to remain in London for the rest of the season."

Longley cocked his head. "Why?"

Vaughan grimaced. "You know I never intended to reside in the same house as my wife."

"I did," Longley acknowledged. "But anyone could see that you and Emma are well suited. I thought you would change your mind."

Vaughan grunted. "So did she."

"Ah." Longley took Vaughan's glass from him and drained it.

"Hey," Vaughan protested.

"You don't need this," Longley told him. "What you need is a clear head so you can tell me everything that happened."

Vaughan tugged uncomfortably at his cravat. He didn't feel like spilling his guts.

"No, thanks."

"Ashford," Longley warned. "Out with it."

Vaughan huffed. "Fine. You were right when you told me weeks ago that Emma wanted love. She told me when we married that she was happy with what I had to offer, but a couple of days ago, she asked for me to be receptive to the possibility of…well…."

"Loving her?" Longley suggested.

"Yes. That."

He nodded. "And you said…."

"I told her about my parents." Vaughan extended his legs in front of himself and crossed them at the ankles.

"You did?" Longley sounded surprised.

"Yes, so she would understand why I don't want the same things she does. I had to make the boundaries clear again."

He had to protect himself.

Longley shook his head. "You're a fool, man. You're allowing your parents' unhappy marriage to interfere with your own happiness."

Vaughan shrugged. His friend couldn't understand. He hadn't been there. He hadn't seen what Vaughan's father had endured or what a disaster the marriage turned him into.

"God's teeth, you're an idiot sometimes." Longley swirled Vaughan's brandy. "Just tell me this: do you love her?"

"I don't know." It was the most honest answer Vaughan could give. "I don't know what love looks like when it isn't warped and twisted. Now, may I have my drink back?"

"No, you may not." Longley watched him steadily. "Do you care for her at all?"

"Of course I do." Vaughan considered whether he should

just get up and leave. He didn't want to mull over his feelings with Longley. He'd rather go for a midwinter dip in the Thames.

"Why?" Longley asked.

"Because she's an incredible woman." As should be apparent to anyone who interacted with her. "Her hair is like spun gold, and it's so soft."

He recalled how it had felt slipping through his fingers and willed himself not to harden.

"I could look into her eyes forever, and she has the sweetest sprinkle of freckles over the bridge of her nose. She's thoughtful in ways I never expected. Did I tell you she brought gifts to our tenants on her first day there?"

Longley ran his finger around the rim of the glass. "You didn't."

"They adore her," Vaughan said. "But being kind doesn't make her timid. She can hold her own against unpleasant company. She even got the better of Miss Snowe."

"Did she?" Longley grinned. "Well done."

"She's patient, and clever, and—"

"Good heavens, Ashford." Longley cut him off. "You're absolutely smitten."

Vaughan gaped at him. "I am not."

"Oh yes, you are." Longley seemed delighted. "Now you just need to get a bloody hold of yourself and do something about it."

"No."

That wasn't the message his friend was supposed to have taken from this conversation. Vaughan picked up a pack of playing cards and began shuffling them so he had something to do with his hands. He glanced around the room, wondering if anyone might be up for a game. Anything to take the focus off his marriage.

"Anyone for whist?" he called.

Longley narrowed his eyes. "This conversation isn't over."

"I beg to differ."

At that moment, Mr. Henry White, a companion of their occasional playing partner Mr. Falvey, dropped onto the chair beside Vaughan's.

"I say, Ashford," he drawled, clearly tippled. "My condolences."

Vaughan's grip on the cards faltered and he dropped one. Longley bent to retrieve it from the floor.

"Whatever for?" Vaughan asked.

White looked surprised by the question. "For being saddled with the plainer Carlisle chit."

Vaughan's chest tightened, and his gaze snapped to White in an instant. His eyes narrowed, and the words echoed through his inebriated mind, bouncing off one another in all their offensive glory.

"Don't ever speak about my wife like that again," Vaughan growled.

And then he reeled back his fist and punched White on the nose.

White shouted in surprise, falling off the chair and crashing to the floor. Blood burst from his nose, immediately soaking his shirt, and a server rushed forward and offered him a handkerchief.

Vaughan's hand throbbed, and a rushing sound filled his ears as he realized that everyone was staring at him. He looked down at his hand, startled by the flecks of blood on his knuckles.

"I hit him," he said to Longley.

"That you did," his friend said, grabbing him by the shoulder.

"He deserved it," Vaughan said, getting to his feet and nudging the sniffling White with his toe. "You will refer to the Duchess of Ashford with the utmost respect."

White glared up at him. "You've lost your mind. Gone soft in the head over a woman, just like your cuckold father."

Vaughan's fingers twitched, eager to lay into him again, but Longley pushed him toward the exit. Somewhere behind them, he heard the manager calling after them.

Vaughan didn't think they would kick him out of the club. He was a duke. More likely they'd remove White. But he wasn't in the mood for socializing anyway, so he let Longley lead him away.

Once they were outside, Longley took his handkerchief from his pocket and wiped Vaughan's knuckles, then tucked the cloth away again.

"Well, I wasn't expecting that," he said. "I don't think Henry was either."

"Ass," Vaughan said.

"He is, rather." Longley eyed Vaughan with a combination of fascination and something else that Vaughan couldn't put his finger on. "Now, keep in mind that I don't agree with him, but I do think you're being a fool when it comes to Emma. Go and talk to her. Running away isn't going to solve anything."

"Talking to her won't either. It will only hurt her more."

He didn't want that.

"Staying away from her is hurting *you*," Longley replied. "Probably her, too."

"I'm not hurting," he protested.

"Yes, you are." Longley summoned a carriage and helped Vaughan into it. "You're smitten with your wife, and you miss her."

"No, I don't."

It was a lie. He did miss her.

His heart ached from it.

CHAPTER 25

Essex,
January, 1820

AN UNSEASONABLY WARM BREEZE STIRRED THE AIR AS EMMA strolled through the gardens with Violet. The sky overhead was gray, but she felt no need for a coat as they explored the shrubbery.

Whereas the grounds of Ashford Hall were expertly manicured, the Mayhew's estate was wilder, with fewer culti-vated flowers, but no less beautiful. It was the sort of place Emma imagined could be a faerie glen.

"So, tell me how you fell in love with Mr. Mayhew," Emma said. She had bits and pieces of the story, but not the whole thing, and she would like to know.

"I met him at a ball," Violet said, lifting her skirt to step over a damp patch of grass. "It was the evening that you remained at home with a headache. I danced with him and found him charming."

"But?" There must be a "but," otherwise Violet would have declared her preference for him then.

Violet sighed. "But I'm selfish, and he was a handsome but

untitled gentleman without a great fortune. I was enchanted by him, but I believed that I could just as easily become enchanted by someone with wealth and a title. When I met Ashford and we didn't bond, I was surprised."

"I thought you were quite enamored of the duke," Emma admitted.

"I was enamored with the idea of him." They rounded a hedge and emerged in front of the orchard. "I liked the prospect of being a duchess, and he fulfilled all the requirements I thought I had. He's an attractive man—and I say that with no designs on him whatsoever—but nothing about him sang to me."

Interesting.

Even when Emma hadn't thought she liked Vaughan, she had been intrigued by him. His stern countenance, striking silver eyes, and his seriousness had made her want to know more about him.

"Ashford is not romantic like Mr. Mayhew," Violet said. "He seems so... dispassionate. When I saw Mr. Mayhew again, I realized that the connection we shared was uncommon and that I'd been too quick to dismiss it."

Emma nodded. Her sister had never been the most emotionally cognizant person, so she could see how she hadn't immediately realized what she was feeling.

That didn't mean Emma approved of her actions.

"You are happy now?" Emma asked.

"I am." Violet stopped walking and turned to her. "I apologized for creating the situation you've found yourself in—although you may choose not to forgive me—but I owe you another apology. I knew you were interested in Mr. Mayhew, and yet I didn't reveal my own interest in him. I hope we didn't hurt you by eloping."

Emma bit her lip. The apology was long overdue, but she found it mattered little.

"I appreciate that, but it's just as well things turned out as they did. I would not have been well suited to Mr. Mayhew."

Yes, Mr. Mayhew was romantic. There was no denying that. After all, he'd interfered with a duke's engagement and risked the ton's ire to win his bride, but he was too self-centered and self-congratulatory for Emma to have been happy with him.

She needed a kind man. One like Vaughan.

"I'm so relieved to hear that," Violet said, touching Emma's upper arm. "I have behaved poorly, but I do love you."

Emma smiled, though it was strained. "I love you, too, sister."

Violet pulled her into a hug. When she drew back, she was grinning with twin dimples in her cheeks and her eyes dancing. She hooked her arm through Emma's.

"Let's see if there are any apples to be found," she said, guiding Emma toward the orchard. She glanced over her shoulder, then lowered her voice. "So, you used to believe Ashford was cold, as I did. I've begun to change my assessment after seeing him with you. Do you still believe him to be cold?"

Emma's heart filled with bittersweet affection. "No, he isn't. He has a very warm and loving soul, but he keeps it locked up where nobody can reach it."

"I think you're mistaken about that," Violet told her. "You've endeared yourself to him, even if you don't want to believe it."

Emma shrugged. Perhaps she had, but it hadn't done her any good. He wouldn't change his mind.

"I'm glad I got to know who he really is," she said. "Though I wish he were willing to give me more."

Violet pulled a face as if she didn't like that response, but she didn't push the matter. She pointed at a tree up ahead.

"Look, there's a large apple," she said.

It was only once they were standing beneath the apple that they realized how far up it was. Violet seemed inclined to walk away, but Emma hitched up her skirts. It had been years since she'd climbed a tree, and this seemed as good a time as any to start again.

After all, no one was about, and even if they were, who would judge her? She was a duchess. There had to be perquisites.

"Emma, are you sure that's a good idea?" Violet asked.

"Perfectly."

Emma wedged her booted foot into a space between branches and hefted herself up. She climbed upward, getting closer to the apple, but before she could reach it, she spotted a figure hurrying toward them from the direction of the house.

"Who is that?" Emma called down.

Violet spun around. "One of the maids."

Emma rolled her eyes. Yes, she'd been able to observe that much from the uniform.

"Mrs. Mayhew," the maid called, panting as she closed the distance between them. Her eyes widened as she noticed Emma up the tree.

"What is it?" Violet asked.

"Um." The maid didn't seem to know how to react to the sight of a duchess with her skirts hiked up, climbing a tree. "The Duke of Ashford is here to see the duchess."

Vaughan rested against the back of the sofa, grateful for the physical support as he waited anxiously to discover whether Emma would grace him with her presence.

They'd been polite to each other when she'd departed, but it hadn't been under the greatest of terms, and the knots in his gut were tangling themselves ever tighter because he feared she'd refuse to see him.

He shouldn't be here.

He was supposed to stay away from Emma. But perhaps he was taking after his father, as Henry White had suggested, because he'd been unable to keep his distance. He missed her too much. He longed to see her pretty face and hear her soothing tones.

His mouth tasted of brandy from the flask he'd left in the carriage, and the wait seemed to go on forever. Yes, that was a slight exaggeration on his part, but as he watched minutes tick by, he grew more certain that Emma planned to just leave him waiting here.

When she appeared in the doorway, her cheeks flushed, her eyes shining—and was that a twig caught in her hair?—he'd never seen anything more breathtaking.

Relief engulfed him.

Perhaps he hadn't completely ruined whatever was between them. Suddenly, he realized he ought to be standing. He wasn't showing his wife the proper respect. If anyone else disrespected her, he'd gut them, so why should he be any different?

He lurched to his feet, but his vision swam, and he stumbled. Emma caught him and steadied him.

"What's happening?" she asked. "Is everything all right?"

"It is now that you're here," he said and leaned down to plant a kiss on her mouth, except she sidestepped at the last moment, and he landed on his ass. His tailbone throbbed, and he grunted as pain shot up his spine. That would hurt later.

But then his gaze flew back to his wife as the meaning of her actions sank in.

She'd rejected him.

He'd tried to kiss her, and she'd rejected him.

He stared in disbelief, a fissure forming in the walls of his heart. In a moment of perfect clarity, he saw himself as if he were hanging from the ceiling, looking down. There he was, sitting at the duchess's feet, making a fool of himself over her.

He'd never felt more like his father, and he'd never been so ashamed.

Yet even that couldn't make him leave.

He levered himself upright and grabbed the back of a chair for balance.

"Violet, will you give us some privacy?" Emma said, and it was only then that Vaughan noticed the other woman standing behind her.

Violet glanced at Emma, obviously uncertain what to do. "Are you sure?"

"Yes," Emma said firmly.

"Fine, but I'll be nearby. If you need me, just call out." Violet backed away, narrowing her eyes at Vaughan.

Wonderful. Emma's sister thought she needed protection from him.

Emma turned those big blue eyes on him. "Why are you here?"

"I missed you," he said, swaying closer, hoping to catch a whiff of her familiar vanilla scent.

Emma scrunched her nose. "Have you been drinking?"

He winced. He'd hoped she wouldn't notice, but supposed he hadn't hidden it well, given the stumbling.

"Only a little." He reached for her hand, and to his surprise, she let him take it. "I've been thinking. I-I'm willing to see if there could be more between us than a convenient marriage."

He was terrified, but surely facing the fear was better than continuing to be without her.

Her expression softened. For a moment, he thought he had her.

"Why are you drunk in the middle of the day?" she asked.

Oh no.

Answering that question would lead them nowhere good, but he also couldn't think of a decent explanation other than the truth.

He dropped her hand and slumped onto the chaise, needing the comfort of something solid beneath him.

"I feel like I've become my father," he confessed, his stomach roiling. "All twisted up over a woman. It was only after I'd had enough brandy that I was able to convince myself to come here."

Her face fell, and he knew he'd said the wrong thing.

"Please come with me," he said, desperate to get the words out before she became so angry, she wouldn't listen. "I don't like being apart from you or at odds with you."

With a sigh, she sat beside him and looked him in the eyes. He could hide nothing from that searching gaze.

"Are you comfortable with your feelings for me?" she asked.

He hesitated. Obviously, he wasn't. The fact he'd gotten soused in order to come here proved that. But that wouldn't help his case.

Unfortunately, it seemed like the hesitation was enough of an answer for her.

She nodded once, then took his hand. He gripped hers tightly, feeling as though she might slip through his fingers.

"I can see you're trying," she said. "But I don't want you to make a decision you'll regret because you're impaired. When you can return and give me this same proposition, sober and clear-minded, then I'll consider it."

The fissure in his heart cracked and widened.

"But…" He trailed off.

She was making the sensible decision, and they both knew it. Yet she was also rejecting him.

"Are you able to get home safely, or would you like to sleep it off in a spare bedroom?" she asked.

"Longley is waiting in the carriage," Vaughan said dully. "So, yes. I'll be safe."

Emma arched an eyebrow. "He didn't want to come in?"

Vaughan sank even farther into the chaise. "He said I was going to regret this and that he didn't want to see it."

"But he didn't stop you?"

Vaughan didn't reply. Honestly, when he'd gotten into the carriage earlier, there had been no stopping him. He'd have ignored anyone who tried.

"Would you like a drink or food before you go?" she asked.

"No." He stood, trying not to wobble. "I'll just be on my way now."

He couldn't even look at her. He understood her position, but he'd also never felt so dismissed in his life.

He was a duke.

People didn't treat him like an errant toddler. But perhaps in this case, it was what he deserved. After all, she'd only sent him away once. How many times had he shot down her ideas of love?

He deserved this.

In the days that followed Vaughan's visit, Emma distracted herself by exploring the grounds of the estate and reading in Lord Mayhew's library in the main house, which he'd kindly allowed her to use.

Nothing she did could erase the memory of Vaughan's forlorn face from her mind, though. Yet he didn't return, and nor did he write. Perhaps he'd come to the conclusion that he didn't want to pursue a romantic intimacy with her after all.

Maybe, once he was sober, his fears had won out.

"Your Grace," Daisy said hesitantly as she dressed Emma's hair.

"Yes, Daisy?"

In the mirror's reflection, she could see Daisy press her lips together, hesitating for a moment before she continued.

"It's been a while since you've had your courses," she said.

Emma frowned. Surely it hadn't been that long. But when she thought about it, she'd last had them prior to her marriage. Well over a month had passed. Closer to two.

"Does that mean...?" She'd heard rumors that a woman's courses stopped when she was with child, but no one had ever confirmed it for her.

"You might be increasing," Daisy said quietly. "I couldn't say for sure. I've heard the other maids speak of such things. Your courses could just be delayed though."

Emma's stomach fluttered. She placed her palm over the softness of her belly. Could a baby be growing inside her at this very minute? A son or daughter she could cherish?

Someone into whom she could pour all of the love that no one else had ever wanted.

Hope swelled within her.

"A baby," she whispered.

"Maybe." Daisy sent her a secret smile. "You should call for a doctor to make sure."

"I will."

Emma sent word to Violet, and within a few hours, the local surgeon came by. He poked and prodded, asking questions that made her blush, but it was all worthwhile when he confirmed that she was likely with child. She couldn't contain her smile and thanked him profusely as he left. He promised to call again soon to look in on her.

After he was gone, Emma and Violet shared a pot of tea in the drawing room, and for once Violet didn't make a fuss when Emma requested scones with jam and cream.

"I need to tell Vaughan," Emma said, still hardly able to believe the news. They might have been trying to beget an heir, but she'd never stopped to imagine how it would feel once they succeeded and the baby was growing inside her. She'd mentally skipped forward to after they were born.

Violet cocked her head. "Vaughan?"

"Oh, the duke." Emma had forgotten that her sister didn't know his Christian name. "But I'm not sure I want to see him face-to-face right now."

"Why not?" Violet asked. "You can't withhold news like this."

"I know." Emma sighed. "But my pride was injured because he felt the need to drink so much brandy in order to face me the other day. Am I really that terrible?"

Violet hid her grin. "Of course not."

"Perhaps I should write him a letter."

"No."

Emma stared at Violet, shocked by her abrupt response. "No?"

"That would be a cowardly approach, and you aren't a coward. Are you?" Violet arched one of her eyebrows.

"I'm...not?" Emma hadn't realized Violet considered her plucky.

"You're not," Violet confirmed. "You're the sister who always knew what you wanted and weren't afraid to let others know. You were courageous enough to marry someone you didn't care for in order to protect the family. You're brave, Emma. So be brave now."

Being brave sounded like a lot of effort.

But she couldn't deny that it was nice to hear Violet speak about her this way, and she didn't want to give her sister a reason to change her opinion.

"Perhaps I will visit him soon," she grumbled.

"That's the proper attitude," Violet said. "Besides, you must remember that not everyone is as certain of themselves as you are. I am sure the duke didn't mean to cause you offense. He may have needed fortification, but I'm certain he meant everything he said."

"You're right." Shame curled through Emma. She'd gotten caught up in her own feelings and hadn't thought about how difficult it must have been for Vaughan to reach out to her. Perhaps he'd gone about it the wrong way, but he'd still tried.

"I will do it," Emma said. "Tomorrow."

CHAPTER 26

London,
January, 1820

HER INSIDES A TANGLE OF NERVES, EMMA KNOCKED ON THE door of Vaughan's London residence. A thin older man opened the door. His eyes widened at the sight of her.

"Your Grace," he said diffidently.

Emma cocked her head. She didn't recall having met him before, but in her new role, she supposed she would have to get used to people recognizing her.

"Good afternoon," she said. "I'm here to see the duke."

"Please come in." The man stepped aside and held the door while she entered. "I am Gladwell. Allow me to show you to the drawing room."

Emma looked around as she followed him. She hadn't visited Ashford House prior to marrying the duke, so she'd never been inside before. The ceiling towered above them, and sconces lined the hall, although few of them were burning at this time of day.

"Through here," Gladwell said.

"Thank you." The drawing room was decorated in masculine shades of green and white and contained two forest green chaises, several other chairs, and a marble fireplace that occupied most of the end wall and threw out a wonderful warmth.

"I will call for tea and inform His Grace of your presence." Gladwell bowed and backed out of the room.

Emma removed her gloves and went to the fireplace to warm her hands at the hearth. They tingled as the numbness dissipated, but she still looked forward to wrapping them around a hot teacup. Nothing warmed the hands quite like a cup of tea.

Unfortunately, Vaughan arrived before the tea did.

He strode into the room, his back determinedly straight, his complexion somewhat waxy. Judging from the lack of wobble to his steps, he was sober, but he didn't look well. Semicircles darkened the skin beneath his eyes, and his hair was ruffled as if he'd been riding in the wind.

He smiled at her, and despite his ill appearance, his smile, at least, was genuine.

"I'm so pleased to see you," he said as she rose to her feet.

He took her hand and, to her utter amazement, kissed the back of it. She blinked dazedly. He'd never kissed her hand before. What did it mean? And why now?

"Please, sit," he said, gesturing toward the chaise.

She sat. She expected him to take the chaise kitty-corner to this one, but instead he parked his bottom right next to her.

A woman Emma assumed was the housekeeper bustled in, carrying a tray laden with tea. She set it on the table in front of them and straightened.

"Will there be anything else, Your Grace?" she asked.

"Cake, please, Mrs. Williams," Vaughan said, winking at Emma.

Winking.

What was the world coming to?

As the housekeeper left, he turned to Emma. "May I pour your tea?"

She hesitated. In all her life, never once had a man poured tea for her. But then, this wasn't just any man. This was her husband.

"Yes, please." Her voice was husky, but she couldn't help it.

Vaughan picked up the teapot and carefully filled one teacup and then the other. He added a teaspoon of sugar to hers and stirred. When he passed it to her, Emma took it automatically.

She placed the teacup on the table and adjusted her skirt. Then, having nothing else to do with her hands, she picked it up again, raised it to her lips, blew across the surface of the tea, and sipped.

"Did I make it the right way?" he asked, uncharacteristically hesitant.

"It's perfect," she assured him.

"Good." His face brightened. "So, what brings you to London?"

Emma almost laughed at how ridiculous it was that they sounded like polite strangers. Only a couple of weeks ago, she'd fallen apart in his arms.

She put her teacup down. "I believe I may be with child."

His smile broadened, and his entire being seemed to light up. She reared back, surprised. She'd expected him to be pleased because the purpose of marrying had been to obtain an heir, but he seemed more than pleased. He looked delighted.

And not just for the sake of continuing the ducal bloodline.

He shot to his feet and swept her into his arms. Then, before she could react, he peppered her face with kisses. She giggled, unable to contain the joy that his reaction brought her.

"This is the best news you could have given me," he said, easing his hold on her but not letting her go entirely. "When will we know for certain?"

She gazed into his pale eyes, which were crinkled at the corner and shining with emotion.

"My courses are a few weeks late," she said. "Another couple of weeks, and we can be reasonably sure. Especially if I begin to experience sickness."

"I hope you won't suffer much," he said, his worry warming her. The corners of his mouth lifted as if he couldn't help it. "You have made me a very happy man."

"I'm glad."

He released her, and for some reason, she was disappointed by that. What did it mean that she wanted him to kiss her—properly—and show her to his bedchamber?

No, she told herself. *Give him a chance, but protect your heart and don't fall straight into bed with him.*

Lord, it was hard to recall why she needed to be cautious when he gazed at her with such affection.

"You will be a wonderful mother." He reached toward her belly, but then dropped his hand.

Emma started to speak. "I—"

The housekeeper appeared, nudging the door open with her foot and carrying a tray containing two small plates each laden with a sizable piece of cake. She glanced between them and colored, appearing to realize she'd interrupted. She quickly placed the tray on the table and left again.

"That looks delicious," Emma said, her stomach rumbling right on cue.

"Have some." Vaughan waited for her to sit before passing her a plate and fork.

"Thank you." She cut off the corner of her slice and scooped it into her mouth, savoring the combination of sweetness and tart lemon. "Mm. Divine."

When she looked at Vaughan, it was to find him staring at

her lips. He cleared his throat and grabbed his own cake, moving so quickly that he knocked his teacup, and tea sloshed over the rim.

"Drat." He wiped the spilled tea with a napkin. "Would you like another piece? I'm sure there is plenty, and you're eating for two now."

"I may have another slice," she said, a wave of love washing over her that was so intense, she could hardly breathe. Not only was he indulging her sweet tooth, but she could already tell he was going to be a doting father.

She'd never have expected that the icy Duke of Ashford would be the embodiment of all of her wildest dreams.

Well, except for the part where he didn't want love. Unless he really was willing to reconsider.

"By the way." He glanced at her, looking suddenly unsure. "I must apologize for my behavior at the Mayhew estate. I shouldn't have turned up soused. You deserve better than that, and you were right to send me away."

She froze with a piece of cake in her mouth, the lemony flavor bursting on her tongue. If she'd realized the topic was to become so serious, she might have waited before stuffing herself.

He was clearly anxious for a response, so she chewed frantically and swallowed the lump down.

"Thank you for the apology," she said. "I have to admit, your visit was a bit... emotionally confusing."

He grimaced. "I understand why, but that wasn't my intention." He set his plate on the table, the cake untouched, his expression determined. "I meant what I said. I want more from you than an heir. The truth is, that scares me, but the idea of being without you scares me more."

Emma moistened her lips. "Tell me what you do want."

A ghost of a smile crossed his face. "I told you once that you were an inconvenient bride, and that is exactly what I want. All of the complications. All of the inconveniences. All of those complex emotions I swore I'd never need."

Her breath hitched. "Love?"

"Yes," he replied. "A wife whom I can love and who will love me in return. But not just any wife will do."

"No?" Emma's heart beat rapidly, and with one last glance at the cake, she set it aside. She couldn't give him the attention he deserved if she kept eating.

"No." His smile grew. "I need a wife who is strong but also gentle. Kind and clever. Loving but not meek."

She leaned closer until their faces were only inches apart. He brushed a stray lock of hair behind her ear, and shivers rippled over her in response.

"I need you," he said. "I know I have been slow to open my mind to the idea, but please allow me to make up for my prior actions."

Their lips touched in the briefest of kisses, but then he pulled back. She instinctively moved toward him, but he stopped her with a hand on her chest.

"Where are you staying while in town?" he asked.

She blinked, trying to clear her head. "Um. I thought I would visit with my parents."

Although now she was wondering whether she might entice him into inviting her to stay here.

"Very well." He smoothed his hand up her chest to the curve of her neck. "May I call on you tomorrow?"

Breakfast at Carlisle House was exactly as it used to be.

In fact, Emma slipped into the routine so seamlessly that she had to stop to ponder whether the past weeks had happened at all or if they'd been a mad dream.

Lord Carlisle sat at the head of the table with a newspaper in front of him, buttering toast while Lady Carlisle picked at her eggs and warned Sophie that she ought to drink more water if she wanted to improve her complexion.

Emma watched them with barely concealed amusement, grateful for the reminder that no matter the upheaval in her personal life, some things never changed.

"Do tell Mother that drinking ten cups of water per day will not magically clear my skin," Sophie said plaintively.

Emma made a face. She'd never suffered from the unpleasant breakouts that aggravated some of her peers, so she had no experience in the matter.

"I can't imagine it will do anything other than give you an incessant need to use the privy," she said. "One can never be sure, though."

Sophie pouted. "You're no help. What good is being a duchess if you don't use it to save your youngest sister from the perils of overconsumption of water?"

"I'm sure there are a host of other benefits," Lady Carlisle said loftily. "Perhaps you will win a duke of your own if you drink enough water."

Sophie seemed baffled by this. Honestly, Emma didn't understand either, but nor did she feel the need to. She wasn't subject to her mother's whims anymore.

"Tell us, Emma. How do you find life as the Duchess of Ashford?" Lady Carlisle asked.

Lord Carlisle glanced up from his newspaper, clearly listening.

"It is… good," Emma said.

"Just good?" Her mother sounded disappointed.

"What did you expect given she married a man she doesn't love?" Sophie asked.

Lady Carlisle shot her a quelling look. "Not everything is about love. Lord knows it caused enough problems for Violet."

No one could argue with that.

Lord Carlisle cleared his throat. "Are you happy, dear?"

Emma looked down at her toast, which was rapidly going cold. "I am not unhappy," she said. "The duke is a good man, and I believe he cares for me."

She still could not get the words he spoke yesterday out of her mind. But she wasn't certain what he intended. As such, she'd hardly slept and was all befuddled now.

"What is his country home like?" Lady Carlisle asked.

"It's lovely. The house itself is easily twice the size of ours in Surrey, and the grounds are extensive. Everyone has been most welcoming."

"Good." Was it Emma's imagination, or did her mother seem relieved? Perhaps she'd harbored some guilt over pressuring Emma into marrying the duke. Not that they'd forced her to. She'd made her own decision.

After breakfast, Emma went to her room to find a book. As she was searching through her bag, there was a knock on the door, and Sophie entered. She hovered in the doorway, her hair gleaming bronze in the sunlight.

"How is everything really?" Sophie asked. "I feel like there is a lot you didn't tell Mother and Father."

Emma withdrew the book and placed it on her writing table, then sat on the chaise and gestured for Sophie to join her.

"I think I love the duke," Emma said quietly. "Or if I don't yet, then I certainly could love him."

Sophie brightened. "That's wonderful."

"Except that... well, I'm not completely certain that he actually wants love." His words said that he did. Now she was waiting for his actions to back them up.

"Oh." Sophie nibbled her lower lip. "I did think it strange that you're staying here rather than at Ashford House."

"He told me he wished for us to have separate residences."

Emma explained everything, from her first proper conversation with Vaughan through to yesterday afternoon, in his drawing room. But before Sophie could respond, someone rapped on the door, and then Daisy stuck her head through.

Daisy grinned impishly. "You have a caller, Your Grace."

Emma rose to her feet. "Please excuse me, Sophie."

She followed Daisy down the stairs. It must be Vaughan. She hadn't told anyone else she was in London. But was she ready to see him?

The instant she stepped into the drawing room, her uncertainty fled. There he stood, handsome and upright as ever, clutching the largest bouquet of blue irises she had ever seen. He offered them to her as she approached.

"They reminded me of your eyes," he said, a splash of pink spreading across his cheekbones. "They're the same shade of deep blue—like a lake on a sunny day."

Behind her, Daisy giggled.

"They are beautiful," Emma said. "Thank you."

She couldn't stop the smile that stretched across her face. She'd always imagined how it might feel to have a man give her flowers and spout poetry inspired by her. Vaughan's words wouldn't be considered poetic by actual poets, but coming from him, they might have well as been a sonnet.

"Will you come for a drive with me?" he asked as she took them from him.

"I will." Even if she had no idea where they were going. When he was like this, she wasn't sure it mattered. "Daisy, will you put these in water?" she asked as she passed off the flowers.

"Yes, Your Grace. Enjoy your drive."

Vaughan took Emma's hand, pressing his large palm against her gloved one, and led her out of the drawing room, past the butler, who watched approvingly, and through the front door. His carriage waited on the roadside, a box already in front of it to help her in.

"You wouldn't prefer to drive the curricle?" Emma asked as a footman closed the carriage door, giving them privacy.

"A carriage is safer for a lady in your condition," he said, glancing at her abdomen.

She warmed, instinctively knowing that he cared for her as well as for the child she might be carrying.

"Where are we going?" she asked.

His face relaxed into a smile for the first time since she'd seen him today. "It's a surprise."

"Oh, really?" She searched his gaze, wondering what he was planning. "A good one?"

He twined his fingers through hers. "I hope so."

They made small talk as the carriage drove through Mayfair. Emma kept an eye out the window, noting when they passed the most popular shopping district. Soon after, they pulled up outside a stone building with a sign attached to the roof.

Excitement stirred Emma's gut. "A bookshop?"

Vaughan nodded. "A shop that specializes in fiction and poetry. Let me show you."

He preceded her out of the carriage and, arm in arm, they passed through the shop doorway. A bell tinkled above them, and a plump woman in a navy dress emerged from the back. Emma's mouth fell open. Not only was this a bookstore, but it was one with a female proprietress.

"Do you like it?" he asked.

"I believe I do." She surveyed one of the shelves, seeing several titles she'd already read and many others she would like to. Her fingers itched to pick them up.

"Go," Vaughan murmured. "Get as many as you like."

She hesitated. "Really?"

Perhaps he didn't realize how many books they would be taking home if she had free rein. But he just grinned.

"I'm a rich man, and I emptied the box in the carriage

before I called on you. I mean it, Emma. You may buy whatever takes your fancy."

Emma had always thought that if there was one moment in her life when she'd feel like a fairy-tale princess, it would be her wedding. But she'd been wrong. Now, surrounded by books—whole worlds she could dive into—with a husband willing to indulge her, she could believe she'd stepped into a fairy tale.

"May I help you?" the proprietress asked.

Emma shook her head absently. "I'm happy looking, thank you."

In fact, she spent the next hour doing just that. Fortunately, Vaughan didn't seem to mind, and when they left with a stack of books practically taller than he was, he just smiled and carted them out to the carriage.

Emma was buzzing, eager to get home and explore her new finds, but she was also torn about where to put them. She loved bookcases, and she needed to set one up for her books, but not at Carlisle House. She wasn't sure where the best location would be. Perhaps Ashford Hall. She should discuss it later with Vaughan.

"Where to now?" she asked as they rolled down the street, away from the bookstore.

"To get ice cream," he said.

If she'd thought the day couldn't improve any, she'd been wrong.

"I remember how much you enjoyed it when we went to the confectioner's for ice cream while I was courting Violet," he said. "I should have known then that I was pursuing the wrong sister."

"It didn't put you off me?" she asked. "Mother always said that men don't like greedy women."

Vaughan laughed. "Any man who'd seen you eating that ice cream would be the opposite of put off." He sent her a sidelong look. "It was strangely erotic."

Her cheeks heated. She'd had no idea he'd even noticed her then, beyond her role as a chaperone, but to know he'd found her enticing even while near the renowned beauty who was her sister... It was balm for her self-esteem.

When they arrived at the confectioners, Emma eagerly reviewed the options as they waited to be served. She chose a raspberry ice while Vaughan chose lemonade. They sat in the dim back corner of the establishment and smiled at each other across the table while they enjoyed their sweets.

Emma's ice cream was sublime, that wonderful combination of tart and sweet she so adored. When it was gone, and her mouth was no doubt dyed red on the inside, she placed her hands one on top of the other and met Vaughan's gaze.

"What are you about with this outing?" she asked. He was enacting some kind of plan, and it made her nervous not to know what it was.

His gray gaze softened, and he laid one of his hands on top of hers. "I was remiss before we got married. I never wooed you as I should have. Frankly, I behaved like an entitled ass, so I'm rectifying the situation."

"You're...wooing me?"

"Yes."

She frowned. "But we're already married."

He stroked his thumb along the side of her hand. "That doesn't mean I own your heart, and I want it. Freely given. Just as I intend to give mine to you."

As if it knew he was talking about it, her heart squeezed. She bit her lip. If she wasn't careful, this man would be the end of her. But maybe that wouldn't be so bad.

He straightened and removed his hand from hers. She silently mourned the loss.

"May I escort you to the opera tomorrow?" he asked.

A smile spread across her face.

CHAPTER 27

When Emma appeared at the top of the stairs in Carlisle House, wearing a luscious blue velvet dress, Vaughan forgot how to breathe. With her golden hair, porcelain skin, and those eyes that could look directly to the heart of him, she was undoubtedly the most stunning woman he'd ever seen.

How had he ever seen her beside Violet and considered Violet to be the better prospect?

She made her way gracefully down the stairs, and he met her at the bottom, automatically taking her arm. He inhaled, and the scent of vanilla tickled his nostrils.

Damn, she was tempting.

"You are beautiful," he said.

She looked away.

He frowned. That wouldn't do. Gently, he gripped her chin and tilted her face toward him.

"I mean it," he said. "You're the most captivating woman I've ever known."

The skin beneath those freckles over her nose turned pink.

"You look very handsome too," she said softly, finally

288

raising her gaze to his. "I shall be the envy of every woman at the opera."

"And I the envy of every man."

Her lips curled in a way that said she didn't quite believe him, so he'd just have to prove her wrong for doubting him.

He walked her out to where the carriage waited and helped her in, then followed her inside. The door closed, encapsulating them in the dim interior, the low light somehow making it seem more intimate.

As the carriage began to move, Vaughan took Emma's hand.

"I wish I had done this right from the beginning," he told her. "I should have taken you to balls and opera, and allowed the ton to see me courting you."

Her breath stuttered between her lips. "Things were different then."

"I know. But that doesn't stop me from imagining how it could have been."

He held her close until they arrived at the opera house. They joined the queue of carriages waiting outside. When it was their turn to disembark, Vaughan tucked her hand into the crook of his arm and led her through the ten-foot-high doorway and into the building.

He'd forgotten just how golden everything was. The walls were gilded, as were the painting frames, and he suspected they'd have used gold thread for the chairs if it had been within the budget.

People turned and stared. He was used to prolonged glances. It was part of being a duke. But tonight, there were even more than he was accustomed to. Perhaps because this was the first time he'd attended an evening event with his duchess.

Whispers started nearby and spread quickly. He couldn't make out the words, nor did he care to. Hopefully Emma wouldn't be distressed by the gossip.

She leaned closer to him. "Do you get the impression they are talking about us?"

His lips twitched. "I do."

"What do you suppose they're saying?" she asked.

He dipped his head and breathed her in. Delicious.

"I suspect they're saying that I'm the luckiest fool in all of London to have taken you off the market," he said.

She chuckled. "I think it's more likely they're wondering how I persuaded you to swap one sister for the other."

"It doesn't matter what they're saying," he told her. "All that matters is the fact that I'm with you."

He puffed his chest as they passed through the foyer. This stunning woman was his duchess, and everyone here knew it. There were times when being the center of attention—especially in a crush such as this—would put him on edge, but for now, he couldn't feel anything other than pride.

They took the stairs to Vaughan's viewing box, where Longley was already waiting with his mother. The dowager countess's eyes crinkled as she greeted Vaughan warmly. He'd always liked her more than his own parents.

"This must be the duchess," the dowager countess said, sweeping into a curtsey. "It's an honor to meet you properly, Your Grace."

"The honor is all mine," Emma said, looking charmed. "I beg your pardon for saying so, but you're awfully young to have an adult son."

"How sweet of you to compliment an old woman." The dowager countess's eyes twinkled. "I was only eighteen when Andrew was born."

"So young," Emma said softly.

Although, really... was it?

Emma herself was only twenty, and she was with child. At least, he dearly hoped she was. She would not even be forty before their first son or daughter was grown.

A disturbance on the stage captured their attention, and

they took their seats, since it seemed the performance was soon to begin.

"I understand that I have you to thank for ensuring my husband got home safely after his jaunt to Essex," Emma murmured to Longley.

One side of Longley's mouth hitched up. "He would have been fine anyway. His coachman takes good care of him."

"Nevertheless, thank you. It was a relief to know he wouldn't be alone."

Vaughan squirmed. He knew he'd behaved poorly that day, but he hadn't realized how worried Emma had been. He was ashamed to have been the cause of it.

"I won't alarm you like that again," he promised.

To his surprise, she laughed. "I'll admit that I don't know a lot about men, but I know enough to suspect that you certainly will be driving about soused at some point in the future. It's enough to know that you will be careful and have someone with you who can watch over you."

"I'm always careful." Except, perhaps, when it came to people's feelings. "You never need worry about my safety when traveling. I take the necessary precautions."

She turned to him, her expression soft. "Thank you."

At that moment, the performance began, and they fell silent.

Vaughan watched without speaking, but beside him, Emma and the dowager countess conversed quietly throughout. Emma made insightful comments about the performance and the play itself. He was so proud to call her his.

He took advantage of the dim lighting to touch her as often as he could. When he shifted position, his arm brushed hers. When he moved his legs, he rubbed his thigh against hers. And when he couldn't resist for any longer, he raised her hand to his lips.

They spend the intermission talking among themselves, and after the opera drew to a close, they parted ways from

Longley and the dowager countess and drove back to Carlisle House. He escorted Emma to her front door and paused on the threshold. She tilted her face toward his, her eyes shining in the dark.

He was tempted to pack her back into the carriage and take her to his home where she belonged, but he needed to be patient. Instead, he cupped her face and gave her the gentlest of kisses.

She pressed against him, silently begging for more, and he obliged, dipping his tongue into her mouth, tasting her unique flavor, and rocking against her abdomen. His pulse picked up, and with a groan, he drew away.

He wasn't going to defile his wife tonight. Not out here where anyone could see, and especially not after he'd promised he'd woo her.

Resting his forehead on hers, sharing breath, he asked, "May I call on you again tomorrow?"

~

AFTER TWO WEEKS ON THE RECEIVING END OF VAUGHAN'S courtship, Emma could barely think straight around him. He called on her every day and escorted her to balls, the park, and to the gardens. He gifted her enough flowers to fill the drawing room—and, when no one was looking, he slipped her a box of the most exquisite chocolate she'd ever tasted.

He'd even returned with her to the bookshop, where they'd perused the shelves and discussed what they'd each been reading. He'd been the perfect gentleman. Every day, she craved him more, yet he always bid her farewell with nothing more than a kiss. It was driving her mad.

He was treating her as if she were a virginal miss, and she wasn't sure what to think of that. She ached for his skin against hers and his cock inside her. He'd introduced her to a world of pleasure, and now she missed it.

Still, she had to admit that she enjoyed his attention. There wasn't a moment she spent with him when he didn't make her feel cherished, but she wouldn't have minded if he'd taken her to the bedchamber and ravished her either.

She tried to corral her thoughts—and desires—enough to concentrate on the present moment. It was a sunny but cold afternoon, and they were walking in the park. The breeze carried the scent of damp earth and the ground was dappled with sunlight and shadow.

It was cool enough that she was tempted to close her eyes and bask in the slight warmth every time they passed through a sunny patch. She kept them open, though, because really, one ought not to walk around without being able to see where they were going.

Their conversation about a ball they'd attended the previous evening tapered off, and they walked in amiable silence.

Emma's stomach fluttered. She'd been intending to broach a subject with him for several days now, and she wouldn't get another opportunity as perfect as this. She hesitated, though, because she'd been enjoying their time together and didn't want to cause any awkwardness.

"What is it?" Vaughan asked, glancing over at her. "You seem anxious."

Emma sighed. They were arm in arm, and his warmth permeated the layers of fabric between them, oddly reassuring.

"I just wondered why you haven't tried to do more than kiss me since we arrived in London," she said, her insides curling tighter as she waited to hear what he'd say.

He blew out his breath. "That's all?"

He said that as though she hadn't been working herself into a lather over it for days.

"Yes."

"Then I have an easy answer for you." He bumped against

her as if wanting to be closer. "I want to take my time and court you properly so you have no reason to doubt how much I adore you."

Her insides melted. If not for his support, she might have stumbled. She wished she could throw herself into his arms right here in the park. Well… she could, but then she'd cause a scene, and she knew he didn't like those.

"You adore me?" She sounded breathier than she'd have liked.

He angled himself toward her. "Of course I do. I'm sorry you even had to ask." He hesitated. "I have never experienced romantic love before, but I believe I might love you. My heart expands every time I see you or think of you, and any minute when we're apart seems to pass twice as slowly."

Her heart leaped. "Really?"

He smiled. "Yes, Emma. Really."

He subtly shifted their positions and intertwined his fingers with hers. "I promise that I will never overlook you again. I won't ask you to live separately from me, and if you were to make the suggestion—which you may, if you wish— it would sadden me. I know I wasn't what you wanted in a husband, but I hope that you'll let me fill the role anyway."

She shook her head. "Oh, you silly man. Of course you're what I want in a husband. You're kind and honorable. I…."

Her breath caught. She could hardly believe they were having this conversation. Even when in the early days of their marriage she'd hoped he might be receptive to love, she'd always known it was unlikely.

They were two people brought together by convenience. Anything more had been too much to ask.

"I love you." Her tone was full of wonder. "I really do."

Love didn't feel as she'd expected. It didn't burn, as she'd always thought it would. It simmered pleasantly beneath the surface, warming her from the inside out and wrapping her in a blanket of comfort and security.

The way he stared at her now...

How had she ever imagined him to be cold?

"Emma, I want...."

"Yes?" she prompted because he seemed to be having difficulty getting the words out. She didn't blame him. Her own throat was clogged with emotion.

He rubbed his chin, and his smile was delightfully shy. "I'd like to redo our vows to each other. I know it hasn't been long since our wedding, but I want to marry you properly, and to give you the day you always dreamed of. I want to do things right."

Emma's soul sang, and her hands trembled as she turned and placed them in his. Neither of them were walking now, although she wasn't sure when they'd stopped.

"I've... I've never heard of doing something like that," she admitted.

He laughed. "Nor have I. Perhaps it's a madcap thing to do, but it makes me sad that you were robbed of your dream wedding—that we both were—and I want to fix that."

Her smile wobbled. "Then yes, I will gladly redo our vows. I know that it will be even better than my dreams. Even if the *ton*—and my mother—are scandalized."

"I'll do my best to make that so." He spoke with conviction. "And as for the *ton*, they don't matter to me. Not like you do."

"You don't have to try, my love," she told him. "It will already be perfect because you'll be waiting for me at the end of the aisle."

CHAPTER 28

London,
February, 1820

As a hairpin dug into the side of her head, Emma couldn't help feeling as if, in some ways, her wedding day was repeating itself.

Here she was, once again, seated in her former bedroom with Daisy dressing her hair while Emma watched in the reflection of the massive, gilded mirror. Daisy had promised nothing too elaborate, and Emma was enjoying the process of seeing her creation take shape.

"Daisy, are you sure you don't wish to remain in London?" Sophie asked from where she said beside Violet on the chaise. "You dress hair so beautifully."

Daisy's reflection beamed. "Thank you, Lady Sophie, but no. I'm perfectly content returning to Norfolk."

Sophie pouted but didn't seem upset. She'd probably known before she'd asked that Daisy would never accept her invitation.

Daisy's cheeks were flushed, and Emma narrowed her eyes.

"Is there something you haven't told me?" Emma asked.

Daisy shrugged. "One of the footmen at Ashford Hall is very handsome, and he has a mind to court me." An impish smile appeared. "I have a mind to let him."

"That's wonderful," Emma exclaimed.

"I can work with Jane next time we're in London," Daisy told Sophie, apparently unwilling to gossip more. "It wouldn't take much for her to be as good as me. Or, if you visit Norfolk, I could teach her then."

"That would be excellent," Sophie said. "Thank you."

"Emma…," Violet began. "Are you sure—?"

"It's fine for you to be at the ceremony," Emma said, not for the first time.

She, too, had worried that Vaughan may not want Violet present, but he'd insisted. He'd assured Emma that he didn't harbor any feelings toward her sister, good or ill, and that he wanted everything exactly as she desired it.

How had she gotten so lucky?

"You're doing it again," Sophie teased. "Your eyes are all moony."

"Leave her alone," Violet said. "She's in love. She's allowed to be moony."

Emma laughed. If someone had told her six months ago that Violet would be defending her right to be a fool in love, she'd have thought they'd lost their minds. Yet here they were.

"I'm glad you're all here," Emma said, affection building in her chest.

"We are too," Violet said.

"And we're glad you're happy," Sophie added.

"Also, your hair is done." Daisy stepped back and held up a small mirror to the back of Emma's head to allow her to see her work. The gold strands were woven into a deceptively simple arrangement that somehow looked both regal and ethereal.

297

"I have never seen a finer arrangement," Emma said, unable to take her eyes off it.

"Now we just need to get you into your gown without mussing it," Daisy said.

Emma stood and turned to study her gown, which was hanging from the railing in the open wardrobe. It was the same gown she'd worn for their actual wedding because it was the one thing from that day she'd unreservedly loved. However, a seamstress had been hired to let out the waist and bodice, since she was beginning to thicken.

Fortunately, pregnancy had not made her horrifically ill. Not yet, at least.

"How about a joint effort?" Violet suggested, crossing the room to help Daisy remove the gown from its hanger.

Daisy glanced at her in surprise. "My lady?"

"It will be easier if we do it together, no?" Violet asked.

"Well, yes." Daisy didn't seem to know what to make of Violet's offer, but she accepted the assistance, and together they lowered it over Emma's head.

Emma slipped her arms through the sleeves and let out a sigh of relief as the skirt settled around her. She'd worried she might have gotten too plump for the gown to fit, even with the alterations, but it seemed that all would be fine.

Daisy moved around behind Emma and began doing it up while Violet came around to her front and fussed with the layers, trying to position everything just so.

"I'm sorry I missed your wedding," Violet said softly.

"It was probably for the best," Emma said. If Violet had turned up, the gossip would have been vicious. Of course, there was still gossip then, and there would be now, but they would surely be far more concerned with the eccentricity of this ceremony than anything else.

"Probably," Violet agreed. "But I'm pleased I can be here for this. Perhaps we too will redo our vows next year, so our families can celebrate with us, and so that I may shock the ton once again."

"That sounds nice." Emma wasn't so sure their parents would feel the same. It was one thing to have their daughter who'd married a duke make a fuss of repeating the event and attracting the attention of all their peers, but if Violet did so, it might not be received so well.

Still, perhaps they could do a private ceremony and hope that nobody caught wind of it.

"Maybe I'll have a wedding soon too," Sophie said, not wanting to be left out.

Emma and Violet exchanged a smile.

"Not too soon, though," Emma said. "Mother and Father have had enough excitement for now."

"Mm." Sophie sounded disappointed, but then she rallied. "If we wait a few years, perhaps my skin will clear up."

"Even if it doesn't, we'll find someone who adores you," Emma assured her. She would accept nothing less for her younger sister—unless, of course, Sophie decided that love wasn't what she wanted. In which case, Emma would support her.

"Ladies." The male voice made them all turn. Lord Carlisle stood in the doorway. Lady Carlisle hovered beside him.

"May we have a moment alone with Emma?" Lady Carlisle asked.

Sophie and Violet both looked intrigued, and Emma had no doubt that she'd be fielding questions from them later, but they left without argument. Daisy followed behind them.

Lord and Lady Carlisle entered together and sat side by side on the chaise. Emma remained standing, since she didn't want to crease her dress.

"What is it?" she asked, unnerved by their serious demeanors. Not to mention how unusual it was for her parents to request a private conversation together. Usually, Lord Carlisle let his wife handle anything of that nature.

"We owe you an apology," her father said, shamefaced.

"For what?" Was there a problem with the ceremony?

"This matrimonial match has turned out well for you," her mother said, taking up the reins. "For that, we're immensely grateful. But the truth is, it could have been very different."

Understanding began to dawn.

"Your marriage could have made you miserable," Lord Carlisle said, confirming her suspicion. He stared down at his hands, which were intertwined on his lap. "I was confident that Ashford was not a known fortune hunter or rake, but I had no way of knowing whether he would be a good husband to you."

"We were scared of what it would mean to be exiled from the ton," Lady Carlisle added. "So we sacrificed your happiness to ensure our return to its embrace."

Lord Carlisle patted his wife's thigh comfortingly. "We've been discussing this since you returned to London. We're ashamed of how thoughtless we were. Just because many women would be glad to marry a duke doesn't mean it's what you wanted. We both knew you had other aspirations."

"We are very sorry," Lady Carlisle whispered. "And regretful. We hope that our support of this…ceremony…goes a little way to showing that."

Emma's eyebrows had climbed her forehead by the time they finished speaking. She stared at them, scarcely able to believe they'd apologized. She'd never expected it of them.

"I… accept your apology," she said slowly. "I was crushed when you made the suggestion—I won't deny that. You pushed me toward Vaughan despite knowing I have always wanted love. But you were in a difficult situation, and I know that if I'd refused to marry him, you wouldn't have forced the matter."

"Of course not," Lord Carlisle sputtered.

"We'd never!" Lady Carlisle added.

"I know." Emma walked closer and sent them a reassuring smile. "Thank you for the apology. But everything turned out for the best, and I forgive you."

Their shoulders slumped, their faces becoming identical masks of relief.

Lord Carlisle stood, wrapped his arm around her, and kissed her forehead. "Let's get you married to your duke."

Lady Carlisle's eyes twinkled as she joined them and kissed Emma's cheek. "Again."

∾

VAUGHAN WAITED IN THE GARDEN BEHIND CARLISLE HOUSE. He was a little too warm despite the overcast sky, and every time he inhaled, he got a lungful of pollen. The Carlisles' gardener was apparently something of a naturalist given the way they didn't seem to believe in trimming or containing anything.

Nevertheless, there was something beautiful about the wildness of the garden.

A string quartet began to play a short distance from Vaughan, indicating that Emma would be arriving soon. Longley winked at Vaughan from the front row, and the dowager countess flashed him a smile.

Emma's sisters appeared, each wearing dresses in a different shade of blue—Violet's was jewel toned and Sophie's more pastel—and sat on the side of the makeshift aisle opposite Longley.

Only a few people were present, including Emma's immediate family, and her maid, who'd been given permission to attend as a guest, although she was lingering in the back. While none of them seemed to know what to think of this ceremony, they were humoring it, smiling and watching with interest.

Lady Carlisle swept across the garden and lowered herself onto a seat beside her daughters.

Vaughan gazed steadily in the direction Emma would be coming from. A sense of rightness bloomed in his chest. When Emma came into view, walking with her hand on her father's arm, a lump lodged in Vaughan's throat.

He couldn't take his eyes off her. Never had he seen anyone so beautiful.

She'd told him that she would wear the same dress she had when they'd wed at St. George's, so he supposed he'd seen her thusly attired, but he hadn't paused to appreciate her then. That was a travesty, and he'd never repeat the mistake. He was now intelligent enough to know that his wife deserved proper admiration.

She moved gracefully, her head held high, and he met her eyes. They sparkled, blue and full of life. He felt a smile tug at the corners of his mouth and was sure he was staring at her like a sappy fool. He didn't care.

When she and her father drew near, Lord Carlisle offered her arm to Vaughan.

"Take good care of her," he murmured.

"I will," Vaughan said.

He walked with her until they reached the celebrant, and then turned and took her hands in his.

This time, when he said his vows, he meant them with every fiber of his being. His words were infused with sincerity, and he hoped Emma could see that he took them as seriously as an oath.

She said her vows, and he watched her pretty pink lips move as she promised to honor and cherish him forever. He ached to cradle her face between his palms and kiss her, but it was more important for him to bask in this moment.

Emma was glorious, and he'd been a fool not to see that from the start.

Once the vows were complete, they exchanged rings for a second time. Vaughan slid his ring onto Emma's delicate finger, filled with a sense of satisfaction at the symbol of possession. She was his, he was hers, and now that they were married twice over, no one could ever doubt it.

As the celebrant declared their vows renewed, he brushed his lips over hers in a featherlight kiss, then intensified it as he felt her mouth curve into a smile.

"I love you, wife," he said.

"I love you, too, husband."

Together, they turned toward their guests.

Lord and Lady Carlisle were the first to congratulate them on a lovely ceremony—and was it just Vaughan's imagination, or were there tears in Lady Carlisle's eyes?

Longley followed suit, and the dowager countess dispensed with formality, dragging Vaughan into a tight embrace.

"You're going to be very happy together," she said softly. "I can already see that."

"Thank you," he replied.

Beside him, Emma hugged each of her sisters. The string quartet played Mozart in the background and Vaughan's inside hummed with contentment.

They accepted well-wishes and said their goodbyes. Today, there was to be no repeat of the wedding breakfast. Instead, he and Emma were to return to Ashford House, where he would finally take her to bed again. They'd held off until now because they'd agreed that it would be nice for their reenactment to be as authentic as possible.

However, as they made their way to the carriage, a familiar —and loathsome—voice called Vaughan's name. He stiffened.

"Who is it?" Emma asked.

"Keep walking," he muttered, determined to avoid his cousin Reginald, who was at this moment trotting along the street toward them.

"I say, Ashford, where are you going in such a hurry?" Reginald called in his nasal tone.

With a sigh, Vaughan turned to face him. "Home. What are you doing here?"

Reginald's rodent-like eyes gleamed with curiosity. "I had to see for myself whether the rumors are true."

"What rumors?" Vaughan demanded.

Reginald glanced from Vaughan to Emma, obviously gleeful about the fact he knew something Vaughan didn't.

"The rumors that you're just as besotted as your pathetic excuse of a father," Reginald said.

Vaughan braced himself, expecting his old doubts and insecurities to assail him, but to his surprise, he didn't feel anything other than annoyance. Reginald was trying to get in one final blow because the possibility of his becoming duke was rapidly dissolving.

Emma stepped toward him. "Excuse me? Who are you?"

"Duchess, allow me to introduce my distant cousin, Reginald," Vaughan said.

"Ah." She curled her lip as if she'd smelled something rotten. "Is this the same Reginald who will never be invited to our social gatherings?"

"The very one," Vaughan replied, a grin stealing across his face.

"And who will not be allowed to visit with our son once he is born?" she asked, rubbing her belly in a way that made her meaning obvious.

Reginald paled. "But you cannot know you carry an heir."

She shrugged. "We intend to have many, many children."

Vaughan's grin grew. God, he loved this woman.

"Let's be on our way," he said, turning away from his cousin. "We have more important matters to address."

Reginald sputtered, but they ignored him as they entered the carriage.

Once the door closed, Emma shook her head. "What an odious little man," she said. "I would never wish social exile on anyone, but he might deserve it."

Vaughan lifted her and placed her on his lap. Her eyes widened, and she giggled.

"Never mind about him," he said. "I want a kiss."

She smiled. "And I am happy to give you one."

Their lips touched... and clung. A puff of breath escaped her, and he inhaled it into his lungs. There was nothing he wanted more than to spend the rest of his days sharing air with Emma.

"I won't be satisfied with just the one," he rasped. "I want all of your kisses."

She curled into his embrace, her lips a mere inch from his. "Then you shall have them. And I shall have all of yours."

"Forever and ever, until our last breath." He nuzzled her. "Now kiss me, my duchess."

EPILOGUE

Norfolk,
Two years later

"Mama!" Lilian toddled toward Emma on her adorably plump little legs with a flower clasped between her hands.

Emma checked the flower quickly to ensure it wasn't a rose—and therefore might have thorns—before focusing on her daughter's sweet face.

"What do you have there, darling?"

"Flower, Mama." She thrust it toward Emma, one of the maroon petals falling off in the process.

Emma's heart swelled with love. "Thank you, Lily. It's beautiful." She took the flower and tucked it behind her ear. "Have you and Daddy been exploring?"

"No." Lilian plonked onto her bottom on the blanket Emma had spread in the shade from a hedge on the edge of the gardens at Ashford House.

"We found all sorts of things," Vaughan said, coming into view from behind the hedge. He was carrying another flower, and he knelt in front of them and smoothed back

Lilian's pale blond hair, then tucked the flower behind her ear.

"There," he said to their daughter. "Now you match your mother."

Lilian clapped her doughy palms in delight. Emma kissed her forehead and breathed in the twin scents of baby and springtime.

"My beautiful ladies." He gazed at them with a softness that had become familiar over the past two years.

"Cake?" Lilian asked.

Emma hid her smile. There was absolutely no denying that their daughter had inherited her sweet tooth.

"Let's see if we have any cake," Emma said, opening the picnic basket that Mr. Travers had packed for them. "Hmm. It looks like we have to eat our vegetables first."

She withdrew a few containers of mashed vegetables and handed Lilian a spoon. Her daughter liked to be as independent as possible.

"Are there scones?" Vaughan asked, sitting beside Emma.

"Yes, with fruit preserves." Emma scooped the berry preserve onto a scone and passed it to him.

He hesitated, watching as she prepared another for herself. "You're sure it's safe for you to eat?"

"I'm certain." She glanced down at her stomach, which was round with their second child who was due to be born in a matter of weeks. "Mr. Travers is very careful with what he gives me."

She'd discovered that her husband could be quite a worrier when it came to her safety and that of their children.

"You must be thirsty," he said, setting his scone down. "Let me get you a drink."

He poured a cold herbal infusion from a flask into a cup. Emma cringed as she accepted it from him. Ever since Mr. Travers had first concocted the brew—intended to settle her stomach during pregnancy—Vaughan had been plying her with it at every opportunity.

The infusion wasn't unpleasant, but it wasn't something she wished to drink constantly either. Unfortunately, she couldn't bring herself to refuse when she knew he only did it because he cared.

She'd never thought she'd have someone who loved her that much.

Tears pricked her eyes.

"Are you all right?" he asked quietly as Lilian shoved a spoonful of mashed potato into her mouth, smearing half of it on her face.

"Everything is perfect," she said. "I love you."

He leaned over and kissed her. "And I you, sweetheart."

At that moment, Lilian pushed herself upright and padded across the blanket. When she reached the grass, she stepped onto it with a sense of wonder. Vaughan and Emma exchanged smiles. Ever since she'd learned to walk, Lilian had loved the feeling of the grass between her toes.

Emma took a bite of her scone, relaxed in the knowledge that Vaughan would chase after Lilian if need be. But then their daughter took them both by surprise. She charged off across the lawn, moving at a faster clip than she'd ever gone before.

Emma gasped. "She's running!"

Vaughan cheered. "Go, Lily! Keep it up!"

He straightened his long form and hurried along behind her, ready to catch her in case she fell. Which she did. Right into the dirt where the grass met one of the rose gardens. Vaughan lifted her into his arms and peppered her face with kisses. Lilian giggled delightedly, apparently unbothered by her fall.

Vaughan carried her back to the blanket and gently placed her on her feet. She started running again, this time along the length of the hedge.

Emma met Vaughan's gaze.

He groaned. "She's going to be so much more trouble now."

"You wouldn't have it any other way," she said.

"I know." He kissed her forehead, then her nose, and finally brushed his mouth over hers. "Our family is more than I ever dreamed of."

Emma kissed him back and snuggled against his body. "I cannot wait to meet our new addition."

She had no idea how she'd been so blessed, but she would cherish every moment with her family, just as she knew Vaughan treasured them.

The same way he treasured her.

She let out a contented sigh. Her story might not be worthy of Jane Austen, but she'd finally found her happy ending.

THE END

ABOUT THE AUTHOR

Jayne Rivers adores regency romance books, especially those by Sarah MacLean and Julia Quinn. She writes feel-good stories with heroines she'd love to befriend and heroes she'd love to sweep her off her feet—if she weren't married, of course.

Made in United States
Orlando, FL
28 April 2024

46294048R00190